THE SURGEON

JOHN NICHOLL

Boldwood

First published in Great Britain in 2025 by Boldwood Books Ltd.

Copyright © John Nicholl, 2025

Cover Design by Head Design Ltd.

Cover Images: iStock and Shutterstock

The moral right of John Nicholl to be identified as the author of this work has been asserted in accordance with the Copyright, Designs and Patents Act 1988.

All rights reserved. No part of this book may be reproduced in any form or by any electronic or mechanical means, including information storage and retrieval systems, without written permission from the author, except for the use of brief quotations in a book review. This book is a work of fiction and, except in the case of historical fact, any resemblance to actual persons, living or dead, is purely coincidental.

Every effort has been made to obtain the necessary permissions with reference to copyright material, both illustrative and quoted. We apologise for any omissions in this respect and will be pleased to make the appropriate acknowledgements in any future edition.

A CIP catalogue record for this book is available from the British Library.

Paperback ISBN 978-1-83561-278-1

Large Print ISBN 978-1-83561-277-4

Hardback ISBN 978-1-83561-276-7

Trade Paperback ISBN 978-1-80656-031-8

Ebook ISBN 978-1-83561-279-8

Kindle ISBN 978-1-83561-280-4

Audio CD ISBN 978-1-83561-271-2

MP3 CD ISBN 978-1-83561-272-9

Digital audio download ISBN 978-1-83561-274-3

This book is printed on certified sustainable paper. Boldwood Books is dedicated to putting sustainability at the heart of our business. For more information please visit https://www.boldwoodbooks.com/about-us/sustainability/

Boldwood Books Ltd, 23 Bowerdean Street, London, SW6 3TN

www.boldwoodbooks.com

The gold of the earth,
The silver of the sea,
My love has brought them both to me;
The golden girdle round my thighs,
But silver scales upon my eyes.

The heat of the sun,
The frost of the moon,
My love has perished all too soon;
The dying flame, faint afterglow,
Burnt out fire beneath the snow.

— PENNED BY MY GREAT-UNCLE,
THEODORE NICHOLL – 1939

1

THE SURGEON

It's time I revealed a little bit about myself in the interests of clarity. Not too much, mind you. No need to rush things and get ahead of myself. But just enough for you to glimpse the man behind the mask I wear so very well.

My name is Professor Sir Alexander Aitken MBBS FRCS, if we're being formal. And once, not so long ago, I was a consultant surgeon at a Welsh hospital – very much respected, and envied even. But now, the filthy red-top papers prefer names like 'Monster', 'Dr Death', or even 'The Cannibal'.

What utter fools those journalists are, with their tired moral clichés. What ridiculous, hysterical nonsense they write for the moronic masses who lap it all up, as if those articles were worthy of even a moment's consideration. They spew their venom, as though humanity isn't inherently violent. That's the worst of it for me. Their level of ignorance is truly mind-boggling. Strip away the facades, and we're all predators, every single one of us. Given the right circumstances, the right pressures, anyone could kill. Just watch the TV news and you'll find that out. It's laughably obvious, is it not? Or is that just me?

None of us are innocent. Not truly. Beneath our skin and civility, we're little more than clever animals, driven by instincts we can barely comprehend. We're no more than smart apes. And yet the sanctimonious journalists who vilify me can't see past their own hypocrisy. Incapable of understanding the intricate genius behind my work, they call me depraved, a demon.

They don't see the bigger picture – the *truth*. My actions were never random. They were precise, deliberate, and necessary. My research required it, demanded it. Sacrifices. Calculated losses. And always the unwanted, the forgotten. Society's human detritus, whose absence would go unnoticed.

Yet they call me evil. Me, Professor Alexander Aitken – a pioneer in both science and art. Because that's what killing is: art. A dance of flesh and steel, of dominance and surrender. It demands brilliance. A lesser mind would bungle it, leaving chaos in place of beauty. But I... I've perfected the craft. And if I'm honest, I miss it. I yearn for it. My work is incomplete, my findings fragmented. I need more data. I need more... subjects. And I will have them.

There is a purity in death, an unflinching honesty in those final moments. Watching the light fade from a victim's pleading eyes, hearing the trembling whispers of their last words – it strips away the lies we live by. There, in those fleeting seconds, is the truth of humanity. No academic paper or textbook has ever come close to explaining it. Not really. The full, shattering force of terror – how it breaks a person from the inside out. How pain, both physical and psychological, strips you bare and leaves nothing but a scream in the dark. Only I can tell that story. And when the moment is right – when I'm finally given the chance – I will. That day is coming. And the world won't be able to look away.

The clock ticks, a relentless metronome counting down to my

next move. Do you hear it? Tick, tock. A rhythm that never falters. Soon, the lights in this wretched cell will flicker out. Darkness will descend. It always does. My time to write is short, so I must be precise. Clarity is crucial.

Almost five years. That's how long I've been entombed in this concrete purgatory. Twenty-three hours a day locked away, suffocated by steel and stone. The fetid air here reeks of despair, thick and choking. The walls themselves seem to sweat degradation. Even the guards walk with deadened eyes. And yet, even in this place, I command respect. They don't look at me – not properly. The guards avert their gazes, and the inmates mutter my name in hushed tones, as though invoking a curse. Fear. That's what they feel. And I've done nothing to correct them. Fear is a useful thing. It serves my purpose well.

Here, in this pit of human waste, time loses all meaning. The clanging of keys, the endless shouts, the muffled sobs at night – it all blurs into a cacophony of misery. The stench is worse. Sweat, decay, despair. It seeps into your skin, your very soul. It's maddening. And yet, amidst it all I wait. Patient. Controlled. The anger fuels me, but it does not consume me. Not yet.

And as if this place with all of its horrors weren't bad enough, I'm here for a crime I didn't commit. No, don't laugh. I mean it. Yes, I've killed before. Four women in total: three over the border in England and one in North Wales, many miles from my West Wales home. But not her. Not Holly Larkin. That death wasn't mine. I stumbled upon her by chance, a frozen figure in a deserted park. Her blood pooled black in the lamplight, congealing in the icy winter air. I should have walked away. But I couldn't bring myself to do it. Something about her – her stillness, her silence – drew me in.

I knelt beside her, studying her face. Open eyes, staring but seeing nothing. Holly was beautiful in her own way, even in death. No, especially in death. I leaned closer, inhaling the familiar sharp tang of her blood. My lips brushed her fast-cooling cheek, a kiss – reverent, almost tender, my mouth open, tongue darting. A tribute to the art she had unknowingly become. But she wasn't mine. Her death wasn't mine.

And yet, when they found me there, cradling her lifeless body, licking her cheek like a cat lapping milk, who else would they blame?

I was told the research history on my computer was damning, a macabre archive etched into the silicon – a gallery of death dredged from the darkest corners of the web.

And crimson blood – Holly's blood – had painted my lips and teeth like some unfortunate signature. Try spinning that into innocence for a jury. Try swaying them when every breath you take feels steeped in shadows, when your very being murmurs of behaviour they dare not understand.

They did not see a man; they saw an ogre lurking beneath my flesh, a beast they couldn't wait to cage. Even with the absence of a murder weapon, I was convicted. Where is the justice in that?

So here I sit, locked in this rotting purgatory, counting the relentless march of seconds towards the inevitable. The clock becomes my symphony: tick, tock, tick, tock. Each chime promises freedom, sweet and certain. And when the final lock clicks open, I'll finish what I started.

Only one escaped me. A worthless creature named Megan Morgan. My first hurried attempt at killing, long before I perfected my craft and hunted further afield. But Megan's time will come. Oh yes, I'll finish it. And others will die, too, for revenge, for the pleasure it gives me, and also in the name of science. Detective Inspector Laura Kesey first, then quite possibly members of the jury and the judge. All will die at my hand. When I get out of here. None will survive my scalpel.

Even now, as the echo of future triumphs vibrates in my veins, I cling to the dark promise of liberation beyond these concrete walls. Every drop of rain against the barred window whispers of a world teeming with unfulfilled potential – a stage where my genius will unfurl its true colours.

I recall the bitter taste of defeat and the sweet scent of blood, each memory a testament to the art of my craft. In the relentless solitude of this cell, I nurture the anticipation of revenge and perfection, knowing that soon the scales of fate will be rebalanced in my favour. It's a waiting game. A game I'll eventually win.

2

THE DETECTIVE INSPECTOR

My name is Laura Kesey, a DI in the West Wales Police Force. A job that burrows under your skin, follows you home and dwells in the background. But I was on a much-needed holiday – though leave never quite means escape, does it? That's the way it is for me.

The warm evening sun painted the whitewashed buildings of Nazaret in stunning hues of gold and amber that stirred my soul that warm October Canary Island evening. From the villa terrace, I could see Lanzarote's barren, volcanic landscape stretching far into the distance, stark and unforgiving yet oddly beautiful, like nowhere else on earth.

The shadows of multiple dormant volcanic peaks played across the landscape, contours deepening as the sun dipped ever lower, casting a fiery glow that seemed to set the whole island ablaze. And beyond, the majestic Atlantic Ocean glimmered like a blue mirage, its surface shimmering under the gradually dying light. God's creation at its most glorious, right there in front of me.

It should have been a perfect time, the kind that etched itself into the memory bank never to be forgotten. But perfection, as I've learned to my cost, is almost always fleeting. In the briefest of moments, my holiday idyll was gone. Replaced by anxieties that wouldn't let up. Such things – the creeping doubts, the gnawing fears – have always been my constant companions in my law enforcement role, lurking in the corners of my mind, waiting to seize any fragile moment of serenity. No surprise there. Such things, I fear, seem to define me. I'm not a black-and-white kind of woman. Life is more complex than that. For me, there are always shades of grey.

Janet, my loving partner and soulmate, was inside our beautiful rented holiday home, humming some happy tune I didn't recognise as she chopped fresh organic vegetables with an almost rhythmic precision. The faint clink of the knife against the cutting board mingled with the occasional sizzle from the pan. The kitchen's warm light, flickering as the blinds swayed in the breeze, spilled out onto the terrace where I sat. And Ed, our eleven-year-old son, was sprawled out on the black leather sofa in the lounge, his tablet lighting up his face as he immersed himself in some video game of the type he seems almost obsessed with playing. His laughter occasionally punctuated the evening's quiet – a carefree sound that should've been music to my ears. The air smelled of garlic, herbs, and the faint saltiness of the sea carried on the warm breeze. I'd never felt more relaxed, never happier. Work seemed so very far away, almost like another life. It all seemed almost like a pleasant dream. And it stayed that way, right up to the time I watched a TikTok video I should have avoided like the plague.

I sometimes wonder what the hell's wrong with me. It seems I'm my own worst enemy. Police work always claws its way to the forefront, picking at the scabs of cases I can't forget, dissecting my every action as if sheer willpower could rewrite the past. It's an incessant, unrelenting loop, a vortex that drags me down at the slightest provocation, my mind racing like a storm-tossed sea. Even when I'd promised my lovely Jan that this time – this holiday – would be different. Even when I'd longed for this fortnight away, counting the days like a prisoner awaiting release. And yet, there I was, falling into the same well-worn rut, unable to escape myself.

That glorious evening, I should've been content. I should've been present, soaking up the golden glow of the Lanzarote sun as it dipped below the horizon, the gentle rustle of palm fronds serenading our little piece of paradise. I should've been savouring the mingling aromas of Jan's cooking, the faint spices teasing the balmy air. Ed's laughter echoed from inside the villa again, carefree and light, a sound so pure it momentarily pierced the fog in my head. But the weight of the laptop on my thighs was like an anchor, pulling me down into depths I'd sworn to leave behind.

'Don't you dare say the word "work", Laura,' Jan called from the kitchen. 'Not tonight. I can see you're obsessing again.'

I let the breeze kiss my face, said nothing.

'You hear me?'

I smiled faintly, watching the shadows stretch across the terrace.

'Loud and clear.'

'Good. Because if you so much as glance at that bloody inbox, I swear to God—'

'I haven't.'

A beat passed. Then, 'You better not be lying to me.'

'I'm just... sitting. Trying to relax.'

Jan snorted. 'You never just sit. Your brain doesn't know how.'

And she wasn't wrong. So I kept my mouth shut, didn't respond. There was an undeniable tension. And it was my fault. All my fault. A senior detective who should know better but who couldn't seem to break the habit, no matter how hard I tried. I knew exactly what I was doing when I opened that laptop, the cold glow of the screen washing over my face like an accusation. As I scrolled through social media, the whispers of old cases beckoned like sirens. I was a helpless addict chasing a dopamine high, fully aware of the self-inflicted harm and powerless to stop. The familiar pang of guilt was there too, lurking in the background, ready to pounce the moment Jan's voice would cut through the stillness to remind me of the promises I'd broken. And still I clicked. I scrolled. I read. Because maybe, just maybe, self-reflection wasn't only my drug – it was my punishment. And I deserved every bit of it.

The contours of my face no doubt changed, a tapestry of frustration and disbelief etched into my features, as I watched an influencer video that had erupted into virality. I'm sure the glow of the screen cast an unforgiving light, highlighting the weariness carved by years of investigative work, sometimes successful, but all too often chasing shadows. That's how I picture the scene, anyway, as I describe it now. That's how it appears to me.

But enough prevarication. I should move on, get to the point. The young influencer, a seemingly smug, self-assured figure, lives not far from me, just an hour's drive away from my home, in the bustling heart of the Welsh capital, Cardiff.

Her carefully curated image beamed to countless devices, spreading her narrative like wildfire. Her voice, honeyed and no doubt rehearsed in my opinion, dripped with righteous indignation, each word a needle pricking the fragile cocoon I'd tried to wrap around the holiday. Her words weren't just a commentary; they were accusations wrapped in velvet, and they hit closer to home than I'd anticipated.

Her name is Bella, or at least that's what she calls herself – a glossy caricature of modern female vanity with trout-pout lips, teeth so white they probably glow in the dark, and impossibly round, gravity-defying tits that practically shout their artificial origins. Her airbrushed perfection is a spectacle, curated for the millions of followers who hang on her every word as if she were some kind of twenty-first-century oracle. Why she doesn't stick to hawking designer handbags, endorsing overpriced skincare products, or blathering on about the latest vapid trends is beyond me. But no, Bella has chosen crime as her niche – my niche. And she haunts me like some dark spectre determined to make my life as stressful as possible. Prodding and poking at the wounds I've worked so hard to heal, turning my professional life into her personal content factory. As if my job isn't difficult enough without her stirring the pot for clicks and likes.

And Bella seems to like nothing more than finding fault with the investigations my team and I conduct in our search for justice to protect the public. She seems to think she's some kind of true-crime expert. And it drives me mad sometimes, the crap she posts, and yet I look at it all too often like some sort of masochist. In truth, I can't take my eyes away. I hate to admit it even to myself. But maybe, somewhere deep down in my psyche, in Aitken's case for example, I fear some of what she says might be true. Not all crap I'm so keen to dismiss, after all.

Professor Alexander Aitken: The Innocent Doctor Behind Bars

The headline screamed in bold, each word an accusation that practically leapt off the screen, sinking in its claws without mercy as I tensed and twitched. And below that attention-grabbing headline, a high-resolution colour photo of Aitken taken at the time of his trial dominated the page. His still-boyish face had been tempered by the years, faint lines carving stories of hardship into his strikingly handsome features. Those piercing blue eyes seemed to hold the gaze of the camera, sparkling with a mix of defiance and vulnerability, while a thick mane of slightly greying black hair framed his angular face, every strand stubbornly resisting the march of time. It was a face that could have graced a Hollywood poster. And let's face it – would Bella be nearly as obsessed with his case if Aitken wasn't blessed with such cinematic good looks?

Call me cynical, but years of police work have left me with little room for naïve optimism. I've seen too much, and it's taught me one thing: everyone has an angle, even Bella with her perfectly coiffed hair and strategically placed moral outrage.

I sat there on the terrace, my fingers trembling with barely suppressed rage, as Jan continued cooking, the tempting aroma of cumin and coriander doing nothing to quell the storm brewing inside me. Jan continued to hum to herself, seemingly oblivious to the black cloud forming over my head, the occasional clatter of pots and pans a jarring counterpoint to the rising tide of anger surging through me.

My laptop's glow illuminated Bella's words, each one a fresh stab to my professional pride. And the more I read, the tighter my chest felt, like a vice slowly squeezing the air from my lungs. How dare she? Why focus on this one case rather than any other, with such intensity and for so long? This was the sixth video I'd watched in recent months. And like all the others, it was getting to me a lot more than it should have. Because it felt all too personal.

Bella didn't bother to mention the mountain of damning evidence that had secured Alexander Aitken's conviction beyond all reasonable doubt. No, of course she didn't. Why let inconvenient facts ruin her neatly packaged narrative?

Her latest post was a relentless tirade, dripping with self-righteous indignation. She harped on about the missing murder weapon, as if that single absence nullified the overwhelming weight of everything else we'd uncovered. She painted it as the gaping hole in the case, an irredeemable flaw in the investigation that I'd led to the very best of my ability.

Bella's words blazed across the screen, big, bold, and bright, casting shadows over the painstaking work my team and I had poured into bringing Aitken to justice for the bloody murder of an unsuspecting young woman walking alone in Carmarthen Park.

And then there's the petition. Bella's frigging petition, started months before like a siren's call to the misguided masses. Thousands have signed it, a virtual army of armchair detectives and keyboard warriors, demanding Aitken's release with no understanding of the case's intricacies.

And each signature feels like a slap in the face, a dismissal of every hour I spent combing through evidence, every sleepless night haunted by the victim's face.

Bella feeds off the frenzy, I'm sure of that, her followers hanging on her every word, their blind support bolstering her campaign to tear me down.

In every video she posts, it's 'Laura Kesey this, DI Kesey that' – always critical, never complimentary. Every post drips with thinly veiled contempt. No sisterhood here, no professional courtesy, just venom and vitriol aimed squarely at me. Like she's plucked me out of the ether to become the villain in her carefully constructed drama. Does she have a grudge? A vendetta? I don't know, and in many ways, it doesn't matter. What matters is that her words are out there, festering in the minds of millions, poisoning the truth and tarnishing everything I'd worked for. And I know, deep down, that I shouldn't let it get to me. But it does. It always does.

My stomach churned as I watched the video for a third time,

the slickly edited montage playing out like a slow-motion car crash I couldn't look away from. Why was I doing that to myself? Why put myself through it again, dissecting every smug word, every carefully chosen image meant to inflame and provoke?

And yet, as I sat there, staring out at the ocean – its endless expanse swallowing the fading light of the day – something stirred in the darkest corner of my mind. A flicker of unease, a memory I'd suppressed broke free and lit up my thoughts like a flare in the night. A lightbulb moment I didn't want to acknowledge but couldn't ignore.

Bella's rantings were needling me not just because they were loud and relentless, but because, in some twisted, uncomfortable way, they echoed whispers I'd tried to silence within myself. Doubts I'd buried deep, only for them to resurface when the night was at its stillest, when sleep was a stranger, and I lay staring at the ceiling, counting the long hours until dawn.

Back then, at the time of Aitken's arrest, I'd been sure enough – sure enough to compile the file, sure enough to hand it to the Crown Prosecution Service, sure enough to trust that the jury would see what I saw. And yet, was 'sure enough' really enough when a man's freedom hung in the balance? When the blade that carved into Holly's body had vanished without a trace, leaving a gaping hole in the picture we'd worked so hard to construct?

We'd scoured every inch of the murder scene to find the weapon. But nothing. I'd tried to explain it away – maybe he'd tossed it, maybe someone had taken it. But the *maybe* hung in the air, as sharp and cold as the weapon we couldn't find. And, as Bella's accusations scrolled across my laptop screen like a relentless tide, I couldn't shake the feeling that our case had been built on shadows and whispers, when we'd all prayed for something solid and unbreakable.

I swallowed hard, the bile rising in my throat as the what-ifs multiplied in my mind. What if Bella was right to raise concerns all along? What if the petition wasn't just a mob mentality but a reckoning waiting to happen? And worse... so much worse. What if Alexander Aitken had been telling the truth all along?

The ocean's steady rhythm suddenly felt mocking, its endless waves crashing against the shore as though answering questions I dared not ask aloud. And all of a sudden, I wasn't sure of very much at all.

'Laura.' Jan's voice jolted me from the screen. 'Dinner's almost ready. It's going to be dark soon. Are you coming in?'

I looked up. She was standing in the open doorway, a white tea towel slung over one shoulder, her brow furrowed as she glanced from me to the laptop, once, then again.

'In a minute,' I replied, my voice tight.

'You said that half an hour ago.' She stepped out onto the terrace close to me, the tension in her movements unmistakable. The golden light from the setting sun highlighting the worry etched in her expression. 'Laura, we're on holiday. You're supposed to be relaxing, spending time with us. Your mind's obviously somewhere else, as usual. And you know how much that bothers me. You promised, remember?'

I sighed, blowing out air, closing the laptop but not before the image of Aitken's face seared itself into my mind again. 'It's that frigging influencer, Jan. I can't just ignore her.'

She made a face. 'Can't or won't?' Her tone was sharper now, raised in pitch and tone. 'Because there is a difference. This isn't the first time, Laura. Every holiday, every break, you find something to bring you back to your job. And to be honest, I'm sick of it. It's not doing any of us any good, least of all you.'

I felt myself tense. 'It's not just a job,' I snapped, louder than I'd intended. Guilt stabbed at me.

'Then what on earth is it? Because from where I'm standing, it looks a hell of a lot like you care more about that fucking laptop than your own family.'

This time Jan's words hit home. They stung. She very rarely swears. And the unexpected profanity sounded somehow strange coming from her mouth. I stood, pushing past her to set the laptop on the nearby table. 'You don't understand,' I said, my voice low but trembling. 'You've never understood. Cases like this... they don't just go away. They stick. They fester. And when someone drags them back into the light, I can't just pretend it doesn't matter. Because it does.'

Jan rolled her eyes. 'Oh, God, not this again. Aitken was convicted. He's locked up. And it's not your case any more. Let someone else worry about it, if anyone needs to worry about it at all.'

I know I should have let it go. Jan's words were well intentioned. She had my welfare and our relationship at heart. And I was unreasonable, at best. But I was in full flow now. And nothing was going to shut me up till I'd said my piece. I turned to face her, anger twisting in my chest. 'It was my case. My decisions. My doubts. And if Aitken is innocent, then I... I helped put him away. For a very long time. Can you even begin to comprehend what that feels like?'

Jan fell silent, the frustration in her eyes giving way to something softer. Pity, maybe. I hated it. 'No,' she said quietly, almost in a whisper. 'I don't really understand why you can't let this go. But I do understand this: you can't change what's already done. Aitken was found guilty. The case is closed. And letting it consume you now won't help anyone, least of all us.'

For a moment, the only sound was the wind rustling through the palm trees and the distant sound of the sea. I wanted to argue, to defend myself, but the words wouldn't come. Because deep down, I knew she was right. And yet, the doubt remained, biting at the edges of my mind.

'Time to eat,' Jan said finally, with more a groan than a sigh. She turned and walked back inside, leaving me alone with the unanswered questions that clung to me like a second skin. There was a lot of evidence against Aitken. But if I'm honest, there was always that one element of doubt. Where *was* the bladed weapon that killed Holly Larkin? We searched everywhere, with dogs, the lot. And as I said, nothing, nothing at all.

I've relived that reality a hundred times in my head, yet still no adequate resolution. Perhaps that's a mystery I'm never going to solve. One thing I do know – if Aitken is guilty, he deserves to rot. But if he isn't, if he's the innocent man he's always claimed to be, then there's still a killer out there. Someone I didn't catch. A predator who may one day kill again.

3

THE HUSBAND

It was a Friday. A day I'll never forget. The driving rain came down in sheets, rapping against the windows like something trying to get in. The kind of rain that soaks you to the bone, that makes everything feel heavier than it should. I could hear it outside, battering the glass. But inside, the silence between me and my wife was the real storm.

My Lily stood by the sink, scrubbing at a plate that didn't need washing. Her hands moved mechanically, a little too fast, too hard. She always did that when she was nervous, when she could feel the weight of something unsaid hanging between us. I knew she was still thinking about the argument we'd had the previous night, about the way I'd raised my voice, about the cruel things I'd said – critical things she didn't deserve at all. I get so very angry. A rage builds inside me. In a way I can't always comprehend or control. I wasn't proud of my behaviour, but I wasn't exactly sorry, either. The truth is, I hadn't been sorry about much at all in the last five years. Just that one thing, which was so much worse than everything else. Our marital arguments, whatever they were about, paled into insignificance by comparison.

And that was why I was there, standing in the kitchen, staring at her like a man about to pull a trigger. The truth had to come out. It had reached that time. I had no other choice, whatever the cost. Or, at least, that's how it felt to me.

I took a step closer to her, my trainers silent on the red tiled floor. 'Lily,' I said, my voice steady, maybe too steady as I fought to hold it together. 'There's something I need to tell you.'

She didn't turn around. I don't think she heard me at first. But then I repeated her name, a little louder this time, and she paused. Her shoulders stiffened, her fingers gripping the plate as though it might slip from her grasp.

'I don't know how to say this,' I continued, watching the water pool in the white porcelain sink, 'but I need to get it off my chest, before I go mad.'

Lily let out a slow breath and set the plate down, finally turning to face me. Her eyes were tired – tired like mine, like we'd both been carrying something we didn't know how to put down. It was always there. It never went away. I think we still loved each other. But there was something missing. I can't put my finger on what.

'What is it, Tom?' she asked, her voice wary, full of anguished emotion. I could tell she knew something was wrong. She just didn't know how wrong. And it really couldn't have been any worse than it was. Nothing she could have imagined came even close.

I could feel my pulse in my throat, my hands trembling at my sides. I opened my mouth as if to speak, but the words got tangled up inside me, like they were too big to fit through the door. The guilt hit me again, crashing over me like a wave, and I almost turned away, almost told her it wasn't the right time to talk. But I'd promised myself I'd tell her. I'd promised myself I wouldn't carry the burden alone any longer. The nightmares were too regular. The self-reproach pervasive, eating away at me like a rabid dog, dragging me down into the depths of despair. The memories gave me no peace at all.

'It's time for the truth. It's eating me up inside. I... I killed a woman, Lily,' I said, and the words felt like they were choking me. I spewed them from my mouth.

Lily stared at me for a moment, blinking as though trying to understand the simple absurdity of what I'd just said. But there was no misunderstanding it. I'd said it, and now it was out in the open, my confession hanging between us like a dead weight. Once said, I couldn't take it back. Everything had changed forever.

'A woman? You... you killed a woman?' she whispered, her voice barely audible, like she was testing the sound of it. 'Tom... what the hell are you talking about?'

I closed my eyes tight shut, trying to steady myself. It wasn't much of an excuse, but it was all I had. So I prayed she'd understand. 'It was over five years ago,' I began, choosing my words with care as if that would somehow alleviate her angst. 'We'd argued that day. I can't remember about what. And I stormed out of the house and went straight to the pub. I was legless after a couple of hours throwing down one pint after another. And I think someone must have spiked my beer or something. Because it wasn't like I'd ever felt before. I was crazy. Like a wild man. And then there was this woman walking alone in the park after dark. A young woman who had done no real harm to me. She looked a lot like you. Same hairstyle and build. Her name was Holly Larkin. She was twenty-two years old, a hairdresser here in town. Although I didn't know any of that at the time.'

Lily stared at me, stock-still, unblinking, an incredulous look on her face as I continued telling her what I'd started. Maybe, I thought, if I explained everything well enough, she'd finally understand. 'I've been living with what I did ever since,' I said with a frown. 'I'm so very sorry, Lily. I truly am. But I had a knife on me. I don't even know why. I was in a dark place, lower than I've ever been. Then she started on me, shouting, saying I was following her. Told me to leave her alone. Screaming at me like I was filth. So I snapped. Threw her to the ground and... I stabbed her.'

Lily looked as if she might throw up. But she didn't utter a word and I had to fill the silence.

'She provoked me. You know how I get when I'm pushed. You've seen it. She shouldn't have gone at me like that. So if we're being honest – it wasn't just me, was it? It was her fault as much as mine. And I haven't done anything like that before or since and I never will again. That's the honest truth. And I'm praying you can forgive me. And the police aren't going to be knocking anytime soon. So you needn't worry about that. That's got to be a plus, hasn't it?' I laughed, a little amused, trying to lighten the mood. 'Another bloke was convicted. A man named Alexander Aitken. A right creep from what I've heard. I... err, I saw it on the news.'

Perhaps part of me thought Lily would do what she always did – tell me she loved me regardless of my moods and the silly things I sometimes did. But no, her face crumpled, as if I'd slapped her hard. She looked suddenly older, worn down by life, lines where I hadn't seen lines before. 'What the hell are you—' She broke off, her hand shaking as she wiped tears from her face. 'Why are you telling me all this now? After all this time?'

I think at that stage she was in denial. Not wanting or able to accept the awful truth of what I'd shared. But I needed her to know it was real. Because if I couldn't talk to her, who could I talk to? *For better or worse*. That was her commitment, wasn't it?

'Because I can't hide it any more, Lily,' I said with feeling. 'I hate myself for what I did. I'm drowning in it. It's always there.'

Her legs buckled as she fell back into a kitchen chair. 'Drowning? Tom, you – you're scaring me. Tell me it's all a dream. That I'm having some kind of waking nightmare. Or that you're just making it all up to shock me.'

I dropped my chin to my chest, avoiding her pleading gaze as she began to sob, her chest rising and falling with the stress of it all. 'I'm so very sorry,' I said again, the best I could offer, but the words tasted like ash in my mouth. 'I needed you to know. I need you to understand why things have been so off between us for so long. Why I've been so... distant. Why I've been avoiding you. This is why. I... I didn't want to tell you, to give you that burden. I know it's a secret I should have kept. I've agonised over it for weeks. But it's reached a point where I had no choice but to say something. It sometimes feels as if my head's going to explode with the memory. I had to confess to you, whatever the price to our relationship. You've always been my saviour, Lily, and now I need your help. Sometimes, I really think I might be going insane.'

She stood up again, now on trembling legs, then took a single step away from me, her eyes wide, and I knew I'd just shattered everything we'd built. She could hardly breathe, I could see it in the way her chest moved in shallow, rapid bursts. And I could feel it, too – the growing space that was opening up between us, a gulf widening with every word I spoke.

'You – you killed someone?' Her voice shook, her words barely forming, as if the reality of what I'd told her was gradually dawning. It was eating away at her like it does me.

I nodded slowly. 'Yes, just like I said. I didn't mean to kill her, Lily. But I did. I... I stabbed her and kept stabbing, as if I was someone else I didn't recognise. I wasn't myself, not that night. I was totally out of control. As if I was possessed by some demonic power. Like I said, my drink must have been spiked. It wasn't supposed to happen. But it did, that's the truth of it. It did.'

'How? What – what do you mean, it wasn't supposed to happen? What the fuck are you talking about?' She took another step back, her eyes flickering nervously towards the back door, like she might run, like she might leave me alone with my angst and never come back. 'How does someone not *mean* to kill someone? You said you stabbed her. You, Tom, you did that, *you*! Why the hell did you have a knife?'

I could feel my entire body shaking now, the weight of my confession and Lily's reaction pressing down on me like a thousand tons of stone. The conversation wasn't happening like I'd pictured it in my head. Not even close. And I was beginning to regret saying anything at all. What to say? What the hell to say? 'I wasn't thinking straight. Maybe I was thinking of harming myself. I was drugged. My mind wasn't right. I just wanted to scare her. It got... it all got out of hand.'

Lily took another backwards step, her voice taking on a harder tone. She wasn't quite shouting, but it was close – so close I feared the neighbours might overhear. '*Out of hand?*' she hissed. 'What does that even mean?' The pitch of her voice was even higher now, totally frantic, but I couldn't stop talking, even when I knew I should shut my stupid mouth.

I couldn't stop because I knew that if I didn't say it, if I didn't tell her everything, I would never have the chance again. The fear of losing her was nothing compared to the fear of carrying my guilt alone for the rest of my life. 'I was angry. So very angry. There was a rage inside me like I'd never felt before. And she... she was just there. Wrong place, wrong time. If only she hadn't been there.' I paused, my stomach churning, acidic vomit rising in my throat. 'I lost control. I... I didn't mean to hurt her, but I did. And when I realised what I'd done, it was too late to stop. I can't remember where I got the knife. I don't know where it came from. But I must have been carrying it on me, because nothing else makes any sense.'

Lily was silent now, her face pale, frozen, her mouth trembling. She looked as though the earth had just cracked open beneath her feet and she was waiting to fall in. Her hand went to her stomach, like she might throw up. 'You—' she began, but the words didn't come. She still couldn't make sense of it, I could see that. She couldn't reconcile the man she thought she knew with the killer I'd become.

'A kitchen knife went missing, a new one I'd bought in the market with a long, thin blade, I... I remember now. You took it. *You!*'

I ignored her observation because what use were her words? 'I'm begging you to forgive me. I'm pleading with you, Lily, to put all this behind us.'

A deafening silence stretched out again, almost suffocating, and I already knew I'd asked too much. She didn't say anything for what felt like an age, maybe a minute, or perhaps two. And I didn't know if she was going to scream or run. Maybe both. It wouldn't have surprised me if she had.

Finally, she spoke, her voice quiet, barely above a whisper. 'What did you do after? You've told me what you did to her. I want to know the rest.'

'I—' I swallowed hard. 'I looked around. There was no one else there. No witnesses to what I'd done. So I left her there and ran. I made sure no one knew. You were asleep when I got home. Then I dug a hole in the garden and buried all my soiled clothes and the knife, then moved the compost heap to cover it. I thought... I thought I could get away with it. Just forget it, as if it never happened, and get on with my life.'

Lily shook her head slowly left and right, as if she couldn't process the enormity of it all, couldn't take in what I was saying because it was all too much. 'Oh my God, Tom. You... you murdered someone. And you've been keeping it from me all this time!'

'I'm so sorry. I never meant for it to be like this. I never meant to hurt you. I just—' My voice cracked, and I couldn't finish the sentence. I'd said all I could, throwing myself on her mercy. There was nothing more to say.

She stepped back yet again, retreating towards the door, shaking her head more vigorously this time, her mouth opening and closing like she wanted to scream. Her eyes were wide, showing the whites, popping. 'Who the hell are you? Because you're not the man I married,' she said finally, her voice so small, so distant. 'You're not the man I thought I knew at all.'

And just like that, the distance between us – the gulf that had opened up five long years before – widened into something I knew couldn't ever be fixed. I'd said the words, I'd done the damage, and now all I could do was wait for her to walk away.

I didn't even know if I wanted her to stay. I didn't know if I deserved for her to stay. All I knew was that, for the first time in years, I was no longer alone with my guilt. And somehow, that made everything better.

I didn't know what she'd do with the information I'd shared. Keep it to herself, share it with her mother or sister, or maybe even the police. The future was in her hands now. And at that moment, that was just fine with me. Any change is better than no change at all.

I felt the bitter taste of lost chances and knew that redemption, if it ever came, would be the calm after the storm – a fragile promise in an unforgiving world for my shattered soul. Another man had been convicted for my crime. Perhaps now it was me who would have to face justice.

4

THE WIFE

Any semblance of a happy life felt impossibly distant as I perched on the cold, unforgiving bench in Carmarthen town centre, its chipped paint and worn wood as weathered as I felt. The air hung heavy, thick with the scent of damp pavements and exhaust fumes mingling with the aroma of burgers and hot dogs from a nearby vendor. My heart thudded dully in my chest, each beat reverberating through the hollow ache inside me.

Tom and I had once built a life together, a foundation seemingly sturdy, forged in laughter, shared dreams, and the naïve illusion of security. I could still remember the warmth of his smile in those early days, how his enthusiasm had been infectious, lighting up every room we entered. But that was then. Over time, cracks began to form, subtle at first, like hairline fractures in a porcelain vase. His temper flared more often, ignited by the smallest of provocations – a misplaced key, an offhand comment – and the storms that followed left me walking on eggshells.

Then there was his need for control, wrapping tighter around me like an invisible chain, its links forged from subtle manipulations and veiled threats. I hung on trying to rekindle the past, hoping against hope that things might change, that the man I'd fallen in love with was still in there somewhere, waiting to resurface.

But that fragile hope had been shattered by his confession, the words cutting through me like shards of glass. They left me raw, every fragment of trust and love we'd built reduced to jagged, irreparable pieces. And now, as I sat there surrounded by the indifferent bustle of strangers, the weight of those broken dreams pressed down on me, relentless, a reminder that some things could never be mended.

'I killed a woman,' he had said, his voice steady, as if discussing the weather or some other inconsequence rather than revealing the darkest corners of his mind. This Holly Larkin he'd talked about was a stranger to me, and yet the burden of her death pressed down on me like a weight I couldn't bear.

And so I'd quickly gathered some essentials and left our home, never more conflicted, and ran until I reached the centre of Carmarthen, where I sat, panting hard, exhausted. I wrapped my arms around my knees, feeling small and vulnerable, asking myself what the hell to do next. I needed to talk to someone I trusted completely, someone who wouldn't judge me at all, to unravel the knot of confusion wound tightly in my chest. My mother's sing-song Welsh voice echoed in my mind, promising comfort amid the chaos. With a trembling hand, I grabbed my phone from a jacket pocket and dialled her number.

'Hello, cariad,' she said with that oh-so-familiar greeting, using the Welsh word for 'love'. Her cheerful tone felt like a soothing balm, but I could sense the sudden shift when I faltered, silent, unable to form the words.

'Mum, can I come over?' I finally managed to choke out, my voice a whisper barely audible over the storm brewing inside me.

'Of course, no need to ask. You know you're always welcome. Is everything all right?'

I hesitated, choosing my words with care as I began to cry. 'Not really.' A silence fell, pregnant with unspoken worries. I couldn't tell her; I had to find the words.

'What is it, Lily? Has Tom upset you again? I don't know why you put up with him. Come on, start talking. You know you can tell me anything.'

And it was true, usually I could. But not this time. 'I'll... I'll tell you when I get there. I don't want to say it on the phone.'

After what felt like an eternity, I arrived at her third-floor flat with its view of the River Towy, exhausted, out of breath, but relieved to be there. My mother appeared in the doorway as soon as I knocked, her hands clutching each other, eyebrows knitted in concern.

'Come here,' she said, pulling me into a warm embrace I wished would go on forever. I felt tears welling in my eyes again, but I somehow held them back, not ready to drown in the depths of my emotions just yet. I feared that if I started weeping, I might never stop.

'I n-need to talk,' I finally stuttered, sinking into one of her overstuffed armchairs.

My lovely mum poured me a cup of chamomile tea, the steam curling upward like my rising fears. 'What's going on this time, Lily? You look pale. He hasn't hit you again, has he?'

It was now or never. 'Tom... he... he told me that he killed someone,' I blurted out, feeling the weight of the words hanging heavy in the air.

My mother blinked repeatedly, her brown eyes wide. 'What do you mean he *killed someone*? When? Who?' The questions tumbled out one after another.

'It happened about five years ago, in the park, here in town. A woman... He... he murdered her, stabbed her, it wasn't an accident,' I said, an edge of panic rising in my voice. 'I don't know what to do. He only told me today. Talking as if he could explain it all away. Like I can live with this.'

The moments ticked by as she absorbed my words, her face a canvas of conflicting emotions. Finally, she leant towards me. 'Lily,' she began, 'I want you to listen very carefully to what I'm about to say. You need to think about yourself now. About what this means for *you*. If what Tom told you is true, he's dangerous. You're talking murder, not some triviality. In truth, I think there's only one course of action left open to you. You *have* to talk to the police.'

I knew it was true. That she'd said what she had to say. The only thing that made any sense at all. But I wasn't ready to accept that. Not just yet. I shook my head, fear of the future clamping down on my throat. 'What could I tell them? That I'm married to a monster?'

My mother's gaze softened, I know out of love. 'I'll come with you. I'll drive you there. And you can tell them the truth, just like you told me. It's the right thing to do. You can't ever keep that kind of secret. It's much too big for that.'

As evening fell and shadows draped over her home, the weight of Tom's confession pressed heavier on my heart, and my mother's, too. I knew what I had to do, but the thought of turning him in – my husband, my lover – made acidic bile rise in my throat. I needed to confront the darkness, and perhaps find some semblance of light.

About half an hour later, when I was finally ready to act, my lovely mum drove me to West Wales Police Headquarters, a large red-brick building on the edge of town. Each second that passed felt like an eternity, my heart racing faster than ever. I knew once the police were involved there was no going back. I knew that only too well. I could have backed out. And yet, the true horror of Tom's confession consumed me.

My mother waited for me in the car at my insistence, not hers. Because I knew this was something I had to do alone. I walked up the wide steps leading to a smoked glass door and stepped into the sterile environment of the station, the air seemingly thick with tension, as if I was approaching the gallows. But despite all that, a part of me was glad I was there. What else could I possibly have done?

I feared my shaking legs might collapse under me at any second as I approached the middle-aged woman behind the reception desk. And then I asked for DI Laura Kesey in a faltering voice, explaining the reason for my request when a look of doubt crossed the woman's face. I'd seen the inspector only a few weeks before on the BBC Wales evening news. And she seemed nice, a person I could trust.

After picking up her phone, the receptionist said DI Kesey would see me. A small victory. But a victory nonetheless. It would be easier woman to woman. No men involved. I took some comfort in that.

As I stood there in the sterile space, my thoughts swirled in turbulent disarray. The harsh fluorescent lights cast long, unforgiving shadows across the polished floor, echoing the weight of secret sins. Each tick of the clock was a cruel reminder of choices past, each heartbeat a silent drum of my regrets and defiance. I felt the icy grip of inevitability tighten around me, binding me to this moment of reckoning. Amid the distant murmur of police radios, I vowed to confront the truth of my shattered life – even if it meant forever banishing the remnants of the love I once knew.

5

THE DETECTIVE INSPECTOR

I was back from holiday all too soon. Lanzarote just a memory. And I'd barely had time to sit down at my desk after an unwelcome meeting with the chief superintendent before my phone sounded on the desk.

'DI Kesey?'

'Yeah, what can I do for you?'

'There's a woman here to see you. Says it's urgent.'

'Urgent how?'

'Her name's Lily Rees. She says her husband confessed to a murder from five years ago earlier today. She asked for you by name. I suggested the duty officer. But she said it was you or nobody. She isn't prepared to speak to anyone else.'

All of a sudden I was interested. 'Did she tell you who her husband claimed to have murdered?'

'Someone named Holly Larkin.'

The name hit me like a punch to the gut. Five years ago. Holly – Alexander Aitken's victim?

I nodded once then stood, my mind already racing. 'Put her in whatever interview room's free,' I said, smoothing down my jacket and trying to quell the uneasy twist in my stomach. 'Tell her I'll be with her in five minutes. And make certain she doesn't leave before I get there. I need to make a quick bathroom visit.'

When I stepped into Interview Room Three, Lily was standing by the table, looking like she'd seen a ghost. Her face was pale, almost waxy, and her eyes were rimmed red, the telltale signs of too many tears. She clutched her handbag to her chest as if it were the only thing keeping her upright, her weight shifting nervously from one foot to the other as if the floor was too hot to stand on.

'Lily,' I said softly, motioning to the chair opposite, 'please, take a seat. My name is DI Laura Kesey. Tell me what's brought you here.'

Her movements were stiff, mechanical, as she lowered herself into the chair. She drew in a shaky breath, her voice barely audible. 'I need to tell you something. It's about... it's about my husband, Tom Rees.'

The mention of her husband's name sent a chill through me, raising the hairs on the back of my neck. I knew it of old. A history of domestic violence.

I leaned forward slightly, my gaze steady on hers. 'Go on. I'm listening.'

Lily swallowed hard, her hands shaking as they gripped her bag tighter. 'Tom... he... he told me something. Something I can't ignore. I didn't know what to do, but I can't keep it to myself,' she said, her voice breaking. Tears welled up, spilling over as she wiped at them with trembling fingers. 'I spoke to my mother earlier, and we both decided I had to come here. She's waiting for me in the car. I asked her not to come in. I know I'd get too emotional if she was with me.'

I could see she was on the edge of breaking down completely. I forced myself to keep my voice calm, measured. 'You're doing the right thing. Take your time. Please tell me *exactly* what Tom said to you. And leave nothing out. I need as much detail as possible.'

Lily hesitated, her eyes darting to the walls as if seeking an escape, before fixing them back on me. 'Tom said... he said he killed her. A young woman named Holly, about five years ago. He said she was a hairdresser here in town. I don't know what salon. I didn't ask.'

The air seemed to thicken, the room closing in around us. Her words hung heavy, like an accusation I couldn't outrun. My chest tightened, but I forced myself to focus. 'Lily,' I said, leaning closer, 'are you saying Tom confessed to murdering Holly Larkin? I need you to be absolutely clear about this. Can you answer that for me?'

She nodded, her hands shaking so violently now that the bag slipped from her grip, falling to the floor. 'He... he told me this afternoon. He was probably drunk – he drinks too much, always has – but he was so... so insistent. He said he stabbed her. He... he described throwing her to the ground... the anger.' Her voice cracked, and she drew in a long breath. 'I didn't believe him at first. I thought he might be trying to hurt me. He does that sometimes. But then I found this.'

She picked up and reached into her bag, pulling out a folded sheet of paper. It was an article from the *Western Mail*, the national newspaper of Wales, reporting Holly's death. The edges were worn, as if it had been handled over and over. 'This was in his sock drawer. I found it before leaving the house. He hides money in there sometimes. Why would he keep it? Why would he keep it if he wasn't involved?'

I took the article from her, my mind a whirl of possibilities and implications. If what Lily was saying was true, the conviction of Alexander Aitken – a case I'd poured my soul into – was built on sand. 'Okay,' I said, my voice steady despite the storm inside me, 'I'm going to need you to give me a full written statement. We'll need to go over every detail. This is incredibly serious.'

She nodded, a fragile determination in her eyes, though her trembling hands betrayed the storm raging within. 'I'll tell you everything. Every word. Whatever it takes. I just want to do what's right.'

For the next twenty minutes or so, Lily poured out her story, her words cascading like a dam had burst, each sentence laden with pain and regret. Her voice wavered, cracking under the weight of the words, but she pushed through, her resolve unyielding. I scribbled notes furiously, my pen scratching against the paper as her story painted a picture so vivid and damning it left me breathless.

Every detail she provided hammered home the gravity of what she was revealing. By the time she finished, my head throbbed. It wasn't just a statement of her husband's guilt – it was a revelation. Lily claimed Tom Rees hadn't just admitted to the murder; he'd disclosed the location of the bladed weapon. If that knife was buried beneath the compost heap, as she said he claimed, it would seal the truth irrevocably. There would be no room for doubt.

After Lily signed her version of events and left the station, I returned to my first-floor office, staring at the statement. My gaze locked onto the words, my thoughts racing like a train about to derail. If Tom Rees had killed Holly Larkin, it meant only one thing: Alexander Aitken was innocent. The man I'd been so certain of – the monster I'd helped put away, the man whose face had haunted the tabloids, darling of TikTok's true crime aficionados – had been telling the truth all along.

The room seemed to shrink around me, the walls pressing in as the enormity of the situation settled over me like an iron shroud. A chill seeped into my bones despite the stuffy heat of the room. How had we missed this? How had *I* missed this? The echoes of my own conviction, my certainty during Aitken's trial, rang in my ears like a cruel taunt. All those nagging doubts that surfaced so insistently on my recent Lanzarote holiday were becoming true. And now, as that reality clawed at me, I grappled with the only question that mattered: what would I do to make it right?

Alone in the oppressive quiet of my office, I felt the weight of the revelation settle like a curse. Every tick of the clock was a reminder of the lives upended by secrets and half-truths. Shadows danced on the walls, echoing the inner turmoil that threatened to consume me. I recalled the fervour of past convictions and the relentless pursuit of justice that had defined my career. Now, with a bitter taste of failure mingling with resolve, I steeled myself to confront the fallout. There was no turning back; the truth had surfaced, and with it came the unbearable demand for redemption.

6

THE SOULMATE

I rang my older brother this morning. For a catch-up. And if I'm honest, to talk things over. He's always been a good listener. And there were things I needed to get off my chest.

'I love Laura to pieces,' I began, almost as soon as he said hello. 'I always have. You know that. Almost since the first day I met her. She's my soulmate. In truth, I adore her. But her job, policing, well, that's another matter entirely. In fairness, she gave me an idea of what her job entailed long before I moved in with her and we formed a family together. And she didn't sugar-coat it – the long hours, the missed family dinners, the late-night calls dragging her from bed. But no amount of warning could have prepared me for the cold, hard reality of life with this particular West Wales detective.'

'Can't be easy.'

I was in full flow now. I get like that sometimes. It just pours out of me. 'It's absolutely not, Ross. It's not just the antisocial hours that wear me down, though they're enough to fray the edges of any relationship. It's some of the crimes. The truly horrendous, gut-wrenching cases that she throws herself into with relentless determination. Cases that linger in her eyes long after she's closed the file. The kind that cast a shadow over her, over us, and seep into the cracks of our home life, no matter how hard she tries to keep them at bay. Some of the horrors she's faced would unnerve the strongest of souls.'

'That bad, eh?'

'And then there's the danger – the unspoken threat that follows her like a shadow, as much a part of her job as the badge she carries. There are menacing people out there, predators who'd think nothing of striking out to protect their secrets. And, at times, some of them have gotten far too close for comfort.'

'Too scary for me.'

I fingered my bead necklace. 'You're not kidding. A case she's dealing with at the moment has put her – and therefore, to some extent, me – under huge pressure. It's the Alexander Aitken case – you may have heard of it. A particularly brutal murder about five years ago, when a young local hairdresser was stabbed six times late one night and left to bleed out in the park, her lifeless body abandoned like discarded rubbish. The sheer savagery of it shocked the entire community, and the media frenzy that followed was relentless. I knew the case was still bothering Laura even before recent events. She'd mentioned it more than once during our holiday, her brow furrowing as she tried – and failed – to leave work behind. But then, a few days ago, everything really spiralled out of control.'

'Really? What happened?'

I shifted in my seat, making myself comfortable. 'It all started when a local woman walked into the police station, apparently pale-faced and shaking, to report that her husband had confessed to the killing. The claim alone was shocking enough, but when he was arrested, he made a full and detailed confession that left no room for ambiguity. Even then, Laura's initial instinct was scepticism, I think more out of hope than expectation. She'd seen it all before: deluded individuals confessing to heinous crimes they'd read about in the tabloids, desperate for attention or recognition. But this was different. The man knew details that had never been released to the public. And when the murder weapon – a long, serrated kitchen knife – was found exactly where he'd said he'd hidden it, everything changed. That was the moment Laura knew the Aitken case had gone horribly, irreparably wrong.

'Alexander Aitken, the man branded a monster, had to be innocent. And that revelation put Laura in the most impossible of positions. Her voice was heavy with resignation when she explained it to me. There was no escape from what was coming. In her words, a shitstorm of criticism was heading her way, and she'd be right in the eye of it.'

'Oh no, horrendous. But I hope it all works out. We'll talk again. I'd better make a move. I need to pop into town for some paint. Dianne wants the lounge decorated.'

And that was it. Our conversation ended and I was left with my thoughts. Feeling a little better, although nothing had changed.

Laura took a chilled bottle of white wine from the fridge almost as soon as she stepped through the door a few hours later, her shoulders visibly sagging with the weight of the day. I watched as she poured us both a generous glass and sat at the kitchen table, her movements deliberate but heavy, as if the simple act of sitting down required all the energy she had left. The lines etched into her face spoke volumes. Events had drained her completely. And she's been getting a lot more headaches than usual, no doubt down to stress. I joined her at the table, pulling out a chair opposite, the scrape of wood against tiles breaking the silence.

'What's wrong, love?' I asked as gently as I could, my voice low so as not to startle her out of her thoughts. I had a good idea what was troubling her, as I'd told Ross – I'd seen the storm brewing for days now – but I knew Laura well enough to understand that she needed to say it herself. Sometimes, just putting the weight into words could lighten the load. I try my very best to be understanding. I really do. But sometimes, the effort feels like pushing against a tide that's determined to drag me under. This time, though, I managed to keep my cool – even if I say so myself. But it's not always easy. The stresses of our lives, the constant push and pull of responsibilities, weigh heavy. They can creep up on me, filling the gaps between moments of calm, and before I know it, the pressure threatens to spill over. And when it does, when the walls close in, understanding feels like the most monumental task in the world.

But, for all that, I had to put Laura's needs first. Because if I didn't, I feared for the consequences. She's a strong woman physically and emotionally. But there's only so much anyone can take.

Laura's fingers wrapped tightly around the stem of her wine glass, and for a moment, she didn't speak, her eyes fixed on the table as though the swirling wood grain might provide some elusive answer. I waited, giving her the space she needed. Because being the best partner I could meant knowing when to push and when to simply listen. And tonight, she needed to be heard.

Eventually, after what seemed an age but was in reality a few seconds, she looked at me across the pine table and sighed. Her weary eyes found mine with an unspoken plea for understanding.

'Oh, Jan... It's this Aitken thing. No surprise there. I know I don't stop banging on about it. I had to tell the chief super the full facts of the case today, as he sat there gloating in his oversized office, on that elevated seat of his. Like a frigging throne surrounded by his golf trophies. Nigel Halliday, what a total and utter prick that twat of a man truly is. I wish he'd piss off back to the Met. But no luck there. Seems I'm stuck with him.'

Laura's voice was a blend of exhaustion and simmering anger, each word laced with the frustration of someone battling a system designed to deflect blame. She twisted the stem of her wine glass, the golden liquid catching the bright light of the kitchen.

I nodded my sympathetic understanding. I knew full well what Laura thought of the head of the Criminal Investigation Department. She'd told me often enough. And having met the arrogant prat a couple of times socially, she has my sympathy. If he was my boss, I'd have resigned long before now. 'That bad, eh? What did he say?' I ventured, keeping my tone neutral, though I could feel the undercurrent of my own irritation bubbling beneath the surface.

Laura frowned hard, massaging the back of her neck as though trying to knead away the tension that had taken root there. 'Oh, you know how Halliday loves to criticise. His biggest concern seems to be how Aitken's innocence is going to look for the force. And that's all my fault, apparently. Not that Halliday raised any concerns at all when Aitken was arrested and charged. It's only now with hindsight he's got something to say for himself. I'm going to be the scapegoat for this one. That's crystal clear. He's already distancing himself from every decision that was made at the time. Even though he signed off on them all. The man's like a frigging politician. Twisting the truth as it suits him. One blatant lie after another.'

Her words hung in the air like a dark cloud, the frustration etched into every syllable. I took a deep breath, hoping the telling was enough for her. I wasn't feeling at my best. There's only so much I can take, too. 'So, what happens now?' I asked, wishing I didn't have to. That we could talk about ordinary things, not involving criminals or work disputes.

'Tom Rees has been charged with murder and remanded in custody. And as for Aitken, that's where the hassle really starts. I'll have to let the lawyers know about the new evidence. And then Aitken's legal team will no doubt apply to the Court of Appeal for his conviction to be quashed. In some cases there's a retrial. But I can't see that being necessary for Aitken. It's all too clear for that. He'll be out of prison soon enough. And it's going to be all over the news. As will I. That's my hopes of a promotion right out of the window.'

I nodded, taking it all in. 'And you'll have to tell the victim's family.'

Laura groaned, her head in her hands. The gesture spoke volumes, the weight of her responsibilities pressing down on her like a physical force. 'Yeah, yeah, that too.'

I couldn't help myself, my true feelings leaking out despite my best efforts. 'Think about it. You could do something else. You're well-qualified with a degree and plenty of management experience. There's any number of other jobs you could do. Do you remember a few months back when you said as a kid you dreamed of being a teacher? Why not give that a go? Shorter hours and think of all those holidays!'

Laura made a face, then drained her glass with a practised efficiency that spoke of long experience. 'Oh, come on. Not this again. I'm going to be a copper till I retire. You need to accept that.'

I bit my tongue, swallowing my words. I'd had enough. It was a conversation we'd had many times before. 'Okay, I hear you.

Message received loud and clear. Sorry to be a pain. Are you ready for some food? There's a shepherd's pie in the oven.'

Laura's smile was faint but genuine, her tone softening when she spoke in her familiar Brummie accent, now tinged with an unmistakable hint of musical Welsh. 'That would be great. Thanks, Jan. I know I'm sometimes too much. I really do appreciate all you do for me. I don't know what I'd do without you.'

I watched her for a long moment, feeling the layers of exhaustion and fierce determination settle like a heavy cloak. In that quiet interlude, as the enticing aroma of shepherd's pie mingled with the fading light, I realised that our love was our last refuge against the relentless cruelty of our everyday battles. It was a fragile yet defiant flame amid the encroaching gloom – a promise that no matter how harsh the world might be, we would endure together, our hearts intertwined and our souls bound by an unspoken strength that even the darkest storms couldn't extinguish.

7

THE LAWYER

Confidentially, there's something about Alexander Aitken that chills me to the core. I saw the files retrieved from his phone and computer during the investigation – the kind of content that persists in your mind long after you've looked away, like a shadow you can't shake. Guilty of the Larkin murder or not, he exudes an unsettling aura, a predator's cunning just beneath the surface of his otherwise polished demeanour. And then there's the surgical precision of his skillset – an ironic twist that makes my skin crawl. I wouldn't want him within ten feet of me or anyone I care about with a scalpel in his hand, no matter how glowing his reputation might once have been as a surgeon. Because maybe he'll be back in his job at some future date, either here in Wales, or perhaps further afield.

Yet, despite every instinct screaming at me to keep my distance, I found myself compelled by duty to see Aitken at Swansea Prison. The grim, institutional air clung to me as I entered, every clang of metal gates behind me echoing like a warning. I was there to take his instructions, to hear his plea to apply to the Court of Appeal. The words felt bitter on my tongue even before they were spoken. Duty or not, it felt like walking willingly into the lion's den.

I could see the rage simmering just beneath the surface of Aitken's eyes as I sat opposite him in the harshly lit, sterile office reserved for those kinds of encounters. The fluorescent lighting above cast a cold, clinical glow, making every line of tension on his face stand out starkly. His knuckles were white as he gripped the edge of the table, his jaw clenched so tightly it was a wonder his teeth didn't crack under the pressure. But as unnerving as his presence was, I really couldn't blame him for the fury radiating off him like an almost palpable force.

Five years. Half a decade behind bars for a crime that the evidence now proved he didn't commit. It's a staggering injustice, one that would break most people – but Aitken, for all his unnerving demeanour, sat upright, composed, his blue eyes drilling into mine with an intensity that bordered on unsettling.

Being a deviant, as his digital history so clearly painted him, doesn't make him a murderer. And as strange and difficult as the man undoubtedly is, the truth is clear: he's entitled to his freedom. And more than that, he's entitled to financial compensation for the years stolen from him – years labelled a monster, his reputation shredded almost beyond repair.

I could feel the weight of that responsibility pressing down on me as I met his gaze, resolute despite the unease swirling in my gut. I'll do everything in my power to facilitate his release and secure what justice can still be salvaged for him. As quickly and efficiently as humanly possible.

He glared at me with unblinking eyes, eyes that seemed to pierce right through me. The intensity in his stare was oppressive, the kind that makes the hairs on the back of your neck stand on end. His voice had a hard edge when he spoke.

'All right, I've heard everything you've said. But how long's it all going to take? I want out of this hellhole, and fast. Every day here is like a damned purgatory.'

I swallowed twice, my throat dry despite years of courtroom experience and countless tense exchanges. Nothing about his case – or the British legal system – would move quickly, no matter how strong the evidence. But I knew before the words even left my lips that Aitken wouldn't take kindly to the truth. 'I'm afraid it's not as simple as that, Alexander,' I began, choosing my words carefully. 'There's a set process we have to follow. And that takes time.'

His glare darkened, those hateful, ice-cold eyes boring into me, making me shudder. 'Explain yourself, man. And make it succinct for once in your life. None of your usual waffle. Come on, get on with it, I'm listening. And I prefer Professor Aitken to Alexander, thank you. We're not friends.'

I drew in a steadying breath, my voice measured but firm. 'The first stage is to make the application, which I'll begin today as soon as I get back to my office. That application, once submitted, will be reviewed by a single judge, who will then decide if leave to appeal will be granted.'

Before I could even prepare for his reaction, Aitken's hand slammed down on the table with a force that echoed through the sterile room. The sharp sound startled me, and I instinctively leaned back, my chair tilting precariously. His voice erupted, his words propelled by sheer fury. Spittle flew from his mouth, small globules spraying my face. 'You said *if*! What the hell do you mean by *if*?'

I wiped my face with the back of my hand, forcing myself to stay composed. 'I'm sorry, Alexander... Professor Aitken. I should have made myself clear. I'm 100 per cent certain the application will be approved in your case.'

His fists clenched tightly, the knuckles whitening as his

expression tightened. 'Then why the hell didn't you say that in the first place? Get your act together, man. You're supposed to be a professional.'

The temptation to rise to my feet and walk out of there was almost overwhelming. Every instinct screamed at me to escape the oppressive, volatile atmosphere. But I'm conscientious by nature, and despite Aitken's unreasonable behaviour, I was determined to finish what I'd started. For his sake, and for the sake of justice, I refused to let his hostility derail the process.

I sat a little straighter, squaring my shoulders, and resolved to see it through to the end. And then he asked a question I wasn't looking forward to answering at all. The wheels of justice can move agonisingly slowly at times. 'How long before I'm out of this shithole?'

I took a deep breath, steadying myself before answering. My throat felt tight, the atmosphere of the room wrapping itself around me like a noose. The white walls seemed to close in, amplifying the tension that crackled between us. Clearing my throat, I outlined the facts as clearly as I could, my voice measured, deliberate. What else could I do? 'I can only tell you the usual timescale,' I began. 'Although that may differ for better or worse in your case. Many factors not in my control play a part.' I kept my tone neutral, professional, even as I felt the weight of his stare. 'The granting of permission to appeal can take anything from one to three months. Although, in some rare cases, it has taken up to six.'

The contours of Aitken's face shifted, his expression darkening as his eyes narrowed to virtual slits. 'Six months! Are you kidding me?'

His voice was a low growl, the anger simmering beneath it unmistakable. I'd seen that fury in his eyes before, a volatile, barely restrained fire. He snarled his words like a caged animal ready to pounce.

Instinctively, I edged my chair back a few inches, the metallic scrape echoing in the suffocating silence. And then I pressed on, my voice steady despite the tension. 'Once leave to appeal is granted, it can take up to a year or more for the hearing to be listed. I would, of course, stress the urgency of your case and the significant public interest involved. And with luck, we might get your case to the appeal court within three to six months of leave being granted. But if I were you, I'd prepare yourself for the worst. That way, you won't be disappointed.'

For a moment, I thought Aitken might explode. His nostrils flared as his hands gripped the edge of the table. But instead, he fixed me with a glower so intense it made my stomach twist. When he finally spoke, his voice was a hiss, slow and deliberate, each word dripping with contempt. 'I want you to write to every one of the moronic bastards who played any part in putting me here. I want you to tell them *exactly* how badly they cocked up, and that they have the imprisonment of an innocent man on their conscience. Remind them that karma is real and that they'll pay a heavy price for their wrongdoing. I want you to prepare the letter today. And I want to read it before it's sent. Have I made myself clear?'

I swallowed hard, my pulse quickening as his demands hung in the air. 'I, err... I fully understand your motives. And I'm sure I'd feel much the same in your position. But I'd strongly advise against. Best to keep a low profile until your release. I think that's for the best.'

His eyes bore into mine, unrelenting, his lips curling into something between a sneer and a snarl. 'Oh, you do, do you?'

I nodded quickly, grasping for a positive. 'And then, once the court process is complete, we can apply for financial compensation for what has to be considered a serious miscarriage of justice.'

His voice cut through the tension like a blade. 'And you'll get on with all this straight away, will you? No delays, no more screw-ups?'

I nodded again, relieved the meeting was nearing its end. In truth, Aitken scared me in ways I can't quite articulate. There is something about him – a coiled energy, a barely veiled hostility – that sets my nerves on edge. 'As of now, your case is my number one priority.' I'd said it with all the conviction I could muster. But for him, it seemed nothing was ever enough.

Aitken leaned forward, his lips peeling back to reveal clenched teeth, a feral snarl escaping as his voice rose to new heights. 'It had better be,' he spat, 'because screw this up in any way at all, and karma could come for you, too. I suggest you never forget that even for a single second. Carve it in tablets of stone.'

Aitken's words lingered in the air, a chilling threat that seemed to wrap around me like a vice, squeezing the air from my body. The room, already sterile, felt even more oppressive as his voice echoed in my ears, a haunting reminder of the ill-concealed rage I'd just witnessed. My hands trembled slightly as I gathered my papers, trying to maintain an air of professional composure that felt increasingly like a fragile mask.

I told myself his anger was understandable and justified as I left the suffocating confines of the prison building and stepped into the biting wind of the car park. The stark grey sky above mirrored the heaviness in my chest, the clouds thick and foreboding. I rationalised that his implied threats were nothing more than the desperate words of a man pushed to his limits. But as I unlocked my car with the press of a button and slid into the driver's seat, the unease clung to me like a second skin.

My drive back along the M4 to Carmarthen was a blur of rain-slicked tarmac and the rhythmic sweep of wipers against the windshield. Each mile stretched under the weight of my thoughts, the encroaching dusk deepening my inner gloom. Every flash of lightning in the distance seemed to echo Aitken's promise, each rumble of thunder a reminder of the relentless force of fate. I gripped the steering wheel tighter as memories of his piercing glare and harsh words churned in my mind, leaving me with the inescapable feeling that the past was determined to catch up with us all.

8
THE SURGEON

The last eleven months, two weeks, and three days of my prison sentence felt like a never-ending eternity, a relentless purgatory where every minute stretched into an hour, every hour into a day. Time dragged its feet, mocking me with its sluggish pace. But I made the best of it, because that's the kind of man I am. Better than most. Superior. An alpha – physically, intellectually – far more intelligent and productive than the common man or woman. Yes, I used the time to my advantage, pushing the limits of my confinement to plan, crafting revenge in the name of both justice and science.

I pictured their faces in my mind, each who had wronged me, etched with the arrogance of judgement. I made diligent mental records, cataloguing every slight, every betrayal. Each name and face became a chapter in my mental ledger of vengeance. Megan, that first victim – or future lab rat, as I like to think of her – escaped my grasp, slipping away into the night as I hurried off, driven by the fear of discovery. A miscalculation, nothing more. But now her time will come.

And then there's Detective Inspector Laura Kesey. The mindless, sanctimonious Brummie detective bitch, who orchestrated my downfall and played such a pivotal role in my prolonged imprisonment. I don't think I've ever hated anyone more than I hate her. Not even the school predator who shattered my innocence at the age of nine. He's on the list too, of course. I'll find him one fine day, and when I do, he won't die easily. I can promise you that.

But Kesey? She's close to the top of my list. Her name is burned into my mind, her smug face a constant reminder of the injustice I've endured. I've devised particularly interesting and informative methods for her demise. Techniques inspired by the most merciless Gestapo officers who ravaged Europe during World War II. Methods designed to inflict maximum suffering – to educate her on the price of her insolence, to make her regret every decision that led to my incarceration. And I'll study her every reaction – the way her body tenses, the tremor in her voice, the fear in her eyes that she'll try and fail to mask. Every scream, every plea, every desperate attempt to bargain will become data, accurately recorded for my future academic paper. I'll chronicle it all, dissecting her physical and psychological responses like the surgeon I am, peeling back the layers of her humanity to expose the raw nerves beneath.

Because this isn't just personal, though it is undeniably satisfying. No, much of what I do, for all its exhilarating fun, as I've said before, is in the name of medical science. The pursuit of knowledge demands sacrifice, as Joseph Mengele understood better than most. A doctor like me, his methods, for all their controversy, held a clinical brilliance. And now I understand it too. I've come to appreciate the necessity of his work – of my work.

And soon the world will see and understand. They'll read my findings, marvel at the depths I've dared to explore. But first,

Kesey will endure, and I'll learn. Every second of her intense suffering will serve a greater purpose. Science demands no less. And I'll record it all on film, capturing every brutal second in pristine detail so I can analyse and relive it whenever necessary. The flicker of terror in her eyes, the sharp intake of breath as realisation dawns, the guttural screams that echo through the soundproofed room – all preserved for careful study. You see, I've never actually taken a captive before. Never had the luxury of time to fully explore my... interests.

But that's all about to change. Because I've evolved, honed my craft, and embraced my true potential as a scientist and killer. Thinking time behind those prison walls gave me that – hours, days, months to refine my methods and imagine scenarios in excruciating detail. The sterile monotony of incarceration carved out a space for clarity, for focus. The one positive thing to emerge from that hellish experience. Not that I'm grateful, mind you. Gratitude would suggest some form of acceptance or forgiveness. No, I'm not grateful. But I can admit that prison played its part, forcing me to bide my time and sharpen my resolve. And now, with my newfound purpose, the world will finally see the depths of my genius.

Yes, Megan will be first, that one simpering girl who escaped me all those years ago, when I finally acted so impulsively on my longings and interests. That only seems fair. She deserves what's coming, and I'll deliver her reckoning at a time when it best suits my purpose. And then, Kesey. Always Kesey. If the stars align as I hope, she will be the next to pay. Her downfall will be the pinnacle of my revenge, the masterpiece of my retribution. And it's only a matter of time.

But before all that, I have to prepare. The groundwork must be flawless, every detail considered and executed with precision. And now I can move forward with confidence and urgency.

Because last week, I was taken to the Court of Appeal at the Royal Courts of Justice in London. The grandeur of the building, with its towering arches and solemn air, seemed almost mocking at the time. My case, after years of wrongful imprisonment, was finally heard. The new evidence was undeniable, and the decision came swiftly. A day later, at ten fifteen on a grey morning, I walked out of the courtroom as a free man, the weight of the past dissolving with each step I took away from that place.

I caught a train from Paddington after indulging in a vegetarian lunch, the first meal in years that wasn't served on a plastic tray. As the countryside blurred past the train window, my thoughts raced ahead to my sprawling Carmarthenshire country home. The anticipation swelled within me, a thrill I hadn't felt in so long. I'm fortunate to still have a fair amount of cash in the bank, close to a million. Enough to ensure that, even before the compensation money rolls in, I can begin executing my ideas.

The first step is constructing a research lab – a concealed haven of innovation and control – buried deep in my garden. The basic structure was originally installed as a nuclear bunker in the eighties, a relic of Cold War paranoia, but its true potential lies in what I'll transform it into. That work begins next week. Inside, it will be a sanctuary of precision and purpose. My collection of medical scalpels and various DIY tools – saws, drills, and the like – are already waiting at my house to serve a far more profound purpose. But there's still more to procure. Not locally, of course. I'll mitigate the risks. A state-of-the-art camera and sound system will be essential, installed by experts to capture every moment of my research. Every frame needs to be flawless, every detail preserved. A camera phone simply won't suffice; mediocrity has no place in my work.

No more killing in Britain's far-flung towns and cities for me. The days of roaming the country, seeking out prey with the thrill of the hunt coursing through my veins, are over. Now, my focus has shifted, my methods refined. Prior to my incarceration, the idea of utilising the bunker had seemed too risky, too close to home. It felt like an indulgence that could unravel everything. But after countless hours of intellectual deliberation during those long, empty prison days, I've come to a different conclusion.

If I temper my instincts and keep my hunger for death in check, the advantages of the bunker become glaringly obvious. A secure, private haven – a sanctum where I can work undisturbed, dissecting the mysteries of life and death with clinical precision. It's a place where time will bend to my will, where hours will stretch endlessly, allowing me to study, to explore, to indulge in the pursuit of knowledge.

And the possibilities are intoxicating. The thought of uninterrupted hours, of subjects carefully chosen and prepared, fills me with excitement. There's so much to learn, so much scientific value in every cut, every reaction, every last breath. But caution will be my constant companion. Recklessness has no place for me. Every step must be calculated, every move deliberate. Success lies in restraint, in mastering the chaos within. Only then can I truly achieve what I've envisioned.

I've occasionally toyed with the idea of re-establishing my previous role as a hospital surgeon, reclaiming the prestige and authority that came with it. But I'm awaiting a big compensation payout. And for now, my research demands my full attention. Operating has its pleasures, of course, but this... this is something far greater. This is legacy. I can always revel in my newfound celebrity, savouring the intoxicating rush of recognition and the power it brings. Attention, now a constant companion, is mine to summon at will, a flick of my presence enough to command every room I enter.

Finally, before I set my computer aside and head for my bed

for much-needed rest, I thought I'd share another update. The media frenzy surrounding my case has been relentless. My handsome face has been splashed across the national UK and Welsh evening news, the fawning journalists eager to tell my story. They showered me with sympathy and congratulations, their questions laced with admiration. On social media, I've become a sensation thanks to influencers such as Bella, a young lady who never fails to champion my cause, though I have little interest in her world. Still, the notoriety serves a purpose. I've been invited to appear on a morning TV chat show in a few days' time, a ten-minute segment to recount my ordeal. I've agreed, of course. The more I can shape the narrative, the better it will serve me in the long run.

Until my research is complete, and my findings are ready for the world, my activities will remain a secret. And when the time comes, when everything is in place, I'll vanish to some sunny island, far away from prying eyes.

But until then, there is much to do. Getting caught was never a part of my plan. One prison sentence was more than enough for one lifetime. I'm never going back there. It's a joy to be free.

Now, as I settle into the liberating quiet of freedom, a fierce exhilaration courses through me – a promise of retribution and revelation. Every calculated move, every carefully orchestrated detail, fuels the burning certainty that those who wronged me will face their reckoning. I find solace in the thought that each piece of evidence, every stored file, adds weight to my inevitable resurgence. The stark clarity of my purpose shimmers in the silence of my reclaimed life. No longer bound by the chains of past injustice, I am free to pursue a destiny defined solely by my own brilliant, irrepressible will.

9

THE SURVIVOR

It's peculiar, isn't it, how life can hinge on a single, seemingly inconsequential moment? Not the colossal, earth-shattering events – no hurricanes, no terminal diagnoses, no heart-wrenching farewells to loved ones – but the quiet, unassuming instances that barely register at the time. You take a left turn instead of a right. You jump onto a bus that's not your usual, or linger just a few minutes too long in a place you didn't plan to be. And in that small sliver of time, fate sharpens its claws.

That's how it was for me. And this is my story. A tale I wouldn't wish on my worst enemy. I was only sixteen when I crossed paths with the man who turned my world upside down, dragging me into a nightmare I still can't escape. He offered nothing but misery, a shadow that lingers long after he disappeared from sight.

Ten years have passed since then. Yet, no matter how far I try to move on, the events of that time still cling to me, shaping every part of my life like an indelible scar. It all happened around 2 a.m. on a warm June night, just two days after my sixteenth birthday. The world seemed harmless in its slumber as I wandered alone through the narrow, silent backstreets of Tenby after a late-night party. Beautiful Tenby. Once my happy place. But now stained with the memory of events I'd prefer to forget.

The air was thick with the scent of salt and flowers. The lovely walled town was still, shadows cast across the streets, and I thought nothing of it. But then, in the blink of an eye, *he* appeared – a masked figure who would carve himself into my psyche, his presence as cold as death itself.

The sound of his footsteps still echoes in my head. They started slow, deliberate, getting louder as he approached, then faster, faster, a predator's rhythm. I'd laughed to myself at first, clutching my keys tighter in my pocket. *You're being paranoid*, I'd thought. *People walk behind other people all the time. Nothing to worry about.* Until there was something to worry about.

I remember his eyes – blue, chilling, like shards of ice that seemed to pierce straight through me. And his voice, a low, menacing, animalistic growl that crawled under my skin and lodged there, a haunting echo I'll never forget. That was the moment. The one I'll never escape. The one that changed everything forever.

The memories come in fragments now, rarely straight lines. A warm hand clamped over my mouth from behind. The smell of sweat and metal. The flash of a blade catching the streetlight as he pulled me round and faced me. And the pain. Hot, searing, gut-wrenching pain as the blade sunk into my body. I remember thinking, *This is it. This is how I die.* But I didn't die. Somehow, by a strange quirk of fate, I'm still here to tell my tale, the memories biting at the edges of my mind like shadows that refuse to fade.

My name is Megan Morgan, or Meg as I'm known to friends and family. Nothing very remarkable about that, is there? Just another name, like so many others, fading into the faceless crowd. Maybe it stirs a memory – a fleeting whisper of recognition – or maybe it doesn't. It's been a long time since my face featured in the headlines, a decade since my name was spoken with the sharp edges of curiosity, pity, or disdain. Ten long years since the world saw me as something more than a shadow. I'm still young, of course, though I feel like a ghost of the carefree girl I once was, a pale reflection stripped of colour and light. The joy that used to define me is long gone, snuffed out by trauma that clings to me like a shroud.

I opened my eyes in that suffocating Pembrokeshire hospital ward hours after the attack. The walls, sterile and white, seemed to close in. The fluorescent lights blazed with harsh intensity, their electric hum mingling with the sharp, rhythmic beeping of machines tethered to me, whispering that my survival was just another mundane fact.

But it's not. Not to me. For the world, it's routine, but for me, it's still a bad dream with no end. I am alive – when I shouldn't be – and the weight of that truth can be crushing. Why me when so many others die?

His masked face. It's all I see when I reach for sleep. That stare – calculating, and so detached. It was as if he wasn't even human in that moment, like some switch had flipped, and all the warmth and humanity drained out of him. It wasn't supposed to happen like that. The night was ordinary. Moonlight dancing on the pavements. I could have gone home earlier. Or I could have called someone. Hell, I could've just stayed in the caravan and not gone out at all. But 'could've' doesn't change a thing. No one's going to change what happened, no matter how much I wish they could. It's as simple as that – tragically, undeniably simple.

Psychological therapy has helped. To a point. Talking, CBT – all the usual. But not enough. Never enough. And certainly not as much as I hoped. The doctors said my survival was a miracle. The knife missed anything vital by millimetres. Just millimetres! A fraction of space, the smallest margin, and I'm still breathing. How do I make sense of all that? How do I accept that my survival wasn't skill or strength or even some heroic intervention? But just luck. Dumb, blind luck. Nothing more than that.

And then there's the guilt, of course. It's insidious, seeping in during the quiet moments when I lie awake at night grasping for fitful sleep. Why me? Why am I alive when so many others – better people, kinder people – don't get a second chance? I can't stop asking questions. Who was he? Why did he do it? Why me? Did I look like an easy target? Did my masked attacker even care who I was, or was I just... there? And worst of all, will he ever find me again, creeping through the shadows on some dark moonless night, even after all these years?

He slipped through the cracks, you see, evading the grasp of justice, never hauled into the glare of a courtroom to face the enormity of his crime. No handcuffs bit into his wrists, no cell swallowed him whole like the rabid beast he is. Justice turned its back, leaving behind an open wound – a rancid, festering thing that aches in the quiet hours. The lack of closure is a burden that never leaves me, its icy breath brushing my neck, murmuring dark promises that he's still out there somewhere, lurking, his eyes watching, his hunger waiting. And who knows? Maybe he is.

And so leaving my Carmarthen rental flat has become something of a challenge. A task that sometimes requires reserves of strength I don't possess. The walls, once a neutral backdrop to my life, have morphed into a suffocating cage, closing in on me day by day. I work from home, my connection to the outside world reduced to sterile, disembodied exchanges online. My flat, no longer a sanctuary, has transformed into a self-imposed prison. My fears and insecurities are as unyielding as any iron bars, keeping me trapped in a cycle of isolation and dread. Every creak, every distant murmur from the street sets my nerves on edge. I flinch at the slightest noise, my heart hammering against my ribs, each beat a reminder of my vulnerability. When necessity forces me to venture out into the world, it feels like stepping onto a battlefield. My eyes dart from one man to the next, scanning every face, every gesture, desperate to spot him before he spots me. But his presence is everywhere, a phantom haunting every corner of my mind. Any male voice, no matter how friendly or innocuous, becomes his, dripping with menace and malice.

And so, I retreat. Always back to my one-bedroom abode as quickly as my legs will carry me, slamming the door shut and locking it tight against the outside world. The moment the bolt slides into place, I lean against the door, chest heaving, eyes closed, as if the barrier could shield me from the memories that refuse to let me go.

But for all that, I'd been doing reasonably well this week – or at least as well as someone like me can hope to manage. Only two bouts of tears, a small reduction in my medication, and even a fleeting sense of achievement after visiting my lovely sister on the outskirts of town. An hour was all I could bear before making my escape, but even that felt like a victory. Pride accompanied me home, a rare companion, its fragile presence barely noticeable until it was shattered.

I saw him, you see, the man who hurt me. Not in person, but on TV. My pulse quickened, breath catching in my throat as the Welsh evening news played out before me. Because there he was, his face framed in the glow of the screen, speaking to a reporter who was unnervingly familiar.

I stepped closer to the television, my entire body shaking, each movement heavy with dread. His eyes – those cold, piercing blue eyes – burned through the screen and into my soul. I'd seen them before, in my nightmares, where they stalked me relentlessly. And the voice – God, that voice. It was unmistakable, slithering into my ears like a snake, coiling around my thoughts. Threats, promises of violence, whispered words laced with malice. He'd said he'd kill me once.

But hold on. Was it him? Was it *really* him? Was he there now, on my television screen, seemingly haunting my reality as he did my dreams?

My chest tightened, a scream rising in my throat but catching there, strangled by the sheer weight of it all. It was him, wasn't it? The man who'd attacked me? The monster who'd left me for dead?

His image flickered like a ghost from my past, a cruel trick. I could feel the room closing in around me, the walls shrinking, the air thick with dread as though it carried his scent. My body trembled uncontrollably as I dragged my eyes away, my movements jerky and desperate, like a puppet on frayed strings. I fumbled for the brown plastic bottle, snatching it from the counter with a clammy hand and tipping an anti-anxiety pill into my palm.

The pill hit my tongue, bitter and dry, as I leaned over the kitchen tap to gulp down a mouthful of water. I slumped onto the nearby sofa, its fabric rough against my sweaty hands, my mind spinning into chaos. Each thought collided with the next, a mix of panic and doubt crashing through my fragile mind. Never more sure, yet never so confused. What the hell should I do? Dial 999? Have him arrested?

But... no. Hold on! Doubts crept in again like shadows at dusk, insidious and unwelcome. I'd been wrong before. So many times. Seeing my attacker when it wasn't him at all. Perhaps I should do nothing. Nothing at all.

My chest heaved as I fought for control, my breathing shallow and uneven. *Deep breaths, Meg. Out through the mouth, in through the nose. That's it. Steady now. Don't be so silly, girl. Your mind's playing tricks on you again, weaving its cruel little narratives. It can't be him. Of course not. Not a professor, an eminent doctor, with his disarming smile and air of self-assured sophistication. A man so polished he could pass for a saint. Get a grip, girl. Don't be so ridiculous. He's already suffered one miscarriage of justice. The reporter said as much. Don't make a fool of yourself. You're wrong. So very wrong.*

Past discussions with my psychologist came insistently to mind, her calm, measured voice an island of reason amid the storm. 'It's all part of the PTSD,' she'd said when I'd talked of such things before. 'Your mind will conjure ghosts, shadows of trauma that feel as real as the air you breathe. But they're not. They can't hurt you.' Her words wavered, tenuous and distant, like a lifeline fraying at the edges. I clung to them desperately, trying to remind myself that my reactions were symptoms – a cruel trick played by a battered subconscious. *Deep breaths, Meg. That's it. Steady now. Try to relax.*

Yes, yes, best to do nothing at all, I thought, offering myself encouragement, my inner voice uncertain. And yet, the image on the screen, those eyes, that voice, seared into my mind with a vividness that defied logic. Even with my eyes clenched tightly shut, it was there – etched into the darkness like a brand, daring me to believe it wasn't just another phantom born of fear.

And so I switched off the TV and sat in the suffocating quiet, haunted by questions that wouldn't let go despite my internal reasoning. Was Professor Aitken my attacker? He looked like him. He even sounded like him. Or was I doing it again? Seeing ghosts where there were none? Twisting my own memories?

Of course I was. My attacker on the telly? Ridiculous! I was wrong, wrong, so very wrong. That was the only thing that made any sense at all.

10

THE SOULMATE

I'm worried about Laura. So worried I can't sleep, can't even close my eyes without the weight of it pressing down on my chest. The bedside clock ticks on, a slow, hollow rhythm that seems to grow louder with every passing second. It mocks my restlessness, filling the silence with its cold indifference.

Laura's strong – stronger than anyone I've ever known. But even steel can fracture under enough pressure. She wears that brave face like armour, but I see the cracks beneath it. The way her smile falters, the way her shoulders sag ever so slightly when she thinks no one's looking. She carries the weight of her world alone, as if she doesn't want to burden anyone else. Police work can do that to a girl. It can blunt your edges. I know Laura better than anyone. And I can see it's killing her.

When she came through the door this evening just after six, I knew something was wrong before she even said a word. She didn't need to. Her eyes gave her away, glossy and wet, the tears threatening to spill over at any moment. She didn't look at me, didn't even pause to say hello. She just busied herself with the small, meaningless rituals – kicking off her shoes, hanging up her coat – as if doing so might hold her together. But her hands trembled as she reached for the coat hook, and the sight of it made my stomach twist. She's the love of my life, my soulmate, and her wellbeing matters as much as my own.

I so wanted to tell her to stop, to sit down, to let me help. But I knew better. Laura doesn't ask for help, and she doesn't take it well when it's offered.

I'd have suggested another holiday. Somewhere far away, somewhere warm and bright, where the sun might burn away the shadows clinging to her. But even in Lanzarote, her work had followed us. It had seeped into our conversations, lingered in the silences between us. No matter where we go, she can't seem to leave it behind. And the Aitken case still seems to be getting to her more than most. I can understand why.

She needs time off. Proper time – weeks, maybe months. But that's a fight I'll never win. Laura? Take time off? See her GP? Get signed off sick with the worry and stress? The very idea is laughable. She'd sooner walk into a blazing inferno than admit she needs a break.

It wasn't until late – a couple of hours after Ed had finished his homework and gone upstairs with his iPad – that she finally opened up. And even then, it felt like I had to drag the truth out of her, piece by painful piece. It's always the same.

'Come on, Laura. What's wrong? I can tell something's bothering you. Has been all evening. It's written all over your face.'

Her eyes flicked towards me briefly, then back to the TV. 'It's nothing. I'm just tired, that's all.'

I wasn't buying it. I never do. 'Is it work again?' I pressed, not willing to let it go. Because she matters to me, really matters, more than anything. 'Is that what's getting to you? Because I can see you're struggling.'

She sighed – a long, heavy groan like she was trying to let go of all the stress in one breath. 'Halliday's been on my back about the Aitken case again. The bastard never lets up. No surprise there. He saw the same interview we did on the news. Aitken saying I got it horribly wrong. That I'm to blame for his wrongful conviction.'

My jaw tightened at the name. Halliday. Just hearing it made my blood boil. I'd lost count of how many times I'd wanted to storm into his office and let him know exactly what I thought of him. 'Oh, God, Nigel dickhead Halliday. That man's a prick,' I said, my voice low but sharp, brimming with disdain.

Laura's lips twitched into the faintest of smiles. Halliday brings out the worst in me. And in Laura too. 'That's one word for him,' she said. 'I can think of a few more. I've called him most of them.'

I reached out and took her hand in mine. 'All this stress with the Aitken case – it'll blow over. You know it will. These things always do.'

She shook her head, her eyes dimming as the flicker of hope faded. 'I'm not so sure. Aitken wrote to the chief constable. He's suing the force.'

I pulled my head back. 'Can he do that?'

Laura nodded. 'Apparently, seems so.' She forced a quickly vanishing smile. 'And if Halliday had his way, he'd probably make me cover the compensation myself. Deduct it monthly from my salary.'

'Well, thank God he can't, then,' I muttered, trying to lighten the mood. 'We're skint enough as it is.'

Laura stood up, gently brushing my hand away. 'I'm going to make a coffee. Do you fancy one?'

I shook my head. 'Decaf tea for me,' I said. 'Too late for caffeine. I'm awake half the night as it is.'

I followed Laura into the kitchen, where the bright fluorescent light overhead cast long shadows on the walls. I'd been debating whether to bring up what I'd seen earlier, but now, watching her move as if carrying the weight of the world, I decided I had to. Laura hates secrets, always has, so I find honesty is best.

'There's something I need to tell you,' I said hesitantly.

She turned, the kettle in her hand. 'What is it?'

I looked at her sheepishly, a small part of me still wondering if I was doing the right thing. 'I was in two minds about saying anything at all. But I thought about it, and I know you wouldn't want me to keep it to myself. I thought I saw Aitken earlier today. Just before I picked Ed up from school.'

Her hand froze mid-motion. 'Where?' she asked, only the one word.

'Outside the house, sitting in a car,' I said, taking a seat at the kitchen table.

She set the kettle down with a clatter and stared at me, her brow furrowed. 'Our house?'

I nodded twice. 'I'm pretty sure it was him. He drove off as I left.'

Laura frowned hard, eyes narrowing. 'Same direction?'

'Yeah, right up until the time I slowed to park near the school. He overtook me then. And that was it, I didn't see him again.'

Laura's gaze was piercing now, sharp enough to cut. 'Are you sure it was Aitken?'

'Um, yeah, I think so. Ninety per cent,' I said, trying to sound more confident than I felt. It was starting to feel a bit like an interrogation. All of a sudden, I wasn't certain of very much at all.

She didn't sit. Didn't blink. Just stared at me. 'What kind of car?'

'Four doors. Dark blue, I think. Or it could have been black.'

'Did you get the number plate?'

'No,' I admitted, guilt creeping into my voice. 'I didn't think to look. You're the detective, not me.'

Finally, she sat down across from me, her face pale and unreadable. 'If it was Aitken, what the hell was he doing here?'

'Beats me... Does he live nearby?'

Laura shook her head. 'No,' she said tightly. 'He's got a big detached place a few miles out of town past the hospital. We searched it at the time of his arrest. Seven bedrooms and a couple of acres of grounds. Impressive. Must be worth a fortune.'

The silence stretched between us, thick and heavy. I finally asked the question that was playing on my mind. 'You don't think he's dangerous, do you?' I said, my voice barely above a whisper.

Laura didn't answer right away. And when she did, her tone was measured, deliberate, as if she was choosing her words carefully for fear of upsetting me. 'I can't say I like him. The man's a creep. But he was released because he's innocent. There's no law against him being on our street. But if you see him again, I want you to tell me immediately. Promise me.'

Laura's eyes locked onto mine, unflinching. I nodded, but a knot of unease tightened in my chest. Something told me this wasn't the last time Aitken's dark shadow would cross our lives.

And then, as the conversation dwindled back into the heavy silence, I felt a new, quiet determination settle over me. In that charged moment, I vowed to be ever vigilant – for Laura's sake, and for our family's peace.

The spectre of Aitken might haunt our street, but I promised myself I wouldn't let fear dictate our lives. I would watch, listen, and speak out without hesitation if he dared return. Every distant sound, every unfamiliar car, would be noted. A silent oath forged in the dim light of our shared uncertainty.

11

THE DETECTIVE INSPECTOR

It hasn't been the best of days. Jan had a go at me about my working hours again over breakfast, her words sharp enough to slice through the tepid peace of our morning. I sat there with my bowl of muesli, feeling the weight of her frustration settle on my shoulders like an unwelcome guest. The day was already off to a bad start, but it seemed fate wasn't done with me yet. Just as I managed to get into my office, cup of coffee in hand and ready to tackle the mounting pile of paperwork, the phone rang. And not just any call. Oh no, it was the oh-so-difficult and insufferably demanding Chief Superintendent Halliday. His voice, grating and authoritative, filled the room as he barked out his need to see me immediately.

Oh joy of joys – exactly what I needed to worsen the throbbing ache already building behind my eyes. By the time I dragged myself into his office, I could feel the tension winding tighter in my chest. Halliday, perched behind his imposing desk like a king surveying his court, wasted no time diving into his tirade. 'I'm assuming you've seen it, Laura? Professor Aitken's latest interview on the evening news.'

I nodded, blew out air. 'Yes, sir, I have.'

Halliday frowned hard, disdain written all over his face. 'Not good, not good at all. Not good for the force and worse for your career. I'm sure you'll agree this is a low point, even for you.'

Like it needed saying. Every word, every damning accusation, had been etched into Halliday's memory bank, and he was all too eager to recount events to me in excruciating detail. Aitken had laid into everyone – the police (me by name, of course), the courts, the prosecution barrister, the judge, the jury, and even the prison staff. No one had been spared his venom. And now, the chief constable, police and crime commissioner, and the local MP were breathing down Halliday's neck, demanding answers. Naturally, Halliday had deflected it all onto me, using me as his personal human shield against the fallout. The man really is a prick.

I could barely contain my contempt as he rambled on, his tone dripping with self-righteousness and a barely concealed glee at having someone to blame. My jaw clenched tighter with every word, the urge to snap back almost unbearable. I'd love to tell him exactly what I think of him with all his paper qualifications but so little frontline experience. Not a real copper at all. But I somehow held my tongue, my hatred for the man burning quietly beneath the surface. If there's one thing I've learned in this job, it's that sometimes you just have to take the hits and wait for the storm to pass. Even if that storm has a name – Halliday.

I've never been so glad that a meeting was over as I trudged back to my cluttered office to get on with my day. After taking two paracetamol, washed down with a swig of strong instant coffee sweetened with a little local honey, an indulgence I sometimes allow myself, I made a start on the seemingly ever-growing pile of red-tape paperwork sitting on my desk. It's a necessary part of the job I don't particularly like. One of the responsibilities of rank. I was just about to close a crime file and head down to the police canteen for a much-needed lunch at about one when my office phone rang again, breaking the silence. I almost didn't answer it. I told myself that if it was important, whoever it was would ring back. But in the end, my conscientious nature got the better of me. It almost always does. I picked up the receiver, holding it to my face with a resigned sigh. I felt as if I was being pulled in every direction at once. And wondered how far the elastic could be stretched before it snapped.

'Afternoon, ma'am, it's Ben. I've got a Megan Morgan here wanting to talk to you. She says you're her regular contact.'

And he was right – I was. Though, if I'm honest, I didn't hold out much hope of it yielding anything useful. I'd interviewed Megan five times before over the years. Not immediately after her attack – I was still with the West Midlands force back then – but later, when she sometimes thought she'd glimpsed her unidentified assailant on a busy Carmarthen street. I remember the sharp desperation in her eyes as she relayed those sightings, the tremor in her voice betraying both fear and hope. I took her seriously, of course, pursuing her leads with dogged determination, eager for a break in the case. But each time, the thread unravelled all too quickly. Each of the men she'd described had airtight alibis that left no room for doubt, and the trail always ended in frustration.

I have every sympathy for Megan and what she's endured. I can't pretend to fully grasp the horrors she's lived through or the way that single, savage moment forever reshaped her life. The attack wasn't just brutal – it was life-shattering. And even now, ten years later, its shadow clings to her, an inescapable weight. But still, I have to admit – however shameful it might feel – I hoped this wasn't another wild goose chase. My workload was a mountain, every step forward undone by the landslide of demands waiting to bury me again.

'All right, thanks, Ben,' I said, swallowing the sigh that wanted to escape. 'Make her comfortable and let her know I'm on my way down. I'll be there in two minutes.'

I stepped into Interview Room One to find Megan sitting there, her thin arms wrapped tightly around herself, as if she were trying to hold together the pieces of a fractured life. Her eyes, rimmed red and brimming with tears, flicked towards me, a fleeting glance before they darted away. The room felt oppressively quiet, the faint hum of the overhead light the only sound accompanying her silent grief. In that moment, I felt nothing but sympathy. No matter how often I'd seen her like this, it always hit me anew, the rawness of her pain like an open wound refusing to heal.

I took a seat opposite her and met her haunted gaze across the small table. 'Hello, Megan,' I said gently, keeping my tone as soft as the air in the room was heavy. 'It's good to see you again. What's it been? Six, or maybe seven months? How are you doing?'

Megan's lips parted, but no words came at first. Instead, her gaze shifted to the wall, unfocused, as though the very act of meeting my eyes was too much to bear. She looked older than I remembered – frailer, worn down by the weight of unspoken horrors. Her frame, impossibly thin, couldn't have been more than seven stone soaking wet. When she finally spoke, her voice wavering, words spilled out in a staccato rhythm that betrayed her inner torment. 'There's... something I need to tell you, Inspector. I... I wasn't going to come at all. Not after everything that happened before. And you know how much I hate leaving my place. I never feel safe. But I can't... I can't stop thinking about it. It's in my head, all the time, every second of the day. It gives me no peace at all.'

I pressed my lips into a small smile, the kind meant to reassure without forcing cheer, doing my best to set aside the pounding headache that had been my companion since my meeting with Halliday despite the painkillers. Megan needed me patient, steady, even as the undercurrent of desperation in her voice ate away at me. 'Listen,' I said softly, leaning forward just slightly to close the emotional distance. 'I've told you before – call me Laura. No need for formalities here. Please take your time, okay? Start from the beginning. And tell me everything that's on your mind. I've got as much time as you need.'

She raised an open hand to her face. 'It's... it's about that... that doctor guy who was on the Welsh news. I've seen him twice now. There on the screen.'

I nodded. 'Do you mean Alexander Aitken?'

Megan lowered her chin to her chest, focused on the tabletop rather than me. 'Yes, yes, that's him,' she said between breaths.

'Okay,' I said, suspecting I knew exactly what was coming next. 'What about him?'

She seemed increasingly jittery now, shifting in her seat as if she couldn't get comfortable. 'I think it was h-him,' she stuttered. 'I think... I think he was the man who attacked me.'

To be brutally honest, it was the very last thing I wanted to hear. The mere thought of sitting across from Aitken again, forcing myself to maintain a professional composure while knowing the storm it would unleash, made my stomach churn. Interviewing him, especially on the basis of information provided by someone as notoriously unreliable as Megan, felt like walking into a burning building with a petrol can in hand. It was almost unthinkable. I could already picture the fallout – complaints lodged with the chief constable, accusations of harassment. To anyone looking in from the outside, it would appear as if I had some sort of personal vendetta, a grudge I was determined to settle at any cost. And I knew all too well what that kind of perception could do to a career like mine. As if it wasn't already damaged enough.

No, the very idea was awful. If I could steer well clear of Aitken for the rest of my days, I'd count myself fortunate. The very thought of him made me shudder. That smug, self-assured smirk of his, the way he wielded his influence like a weapon, the casual malice he directed towards anyone who dared challenge him – it all made my blood run cold.

But still, despite the dread curling in my chest, I couldn't bring myself to brush Megan off entirely. For all her flaws and frailties, she deserved compassion. Her desperation was as genuine as her fear, and as much as I wanted to distance myself from the chaos she often brought with her, I couldn't deny her humanity. It was that thought – the need to be kind, to offer her some measure of solace – that tempered my reluctance, if only slightly.

I fixed my eyes on hers as she raised her head, steady but firm. 'We've been down this road before. Five times now. So I need you to think very, very carefully before we put another statement down on paper. Because you know what happened those last times – each of the men you identified was innocent. They were questioned and dragged through all that when they hadn't done a thing wrong.'

Megan's eyes darted away, searching for something in the blank expanse of the wall. For a moment, I thought she might get up and leave, that the weight of my words would silence her. But the quiet stretched, heavy and taut, before she finally spoke again, her voice trembling like a fragile thread. 'I know... I know. I'm so very sorry about all that. But... but this time feels different. I can't just ignore my thoughts, no matter how much I've tried. They won't let go. That's why I'm here.'

I leaned forward slightly, my tone softening, but my words

still deliberate. 'The man who attacked you wore a mask. You told us that. And it all happened ten years ago. Do you honestly believe, after all this time, you can be certain Professor Aitken is the one we're looking for? Just because you saw him on the TV a couple of times?'

Her lips parted, her breath catching as a single tear traced its way down her cheek. She wiped at it with shaking fingers, her voice breaking. 'It was his e-eyes. Those cold, piercing eyes. And his voice – it echoed in my head, like it was pulling me back there. Sometimes I'm so sure. When I got the taxi to come here, I thought I was doing the right thing. But now...' Her shoulders sagged under an invisible weight. 'Now my head's full of doubts again. Maybe I'm wrong. Perhaps I've been wrong all along. That would be terrible. I'm so sorry. I think... I think I've wasted your time.'

Relief coursed through me, but I kept my expression neutral. I stood slowly, the interview drawing to a close. 'Are you still seeing your psychologist?' I asked, keeping my tone conversational. 'I remember you saying it was helping.'

Megan nodded as she fiddled with her silver bracelet, preparing to leave. 'Yeah, I am. Not as often as before, though. I stopped for a bit, but then it all started again, after my doctor sent another letter. Talking's better than pills, you know?'

I nodded.

'I've got another appointment at nine next Monday morning, as it happens.'

'That's good, Megan,' was all I could think to say in response. I walked with her to the exit, the sound of our footsteps echoing faintly in the corridor. 'Do you want me to call you a cab?'

She gave me a small, fleeting smile as she pulled out her phone. 'I've got my mobile, ta.'

And just like that, she was gone, her figure shrinking into the grey day outside. I watched her for a moment longer than necessary, the faint chill of uncertainty lingering in the air as the glass door swung shut behind her.

Left alone, I felt the weight of unsolved mysteries press down on me. The fading sight of her departure served as a reminder of the fractures in our past and the relentless pursuit of truth that still haunted us. I trudged back to my office, each movement resonating with a quiet vow: to leave no detail unchecked, no lead unexplored. In that oppressive silence, I resolved to chase every shadow until the elusive truth finally emerged from the darkness. Megan's attacker was still out there. And I'd catch him if I could.

12

THE SURGEON

Three weeks have crawled by since my overdue release, the days blurring into a haze of restlessness and anticipation. My initial euphoria, that intoxicating rush of freedom, has already begun to sour, slipping through my fingers faster than I could have imagined.

But I haven't been idle – far from it. I've been more focused, more determined than ever before. Every moment has been planned, every step calculated to avoid the impulsive mistakes of my past. Megan was a lesson, a stumble I won't repeat. Leaving her alive in that Tenby backstreet was a failure that still bites at the edges of my mind, a festering wound in my otherwise immaculate record. The headlights had appeared out of nowhere, slicing through the darkness and freezing me like a deer caught in their glare. Panic surged, raw and unbridled, and I had no choice but to run – run faster than I ever thought possible, my heart pounding like a war drum, the adrenaline drowning out all coherent thought.

Megan was an act of sheer impulsiveness, a rookie's blunder born of impulse and haste. I hadn't accounted for every variable, every potential twist. And because of that, she survived – left to lie there, bloodied and broken, but alive. It was a humiliation, a blemish on my otherwise flawless discipline. But I evolved after that. I learned. Adapted. Refined my methods with a level of precision that left no room for error. That night in Tenby was a turning point, a reminder of the stakes, of the risks inherent in my work. I promised myself it would never happen again, and I've kept that promise. Mistakes are for the unprepared, and I am nothing if not thorough. It's Megan's destiny to die at my hand.

Then why was I wrongly convicted and imprisoned? Simple enough to answer if you possess my degree of insight and intelligence. Holly Larkin was no more than a deviation from the careful control that defines me. An unplanned, uncalculated anomaly that slipped into my orbit like a rogue comet. So, no, I don't count Holly as a failure. How could I? It wasn't a blunder but rather a moment of exquisite temptation, a tantalising lure that proved even I am not immune to the darker currents of human impulse.

The sight of her, so vulnerable, so unaware, was a siren's call that resonated deep within my core. The allure of her blood was intoxicating, a crimson promise that sang to me louder than reason or restraint. Because blood seduces me, the look of it, the smell and the taste. How could I possibly resist? I'm only human, after all – a man with instincts honed sharp as a blade, with desires that demand satisfaction.

Holly's existence may have been a deviation, but it was not a mistake. It was a reminder of the thrill, the danger that pulses just beneath the surface of my calculated world. Holly Larkin was an aberration, yes, but she was also proof of my humanity – the dark, unyielding part of me that refuses to be denied.

But enough of the past. Time to move on. Lessons have been learned. And there are exciting times ahead.

The need to resume my research, to reclaim my purpose, eats away at me with a relentless intensity, a fire that burns brighter each day. It would be so easy to give in, to act now, but I've held back – barely. Patience. The waiting, no matter how excruciating, is all part of the process. And it will amplify the thrill, magnify the satisfaction when the time finally comes to welcome my first reluctant guest to her new home. The bunker is ready. My freedom secured. And there will be no interruptions this time. No meddling authorities with their misplaced morality. Only time – precious, unhurried time – to explore every possibility, to push the boundaries of pain and fear further than ever before.

I imagine her cries, the frantic pleading that will give way to raw, guttural screams as her voice fails her. She will beg for mercy, appealing to an empathy I neither possess nor desire. Empathy is weakness, a trait of the feeble and unremarkable, those who shuffle through life without leaving a mark. Not for me. My work is meaningful, innovative, and above all, necessary. And if it just so happens to bring me unparalleled pleasure, well, who could fault a man for enjoying his vocation? Three cheers for me. Genius doesn't ask for permission – it simply is.

Each day since my release has been consumed by cautious planning, executed with what I like to consider military precision. Nothing has been left to chance. I began tracking both Kesey and Megan. And now that the work at my generously proportioned home is complete, it's entirely mine once again. Its isolation and sprawling grounds make it the perfect location for my research. The more I dwell on it, the more I question why I didn't seize the opportunity before. I once thought it a breeding ground for risk and exposure despite the trees I planted. Enough to halt me in my tracks, a line I wasn't ready to cross. But now, with time to reflect, I see the truth with startling clarity. The potential advantages far outweigh the perceived dangers. The proximity, once a deterrent, now feels like an asset waiting to be exploited, a calculated gamble that will tip the scales firmly in my favour.

The key, of course, lies in precision – being more cautious, more cunning, and more methodical than I've ever been. Every move must be deliberate, every step part of a grander design. Mistakes are for the reckless, and I am anything but. With the right strategy, the risks can be minimised to the point of insignificance. The game has changed, and I intend to play it to perfection.

The bunker – a masterpiece of clandestine architecture – has been expertly prepared by a discreet firm from Manchester, owned by a criminal contact in the security business, who was happy to be paid in cash. I told him it was going to be a recording studio. That was the reason for the soundproofing and wireless speakers. Better safe than sorry. And it suited him to believe every word I said. Criminals don't tell tales. And no doubt the money came in useful.

Local workmen were never an option, the potential for loose tongues and unwanted attention too great. Instead, I ensured every detail was handled by professionals who would never think to question the purpose of their work. The result? An impenetrable fortress of silence, where even the loudest screams will never reach the outside world.

And at considerable expense, the same people installed a state-of-the-art surveillance system, so the process of creating *music* could be filmed as well as recorded. That's all I had to say. And naturally, I paid well over the odds for discretion. Thousands. But needs must. It's going to be worth it.

High-definition cameras, equipped with night-vision lenses, will capture every movement, every expression. The bunker's every corner is under relentless scrutiny, all wirelessly linked to a large, high-resolution monitor in one of my bedrooms. Nothing my guests say or do will ever go unnoticed. Their terror, their desperation, their descent – it will all unfold before me, an uninterrupted symphony of human fragility. The basis of my scientific paper when I'm finally ready to complete it.

This setup, this brilliant orchestration of power and observation, is another testament to my ultimate genius. I've thought of everything. I've missed nothing. And the thought of my human lab rats being under constant, unrelenting observation, whether I'm entertaining them in the bunker or not, fills me with a deep, visceral satisfaction. How deliciously perfect it all is. I'm so very proud of everything I've achieved so far. Even the small hidden pipe bringing air into the structure. And as if that wasn't enough, there's so much more to come.

I've been revisiting the sequence in which my carefully selected guests will be introduced to their new subterranean accommodation, and I must admit, it's been maddeningly difficult to decide. A significant part of me sometimes yells that pig Kesey should be first – her role in orchestrating the miscarriage of justice that obliterated my life makes her the obvious initial target. But then, there's that simpering little slut, Megan, as I thought before. The idea of finally finishing what I started with her still has an undeniable allure. And this time, there will be no missteps, no unforeseen headlights cutting through the dark to thwart my work. Megan won't escape death again. That much is certain. And she won't die easy. My prerogative. I'll make certain of that.

It wasn't hard to find out where both live in a small town like Carmarthen. It proved a little more challenging in Kesey's case. But I followed her home from work one day. So, problem solved. And for some time now, I've been methodically monitoring their homes, sitting patiently in my car from time to time at each address, taking notes on their comings and goings, mapping their routines with surgical precision. It's the only way to properly decide when and where to strike. Kesey's movements, along with those of her partner and son, have been straightforward to observe, offering plenty of opportunities. But Megan, ever the recluse, is another matter entirely. She barely ventures beyond the confines of her flat, leaving me no choice but to contemplate a night-time intrusion. Not ideal by any means – breaking into her sanctuary under the cover of darkness carries risks I'd rather avoid. Yet, her obstinate isolation leaves me no alternative. Her fault, entirely her fault. Another offence warranting punishment. Such inconsideration, such selfishness! But it's clear what must be done – Megan must come first, if only to rid myself of the persistent worry her elusiveness brings. Lingering uncertainties are distractions I can ill afford.

And then there's Kesey. She'll quickly follow, though not quite in the manner I initially envisioned. Observing her home has revealed a fascinating dynamic – her partner, a woman I'd estimate to be in her early to mid-thirties, spends much of her time there, tending to the child who appears to be their son. Each weekday, she takes the boy to school in the morning and fetches him again in the afternoon, her routine as predictable as clockwork. And therein lies a delicious possibility. Imagine the agony for Kesey if her partner, rather than the pig inspector herself, is the one to grace my newly equipped bunker before her. The psychological torment of such a move would be wonderful to facilitate. The thought deserves serious consideration. But for now, I'll focus primarily on Megan, a decision now cemented in my mind. Yes, Megan, a dead woman walking. Her time has come.

13

THE SURGEON

Even with all my careful preparation, the time since my release dragged. Each second felt like an eternity, stretching and snapping taut with anticipation until, at last, the day arrived. *The* day. The one I'd envisioned a thousand times over, each fantasy more vivid than the last. When all my watching would finally pay off. The day when I'd finally transform my longings into a glorious, living reality – just as I had in my dreams, only better. The experience wasn't just thrilling, it was electric, coursing through my veins, making every moment so deliciously sweet.

I positioned myself early, concealed on foot behind a convenient stone wall, where I could watch Megan's flat without interruption, my car parked three streets away in the interests of security. The morning chill bit at my skin, but I barely noticed, my attention fixed on the two front windows of her home. My eyes flitted from left to right and back again, scanning for movement, my pulse quickening with every flicker of light and shadow. As parents passed by with their children, hand in hand, heading towards the nearby primary school, unwanted memories bubbled to the surface – dark, intrusive thoughts of my childhood. I tried to push them down, but they remained, refusing to let go. For a time, I let them consume me, drowning in recollections as I kept my vigil on those windows, waiting. Always waiting.

I suppose my childhood could be described as unremarkable. At least, that's how I've always seen it. But maybe it's worth delving into, if only to set the scene. My father was cold, distant – a shadow of a man whose affection never extended beyond the occasional grunt or nod. My mother, on the other hand, was suffocatingly attentive, as if her constant doting could somehow make up for my father's indifference. I appreciated neither of them. But I will say this: they encouraged my curiosity. They indulged my fascination with dissection when I turned seven, rightly thinking it was a sign of a budding scientific mind. Frogs and rats became my first specimens, neatly laid out and explored with precision.

Then came the family cat – hit by a car, its body still warm when I carried it inside for closer examination. It wasn't long after that when I moved from finding dead animals to creating my own specimens. The thrill of it was intoxicating, the power of ending a life to feed my hunger for discovery. But even then, I knew deep down that animals wouldn't ever be enough. They were a means to an end, a stepping stone to something far more fulfilling. Something I was destined for.

I became a doctor not out of any noble want to help people. The very idea of altruism makes me smirk. No, my ambitions were far more self-serving. I craved the status, the prestige, the power that came with the title. And, most of all, I wanted access to the scalpel – the sharp edge of control. Becoming a surgeon was the obvious choice, granting me the freedom to cut and slice almost at will, to explore flesh and bone under the guise of healing. For a short time, I toyed with the idea of pathology. Post-mortems held a certain appeal – the quiet of the morgue, the stillness of the dead. But that was the problem, wasn't it? The dead are unresponsive. And my interests are far more... *lively*.

For a while, the work of a surgeon satisfied me to a limited degree. The sterile theatre, the incisions, the quiet awe of colleagues watching me wield my tools with expert precision. But it wasn't enough – not nearly enough. It wasn't just the act of cutting that thrilled me; it was the life beneath the blade, the power to play God over the living. I began to realise that my needs were far greater than the operating room could ever fulfil. My instincts demanded I evolve, push boundaries, explore new terrain. And, of course, there's the simple truth I can no longer deny: the act of killing, the ritual of it, is my only true source of satisfaction. The chase, the fear in their eyes, the final moments – they are the only things that truly turn me on.

That realisation came to me in sharp, undeniable clarity in the early hours after I first encountered Megan. The memory is seared into my mind, every detail vivid. The way the blade slipped into her flesh, the resistance of muscle and sinew, the heat of her blood spilling onto my hands. The thrill of it, the power, was intoxicating. But there was something else too, something deeper – a sense of fulfilment I'd never known before.

Still, even in the midst of that ecstasy, one truth became abundantly clear: if I were to develop my interests further, caution was key. Recklessness would lead to ruin. Control – cold, meticulous control – was the only way forward. Running that night all those years ago – leaving Megan alive, beyond the initial taste of what could have been – was one of the lowest moments of my life. A mistake I've spent years replaying, over and over, imagining what might have been. The wasted potential haunts me, but it's also driven me, sharpening my resolve.

And then, as I hid behind that wall, my gaze fixed on her flat with unblinking intensity, I knew the time had come to make things right. To finally finish what I'd started.

My body reacted to the thought, the anticipation coiling tightly in my core. The mere idea of what lay ahead sent a shiver of pleasure through me, my heart pounding in sync with the blood rushing to places I didn't need to acknowledge. Megan was the only thing that mattered now. My childhood, my past, everything else faded to nothing as the front door of her building suddenly opened.

Oh, the joy. No need for a night-time intrusion after all. So fortuitous. So wonderful. Because Megan stepped out as if it were meant to be, her figure illuminated by the dull, grey morning light, and I felt my breath catch. A white taxicab pulled up, its tyres sounding on the wet tarmac, and she climbed in, oblivious to the eyes that followed her every move. And then she was gone, whisked away. But she wouldn't be gone for long. I was sure of it. Everything was aligning in my favour. I had never been more certain of anything before.

Opportunity had arrived, and it was a chance far too precious to let slip away. The excitement clawed at me, barely contained, my entire body taut with the unbearable anticipation of what was to come. Today was the day. The culmination of years of longing, of imagining. By the time Megan returned, I would be waiting. Prepared. And ready to pounce.

In the silent time before her inevitable return, I would wait in calculated stillness, mapping every possible scenario with clinical precision. My thoughts raced over each precise detail, each contingency crafted to perfection. The thrill of retribution mingled with the cold satisfaction of finally correcting past errors. Every second that ticked by deepened my resolve, sharpening my focus like a honed blade. Soon, the moment would come – and when it did, nothing would stand between me and the continuation of my work.

14

THE SURVIVOR

At first, I felt reassured after my visit to West Wales Police Headquarters. As the taxi went back through the familiar market town streets towards home, I'd clung to DI Kesey's words like that girl in that old movie *Titanic* that you always see memes about, holding on to the wooden door. I told myself she was right. She had to be, right? Over the years, I'd thought of many men as my attacker. Professor Aitken wasn't the first freak to invade my thoughts, and if I'm brutally honest – my honesty being something my psychological therapist seems to favour – he likely won't be the last.

That grim inevitability hangs over me like a storm cloud, oppressive and inescapable. It's a truth I've come to live with, as unrelenting as the echo of my attacker's voice in my nightmares or the feel of phantom hands on my skin when I least expect it. All of it a cruel, relentless by-product of post-traumatic stress. Most people seem to think PTSD is reserved for soldiers, for those who've trudged through the horrors of battle. But survivors like me? We fight battles of a different kind, in a war waged not on foreign soil but deep within the fragile confines of our own minds. There are no medals for people like me, no parades, no commemorative plaques to mark our survival. But the suffering? It's just as real. Just as raw. I know that better than most. My fear is one of the many reasons I rarely step outside any more. The world beyond my door is a minefield of red flags, each one snapping violently in the wind of my troubled mind. Every man I encounter – young or old, harmless or charming – transforms within moments into a potential threat. Their smiles seem sinister; their passing glances feel weighted with intent. It's suffocating, unbearable, and it's why I live the way I do – trapped. My life is a fragile house of cards, built on the ruins of who I once was. The thought of returning to a workplace, of stepping into crowded rooms where strangers brush past and murmur, is totally unimaginable. And so, my life is small. So much smaller than before. So much has changed even after ten long years. I don't think I'll be the carefree, happy young woman I once was ever again.

So, DI Kesey must have been right, mustn't she? The professor was just another freak conjured by my subconscious mind, another face added to the endless carousel of suspicion. It was the psychological damage – that's the only explanation that makes any sense, isn't it? The only answer that fits the shattered pieces of my mind. And yet, even as I tried to cling to the fragile threads of reason, the certainty I so desperately craved slipped through my fingers like smoke. When I saw Aitken on the Welsh evening news again, this time there was no hesitation, no room for doubt – those eyes, so piercing and cold, and that voice, every syllable wrapping around me like a vice. In that moment, I *knew*. I was so utterly convinced he was *the one*. But surely I must have been mistaken. Certainty remained an impossible luxury, the questions crept in again like shadows under a locked door, insidious and unrelenting. What if I was right this time? What if it wasn't another case of crying wolf? The possibility twisted inside me, both hope and terror entwined.

Yet, the deeper part of me, the one warped by years of suspicion and self-doubt, whispered that very little of what I think or say can ever be trusted. Not by others, and not even by myself. There are always doubts at the edges of my thoughts, undermining any momentary conviction. Aitken my attacker? Who knows? Certainly not me. And that's the most tormenting truth of all – being trapped in a mind that no longer distinguishes between fear and reality, where certainty is as elusive as the peace I haven't known in years.

I saw my psychologist at nine o'clock sharp this morning, the clock ticking ominously in the quiet waiting room as I waited for her to call me in. An hour passed behind closed doors, though it felt longer, with me spilling my thoughts into the space between us. She listened, as she always does, her nods and murmurs of encouragement urging me on. Dr Russell is a pleasant enough woman. Always welcoming, always composed. She has that professional warmth, the kind that makes you feel as though you matter, even when you suspect you don't. Or, at least, that is how it is for me. I do think she wants to help – genuinely so – but her efforts always fall short of what I need. What I hope for. And today was no exception. I told her about my trip to the police station, about my conversation with DI Kesey, every detail laid bare under her watchful eye. And though Dr Russell tried to mask her reaction, I caught it. That flicker of disbelief, the faint twist of her mouth. Disdain, disguised as professionalism but unmistakable all the same.

'I really did think the professor was the man who stabbed me,' I said, my voice steady but my mind churning. 'I still do, sometimes. It's as if his guilt is yelling in my head, screaming for attention. Like some invisible hand is pointing right at him. I heard my mum's voice once, after she died, telling me everything was going to work out okay in the end. Perhaps it's her pointing to Aitken now. I even thought I saw him in his black car on the road outside my flat yesterday afternoon. I only got a fleeting glimpse of him before he drove off. But, like, I'm fairly certain it was him.'

Dr Russell's expression faltered – just for a moment. A barely perceptible twitch of the lips, a tightening around her eyes. She didn't believe me. Not a word of it. She didn't say so, of course; she wouldn't. That's not her style. But she didn't need to. Her face said everything her words never would. She leaned forward slightly, her pen poised over her notebook, her tone carefully neutral as she murmured something meant to soothe, to redirect. But her disbelief lingered, a shadow between us, impossible to ignore.

'Megan.'

'Yes?'

'Are you still taking the anti-anxiety medication prescribed by your doctor?'

The question hit me like a gut punch, its unspoken implications reverberating louder than the words themselves. It wasn't just a question – it was an accusation, a judgement, a reminder of everything I couldn't quite explain or defend. The force of it stole the air from my lungs, leaving me winded, as though I'd taken a blow to the chest. I exhaled sharply, trying to steady myself, but the weight of it remained. I'm sure Dr Russell didn't intend to come across as dismissive or patronising – why would she? She probably thought she was treading carefully, but her words still cut deeper than she realised. Or maybe she did realise, and that would be worse.

After that, I barely said a word. What was the point? I gave a vague assurance that I was still taking the tablets – half true, at best – and let the silence hang in the air between us, heavy and suffocating.

When the hour was finally up and my taxi arrived outside, I stood and left without ceremony, not sparing her a glance. Relief washed over me the moment the door closed behind me. I was free. Free to retreat to the safety of my flat, to double-lock the door and block out the world. Back to my sanctuary, where I could keep the whispers of doubt and the questions at bay – at least for a little while.

Tears streaked my face as I stumbled from the car, my breath hitching with every hurried step towards the sanctuary of my front door. Safety – that was all I wanted. The promise of it pulled me forward, the only thing keeping me from crumbling. I'd sought reassurance that morning, a shred of understanding to anchor me in a world that felt increasingly out of control. Instead, I'd been met with doubt, that insidious, creeping doubt that made me question everything. But now I was home. A small mercy, perhaps, but one I clung to like a lifeline.

Relief washed over me as I turned the key in the lock, the familiar creak of the door almost soothing. I stepped inside, sliding the chain into place with trembling fingers. Locked. Secure. Or so I told myself.

The bathroom was my next stop, the small blue tiles cold beneath my feet as I entered. But my relief was short-lived. My heart jolted in my chest as I noticed the window – the double-glazed pane slightly ajar. A small detail, but one that struck me like a bolt of electricity. How could I have been so careless?

My mind raced as I pieced it together: I'd opened it after my shower that morning and forgotten to close it. Stupid. Unforgivably stupid. A wave of disappointment coursed through me as I leaned against the sink, gripping its edge until my knuckles whitened. Note to self: always double-check. Always.

Desperate to steady my nerves, I drifted into the kitchen. Perhaps a cup of calming lavender tea would help, I thought, though the idea felt hollow, a futile attempt to mask the unease clawing at my insides. I was home now. I was safe. I repeated the words in my head over and over again, each repetition quieter, less convincing than the last. As the kettle whistled to life, I forced myself to breathe, but the unease only deepened. It was irrational, I told myself, an aftershock of the morning's events. And yet... it wasn't. I could feel it. A presence, a shadow pressing against the edges of my mind, suffocating and undeniable. My hands shook as I dropped the tea bag into the cup, the faint sound of it hitting porcelain echoing far louder than it should. It was then, in that moment of uneasy stillness, that I heard it. My deceased mother's voice. Clear as day, as though she were standing close behind me, whispering directly into my ear. *Run, Megan. Run now. Get out of there. Run for your life.*

I froze, the breath catching in my throat. The warmth of the kitchen felt suddenly oppressive, the walls closing in, and for a moment, I wasn't sure if I could move at all. Then, as the silence pressed in around me, time itself seemed to slow – each heartbeat a resounding echo of fear and longing. And in that heavy, suspended moment, my mother's voice, soft yet urgent, whispered once more, *Run, Megan. Run now. Run faster than you've ever run before.*

It was as if her spectral urging stirred a dormant resolve within me. My trembling hands gripped the counter as I forced a shuddering breath, determined to reclaim even a fragment of the peace I so desperately craved. But my mind raced.

Was I going totally mad? Hallucinating? The dead didn't speak, did they? Of course not. *Get a grip, girl. Perhaps another tablet will help*, I said to myself. Yes, a tablet. And maybe some self-hypnosis before an early lunch. Self-care. Anything to take the edge off. I was safe now, wasn't I? Yes, yes, of course I was.

15

THE SURGEON

Fortune favours the brave, or so they say. And today it certainly favoured me. The moment Megan's taxi disappeared down the road I made my move, pacing with purpose to the rear of her ground-floor flat. Part of a divided house. My heart hammered in anticipation, though my hands remained steady, every action calculated. The back of the building was a stroke of pure luck or perhaps destiny, tucked away with no nosey curtain-twitchers lurking in their dreary living rooms to foil my intentions. It was almost too perfect, as if fate itself had orchestrated the opportunity. And, you know, I sometimes think it had.

I wore a long, dark, oversized coat, the hood drawn low over my face, shrouding my features in shadow. The cloth hung heavy against my body, its folds concealing everything that needed to stay hidden. It wasn't foolproof, of course – nothing ever is. But it would do, so long as I avoided unnecessary attention. And I would. I always do. The events of ten years ago taught me that.

I moved like a ghost, every step deliberate, every sound muted by the damp ground beneath my shoes. Still, I couldn't shake the awareness of how fragile perfection can be. A single misstep, a glimmer of movement caught by the wrong eyes, and my entire scheme could crumble. And yet, that danger only fed me. It heightened the thrill, sharpening every sense. But even so, there was one rule I wouldn't break: no one could see me in the act itself. Not a single soul.

A jolt of glee shot through me, and I couldn't help but perform a little jig of triumph when I spotted it – a slightly open opaque window on the left side of the end-of-terrace building. The sight was almost too good to be true, a gift wrapped in cracked paint and cheap plastic. I stepped forward urgently, gripping the frame with gloved hands, the cool surface slick with condensation. My breath quickened as I peered inside, my eyes sweeping over the small, dimly lit bathroom.

A white porcelain toilet and sink sat against one wall, functional and unremarkable, while a glass shower cubicle stood in the corner, pristine in its transparency. A large pink bath towel hung over a stainless-steel radiator, its softness almost incongruous in its potential usefulness. I noted it immediately – a tool, if needed, to mop up blood.

With practised precision, I moved the clutter on the windowsill – soap, shampoo, a few items of make-up – shifting them just enough to make room for me to climb in. Every motion was deliberate, careful, my mind noting the placement of each object. Nothing could be left out of place. Nothing to tip Megan off, to ruin the sanctity of this moment. As I clambered through the narrow opening, head first, my hands found purchase on the cool tiles below. And then I was in. Another triumph. One of many.

I straightened, adjusting the window back to its exact original position before returning the items on the sill to their rightful spots. Order restored. Perfection preserved. I really was on top of my game.

The air in the bathroom was thick and humid despite the winter chill, carrying faint traces of jasmine soap and damp fabric. My pulse quickened as I took in the details, my gaze lingering on the towel for a moment longer, again envisioning its role. There could be no mistakes this time. No errors of judgement. I couldn't let her escape death again. Like a god, I decided: now was her time. Her fate was sealed. And nothing – not her, not chance, not fate itself – could stop me.

It took no more than a minute or two to survey the flat, my eyes flitting over every corner, every recess, in search of the perfect hiding place. I'd already decided that her capture would need to wait until after nightfall. Darkness would be my friend, shielding me as I carried her limp, broken form to my car in the small hours of the morning, when potential witnesses were safely lost to their dreams. Until then, I needed somewhere to conceal myself. Somewhere secure, where I could wait undetected for hour after hour until the precise moment to strike arrived.

The waiting would be torture, I knew that. Every minute stretching into eternity as I fought to contain the searing anticipation of what was to come. The thought of it sent a shiver of pleasure coursing through me, igniting the fire that had burned inside me since that first moment I laid eyes on her ten years before. This was all her fault. *Megan's* fault. She'd been the one to escape me, to deny me the satisfaction I craved and my research demanded. But now, as I plotted my triumph, I allowed myself a smile. The prolonged wait would only sweeten the inevitable. Her suffering, her terror, would be all the more delicious when she was finally helpless – trapped in the cold, unyielding confines of my bunker deep underground.

Every second of Megan's torment would make up for the inconvenience she'd caused. And soon, very soon, the bitch would learn that no one escapes me twice.

My slim but muscular frame was wedged into her Victorian wardrobe, cramped amid the faint scent of stale fabric, my muscles aching from the unnatural position. The space was stifling, the air thick and stagnant, but it was the perfect hiding place.

The moment the front door creaked open – a faint, drawn-out sound that sent a thrill coursing through me – I froze, holding my breath. The sound was music to my ears, a signal that Megan was back. Back where she no doubt thought she was safe. Safe, when in truth, she was walking straight into my spider's web, more vulnerable than ever before. How delicious is that?

The minutes crawled by, each one stretching into an agonising eternity as I remained hidden in that stifling, airless space. My limbs ached from the stillness, my joints stiff and painful, but I barely noticed the discomfort. The anticipation dulled the pain, sharpened my focus. I peered through the narrow sliver of space between the wardrobe doors, my breath shallow, controlled.

From time to time, I risked the smallest of movements, shifting just enough to let my eyes scan the room, every nerve on edge as I tracked her. The waiting was unbearable, yet intoxicating – a slow, simmering build to the inevitable climax.

The soft glow of the illuminated clock on the small cabinet to the right of Megan's bed cast flickering shadows across the room, its numbers glaring like a silent witness. Just after 10 p.m. At last. She entered the bedroom with the casual ease of someone who felt utterly safe, moving towards the bed in blissful ignorance. Wrapped in her own little world, she had no reason to suspect that danger lurked mere feet away, watching, waiting.

But, of course, she *wasn't* alone. And that knowledge sent a mouth-watering shiver through me, an intoxicating thrill that curled around my spine like a lover's whisper. The clandestine secrecy of it, the sheer audacity of my presence in *her* space, undetected and unstoppable – it was a high unlike any other. I remained still, hidden in the suffocating confines of the wardrobe, my breath controlled, my pulse steady, savouring the moment. She had no idea. No inkling of the horror that loomed in the darkness, coiled and waiting to strike. And that was the best part of all.

Propped up on three white pillows, Megan read from a Kindle as she listened to modern music of a kind I don't appreciate playing on her iPad. I watched her with a hatred so visceral I could feel it coursing through my veins. It wasn't just her presence that repulsed me – it was everything about her. Her ignorance, her complacency, her audacity to think she had escaped me. Soon she'd learn she was very, very wrong.

An hour passed, the seconds ticking by painfully slowly as she turned page after page, seemingly lost in whatever trivial nonsense she was reading. My jaw clenched, my hands trembling with suppressed rage, as I waited for the moment I'd been anticipating for so long. Finally, she set her Kindle aside with an almost casual air, silenced the music, turned out the light, and shifted under the quilt. Her breathing slowed, her form sinking into the mattress as sleep began to take her.

I watched her in the semi-darkness of the room for a little longer, my loathing giving way to an icy clarity. She thought she was safe now, wrapped in her bed, the night holding no threat. But she was wrong. So very wrong.

I chose to wait until precisely 1.30 a.m. before claiming what was mine. Time can be painfully slow, stretching out like a taut wire, each minute dragging, teasing, taunting. And it did – right up until the moment I was ready to strike.

With the utmost care, I pushed open the wardrobe doors, inch by inch, the hinges whispering their quiet protest. I stepped out into the room, cramping legs aching, the darkness wrapping around me like a cloak. She was there, sprawled across the bed, her chest rising and falling in a steady rhythm, oblivious.

A faint snore escaped her. The bitch had no idea. No inkling of what was coming. In my right hand, I held a bottle of chloroform, its weight solid, reassuring. In my left, a yellow duster, soft and unassuming – until now. My fingers trembled slightly as I unfastened the bottle's white plastic cap, the sharp chemical scent filling my nostrils, electrifying me. I tilted the bottle, letting the thick, volatile liquid seep into the cloth, saturating it, preparing it.

And then, the moment. The thrill. One step. Then another. *Close now*. The time had finally arrived.

I moved fast. Graceful. Precise. In one swift motion, I clamped the soaked cloth over Megan's nose and mouth, pressing down hard, sealing her shrieks before they ever had the chance to form.

She jolted awake with a muffled gasp, her limbs flailing, weak, instinctive, her body fighting without understanding. I leaned forward, forcing all my weight onto her, locking her beneath me. Her hands clawed at my wrist, at the air, at anything.

Seconds passed. Her struggles weakened. Her limbs went limp. A ragged breath. And then nothing.

No blood. No need for the towel. Just stillness.

I stepped back, panting slightly, my pulse thumping with pure, unfiltered exhilaration. A thin line of drool ran from one corner of her mouth, her head lolling, utterly defenceless. Helpless. Such a pretty sight to behold.

My penis was hard now, standing proudly to attention as I studied her face. I'd done it. And this time, there was no escape. She was mine now. My property. Time to take her home.

Megan lay limp, utterly insensate, her unconscious form nothing more than dead weight as I wrapped her tightly in her own quilt. A fitting irony – her sanctuary now her shroud. I lifted her effortlessly, draping her over my shoulder, her head lolling, arms dangling like a broken doll's.

The exhilaration coursing through me was intoxicating, a heady surge of adrenaline and triumph that made her feel almost weightless as I held her. I moved swiftly, my breath controlled, my steps steady, carrying her through the silent flat and out into the night. Jogging towards my car, my pulse sounded in my ears, my heartbeat pounding in perfect harmony with the rush of victory flooding my veins. And no one saw me. Nobody at all. So fortunate. I'm certain of that. She was mine. *Mine.* To do with as I pleased. To break. To mould. To destroy. And I would. I definitely would.

I lifted open my car boot, heaving Megan inside, her limp form folding in on itself as I closed the lid with a satisfying thud. The finality of it sent another delightful shiver through me. There'd be no escape this time. No second chances. Not like the last time. I was in control now. Her master, her god.

Laughter bubbled up, raw and unchecked, spilling from my lips as I slid into the driver's seat. I tipped my head back, my Adam's apple bobbing as I let the sound fill the car, echoing in the confined space. Triumphant. Euphoric. The ultimate high. My hands clenched the wheel, knuckles taut with exhilaration, as I pulled away from the kerb and drove off into the waiting night.

Megan had no idea what awaited her. But she would soon. The moment she surfaced from the drugged haze, groggy and disoriented, she'd come to know the cold, unrelenting reality of her new existence. No comfort. No escape. Just concrete walls and the suffocating weight of terror pressing down on her, hour after agonising hour.

Her new home. Her bunker. Her personal hell. Every detail had been designed with precision, every element orchestrated to perfection. There'd be no missteps, no margin for error. Just pure, calculated suffering. And she would *feel* it – every second of it. The bitch would learn.

I'd record everything, every sob, every scream, every desperate, hopeless plea. No half measures. No mercy. Just raw, unfiltered horror. The kind that rewires the mind, that drags a person into the abyss and leaves them there, broken, begging for an end that will never come.

This was more than pleasure. More than power.

This was *art*. A storm of suffering was coming her way. And I was going to savour every moment of it.

Every tortured breath and silent plea Megan would make soon resonated in my mind like a macabre symphony of despair.

As I drove towards the bunker, my mind was filled with the promise of retribution – a dark, relentless certainty. Soon, when she stirred in that icy cell of confinement, her screams would be captured in every frame, every recorded moment a testament to my absolute control. That was my creation, my ultimate masterpiece of calculated vengeance.

16

THE SURVIVOR

I opened my eyes to nothingness. No light. No shape. No sense of space or time. Just a crushing, suffocating void. Not the comforting semi-darkness of my familiar bedroom, where shadows shift and soften in the dim glow of the streetlights and moon beyond the curtains. No. This was different. This was absolute. The kind of darkness that swallowed you whole, that made you blind even to yourself. I lifted a trembling hand, held it inches from my face. But nothing. Not even a shadow.

A deep sense of panic surged, sharp and electric, sending a sickening jolt through my gut. My head pounded, a relentless, throbbing ache radiating from my skull. I was cold, a deep, marrow-chilling cold that burrowed into my bones. And then, almost the worst realisation of all – my skin. Bare. Exposed. Someone had removed my T-shirt and knickers. I was *naked*.

At first, for the briefest flicker of time, I clung to the desperate hope that this was another nightmare. A grotesque, all-too-real manifestation of fear – some sick trick of my subconscious mind, twisting and distorting reality into something monstrous. But reality came crashing down all too quickly, brutal in its certainty. I was awake. *Oh, God, I was awake!*

I lifted myself upright, my limbs sluggish, my body aching, until I was seated on what felt like cold, hard concrete. The chill of it seeped into my skin, a cruel contrast to the heat of panic rising in my chest. My breath came in ragged gasps, my pulse a frantic drumbeat against my ribs.

Then I screamed. I don't know how long for. Time had lost all meaning in that black void, swallowed whole by the overwhelming terror clawing at my throat. I yelled again. And again. Until my voice fractured, until my cries for help became nothing more than hoarse, desperate rasps.

But no response. Not a whisper. Not a sound.

The silence pressed in on me, thick and unnatural, amplifying the sheer wrongness of it all. My fingers skittered across the floor, blindly searching, needing to feel something – anything – that might make sense of the incomprehensible. But there was nothing but the concrete beneath me. Empty. Unforgiving. Just like the darkness.

I sat there, broken, head in my hands, my body wracked with shuddering sobs. My chest ached, my throat painful from screaming into the void, my tears hot against my ice-cold skin. Minutes passed, or maybe hours. I was swallowed whole by the suffocating dark.

I didn't want to move. Didn't want to confirm what every instinct in my body already knew – that I was trapped. Sealed in. Forgotten. In some kind of unfathomable cell. But staying still wasn't an option. Not if I was going to survive. Not if I was ever going to get out of there.

Somehow, I found it – the will to act, clawed from the depths of blind, animalistic fear. I finally moved, scuttling sideways on my bare skin, crab-like, the rough concrete scraping against my flesh. I hated the way it felt – exposed, vulnerable. But I had to keep going. My breath came in sharp bursts, terror thick in my throat, nausea rising with every inch I covered. And then – *contact*. A wall.

I pressed my palms against it, the coldness of the surface bleeding into my fingertips. I gritted my teeth, forcing myself to stand, my legs trembling beneath me, weak and unsteady as though they no longer belonged to me. I swayed, bracing against the wall, the fear so consuming I thought my body might simply give out beneath the weight of it.

But I couldn't stop. I *wouldn't* stop. I had to drive myself on. I inched to my right, my hands frantically searching, sweeping, desperate to find *something* – a door, a window, a switch. Anything that might break the nightmare, that might let the light in, giving me hope. But there was nothing. Nothing at all. Just endless, unrelenting blackness and that chill that made me shiver.

I ran my hands over the wall, feeling every inch of the surface. Then another wall. And another. My fingers scraped against rough concrete, my breath coming in short, panicked bursts as I searched, desperate for *something* – a crack, a gap, a hinge. Some way out of the hellhole. But there was nothing.

Panic tightened its grip, my body trembling violently. The realisation hit me like a hammer blow – I was trapped. Sealed inside this black void with no escape. My stomach clenched, a sick, twisting sensation taking hold. And then – humiliation. My bladder gave way, warm urine trickling down my legs, pooling at my bare feet. A broken sob tore from my throat as I stumbled, pressing myself against the wall, begging. '*Help! I'm in here! Someone please help me! Mum, Mum, please, where are you? I'm sorry I didn't listen to you.*'

My screams bounced off the walls, swallowed by the emptiness. But there was no reply. No footsteps. No reassuring voice calling back or whispering in my ear. Only silence, thick and merciless, pressing in on me from all sides.

And then – *light*. A blinding, searing beam sliced through the darkness, so bright it felt like fire against my retinas. I gasped, throwing up my hands to shield my face, squeezing my eyes tight shut as white-hot pain exploded behind my lids. The sudden shift from pitch black to unbearable brilliance sent my senses into freefall, disorientating me completely.

And then – *the voice*. Deep. Cultured. Unhurried. A voice that oozed confidence. And power.

'A very warm greeting to your new bunker home, my dear Megan. I'm delighted to finally welcome you as a guest. It's something I've been looking forward to immensely for some time now.'

I froze, my blood turning to ice.

'I'll introduce myself properly in an hour or two, once I've had some much-needed rest. Although…' A pause. A cruel, knowing pause. 'You may remember me from our mutual past. Mull on that to pass the time until my arrival. Something for you to look forward to, wouldn't you agree?'

I bit down on a whimper, nausea clawing at my throat. Please, God, no. I recognised that voice, didn't I?

'Oh, and best think of yourself as a *lab rat*,' he continued, his voice smooth, almost amused, and now I felt more sure. 'That might give you some understanding of your new purpose in life. But first – some music to keep you entertained. I've had a sound system fitted for exactly this reason. Enjoy.'

A beat of silence. And then – *the music*. It blasted through the room, deafening, inescapable. A slow, ominous melody. Chopin, I think. Although I can't be sure. A famous funeral march. My funeral march? The notes vibrated through my bones, the relentless rhythm pounding inside my skull, stabbing at my eardrums like needles. I clenched my teeth, screwed my eyes tighter shut against the glare, and clamped my hands over my ears, but it was useless. There was no blocking it out. No escaping the torment.

It went on for hours. Or maybe it was minutes. Or perhaps days. Time had fractured, spiralling into a nightmarish loop of sound and light and horror. My body ached, my mind splintering under the relentless assault.

I thought my torment couldn't possibly get any worse. But I was wrong. So *terribly* wrong. I would find that out soon enough.

As the mournful strains of the funeral march finally stopped, a deliberate clang resounded from above – the metallic sound of a roof hatch slowly opening.

And that unfamiliar noise sent a fresh jolt of fear through my heart, as if heralding the arrival of yet another horror. It was a chilling reminder that my ordeal was far from over, that the trial still held secrets waiting to be unleashed.

17

THE SISTER

I ring or text Megan almost every day. Just to check in. Just to make sure she's coping – or at least, as well as can be expected under the circumstances. It's what big sisters do, isn't it? A duty. A promise I made to Mum before she died. *Look out for Megan, love. She'll need you.* And she did. She still does.

There's only two years between us, but it feels like a lifetime. I moved forward – university, a husband, children. Life carried me away, sweeping me along in its steady current. But Megan... Megan got stuck. Trapped in the past, in the moment she was attacked. Sixteen forever. A shadow of the person she should have been. A ghost of the bright, fearless girl I once knew.

Megan's been fragile ever since. A whisper of a woman. A mouse of a person, timid and wary, always looking over her shoulder, waiting for something – *someone* – to come back for her. And who could blame her? When you've been hunted once, the fear never truly leaves, does it?

I tell her to move on, to let go of the past, but even as I say it, I know how hollow the words sound. Easier said than done. But what else can she do, though? She either breaks free from the seemingly never-ending nightmare, or she lives in its shadow forever – trapped, paralysed, still bleeding from wounds that should have long since healed. And that's no life at all. She still goes for therapy. Still! But I think all it does is remind her. I don't think she's moved on at all.

This morning marked the third day in a row that Megan hadn't answered her phone. No reply when I rang. No response to my texts. Nothing. Silence. And that wasn't just unusual – it was unheard of. A one-off. Something she'd *never* done before.

Megan isn't the type to just vanish. She doesn't shut people out, not like this. She's never self-harmed, never spoken of suicide. But she's fragile, always teetering on the edge of something dark. Anxious. Sometimes depressed. Popping pills doled out by her GP, papering over the cracks but never quite fixing them.

And as I gripped the steering wheel, more concerned with every turn, I couldn't shake the fear that clawed at my insides. What if something had happened? What if I was too late?

The thought stuck itself in my throat, thick and unrelenting. I pressed my foot down harder on the accelerator, my heart hammering in time with the rhythm of the tyres against the road. I was going too fast. I knew that. But I didn't care.

Because, truth be told, as I sped towards Megan's flat, every nerve in my body braced for the worst. For the unthinkable. For the possibility that when I finally reached her, I might find her cold, still, and beyond saving. And I knew I wasn't ready for that.

Megan didn't answer when I banged on her front door, my fist landing hard against the plastic, the sound echoing down the empty hallway. I leaned in, pressing my lips to the cold metal of the letterbox, shouting her name, the desperation bleeding into my voice. But nothing.

The silence sent an icy shiver down my spine, but it was

nothing compared to what I felt when I hurried round to the back of the building. My pulse spiked, a sharp, gut-twisting fear taking hold as I spotted the back door. Not just unlocked – *open*. Slightly ajar, just enough to expose the room beyond.

Megan would never leave it like that. *Never.* She was far too careful, too fearful, always double-checking locks, peering through the peephole, jumping at shadows. Something was wrong. Badly wrong. I was sure of it. And I had to know more.

I hesitated for only a second or two before stepping forward, pushing the door wider, wincing as the hinges groaned. The familiar kitchen was dimly lit and eerily still. My own breathing sounded too loud in the hush that dominated the room. I swallowed hard, then called Megan's name. Once. Then again, louder the second time.

But still no response. Only silence. A thick, suffocating silence that pressed in on me from all sides, amplifying the dread curling in my stomach like a living thing.

I forced myself to move, to search, though every instinct screamed at me to turn back, to get out of there and run. My stomach churned, twisting itself into knots as I pushed open doors, peering into rooms that felt too empty. For a moment, I thought there was nothing to find – until I stepped into my sister's bedroom.

And then, the alarm bells in my head got louder. Red flags at the forefront of my mind. The bed was stripped bare. No quilt, only pillows and the sheet covering the mattress. A cold dread slithered through me. Megan was obsessive about making her bed. Forever tidying. I think such things give her the illusion of a control she doesn't possess. So, the sight of the bed in such disarray sent my thoughts spiralling. But that wasn't all.

Her Kindle. Lying on the floor, facedown, as if it had been

dropped – or knocked from the bed. She always put it on the bedside cabinet. Always.

I turned in a tight circle, scanning the room, my breath coming fast and shallow. Something was wrong. My nostrils flared as I inhaled, catching a strange, acrid scent hanging in the air. Sharp. Unfamiliar. Chemical. It clung to the room, curling into my lungs, setting my nerves even further on edge. I couldn't place it, but I knew it didn't belong.

By the time I stepped into the lounge, my hands were already shaking as I reached for my phone, my mind set – I was calling the police. And then I saw it.

Megan's mobile. Sitting on the table. Still. Silent. A glaring contradiction in a reality that made no sense.

A wave of cold washed over me. No wonder she hadn't answered my calls. The phone was practically an extension of her hand, never out of reach, a lifeline to the outside world. She wouldn't leave without it. Not ever. It was time to summon urgent help.

I bolted from the flat, lungs burning as I stumbled into the street. The cold air hit me like a slap, but I barely felt it. My only thought was to get out. To escape that suffocating silence, that chemical stench, that morale-sapping certainty that something was very, very wrong.

I pulled open the car door, throwing myself into the driver's seat, hands trembling as I fumbled for the keys. My mobile was already clenched in my other hand, thumb hovering over the keypad, ready to dial 999. But then, a thought – sharp, insistent – entered my mind. *Kesey. DI Laura Kesey.*

Megan liked her. She trusted her. And trust didn't come easily to Meg – not any more. If anyone would take my concerns seriously, if anyone would understand the significance of Megan's disappearance, it was Kesey. Not some faceless call handler at the other end of a switchboard. Not an officer who didn't know the history, who'd likely make a report and dismiss my fears as paranoia. No. Kesey was the one I needed.

My decision was made in an instant. I put the phone aside, jammed the key into the ignition, and twisted it hard. The engine roared into life, a low, growling snarl beneath my grip. I shoved the car into first gear, foot pressing down hard on the accelerator, tyres screeching as I shot forward into the road.

West Wales Police Headquarters wasn't far. Minutes away, if I pushed the speed limit. And I would. Because something wasn't right. And if I was correct – if that empty flat, that unlocked door, that abandoned phone meant what I thought they did – then every second counted. Megan was in danger. Every cell in my body screamed it, a deep, instinctive certainty that clawed at my insides and refused to let go. It wasn't paranoia. It wasn't overreaction. It was cold, hard truth. A gut-wrenching, inescapable fact that settled like lead in my stomach. My poor sister! I'd never been more certain of anything in my life.

I pushed my car faster than was sensible as I raced towards help. Each second became a desperate prayer that Megan was still safe, that her absence was only temporary and not the prelude to some unspeakable tragedy. My heart pounded like a drum, each beat echoing with the promise of a silent vow I'd made long ago – to protect my sister at any cost. The burden of her likely peril grew heavier, and I steeled myself with grim determination. I wasn't just her sister any more – I was Megan's last lifeline in a world that had turned cold and merciless.

18

THE DETECTIVE INSPECTOR

I exhaled sharply, rubbing a hand over my face as I forced my eyes back to the computer screen. The numbers blurred for a moment before snapping into focus – row upon row of dry, mind-numbing figures. Overtime budgets. The very phrase makes my skin crawl. I couldn't think of anything more tedious, more infuriatingly pointless. Another bureaucratic box-ticking exercise. Another part of the job I loathe.

But Nigel Halliday? Oh, the man loves that shit.

Anything to avoid real policing. Anything to keep himself buried in spreadsheets and policy documents while the rest of us wade through the filth out there. The bastard thrives on it – feeding off the paperwork, twisting it into some perverse sense of control. And now, thanks to him, I had to waste my time on that nonsense – every bloody week. An overtime report. With full costings. Every single week.

I shook my head, jaw clenching as frustration clawed at my ribs. A ridiculous, bureaucratic charade. The kind of thing that made me wonder if I'd chosen the wrong career entirely. What a crazy, infuriating, soul-destroying waste of time.

I welcomed the distraction when my phone rang, relieved to drag my eyes away from the soulless figures on the screen. 'DI Kesey.'

'Morning, ma'am. It's Ben on the front desk.'

I sighed, pinching the bridge of my nose. *Here we go.*

'I've told you before, Ben. It's guv or boss. Ma'am makes me feel ancient.'

'Sorry, ma'am. I'll try to remember.'

I shook my head, accepting defeat. There was no winning with him. *Ben was Ben.* 'What's this about?'

His response came with his usual boyish enthusiasm – like an excitable puppy desperate for praise. No jaded cynicism, no world-weary sighs. Not yet, anyway. 'I've got a Rhian Thomas here with me, ma'am. A local social worker. She's Megan Morgan's sister, and she's asked for you by name. Do you want to come down, or shall I get the duty officer to see her?'

I stilled. First Megan the previous week. And now her sister. A coincidence? Maybe. But something about it bothered me, setting my instincts on edge. 'Did she say what it's about?'

Ben's tone shifted, losing some of its usual eagerness. There was an urgency now, a note of something that put me instantly on alert. 'She says her sister's missing.'

I was already on my feet when I replied. 'Make her comfortable. I'll be there in two minutes.'

The overtime report was forgotten before I'd even put the phone down. I moved quickly, taking the stairs two at a time – faster than waiting for the lift, my shoes echoing against the hard floor. A dull, sterile hum filled the station, the usual background noise of ringing phones, muffled voices, and the distant clatter of keyboards. But none of it registered. My focus was locked on the woman waiting for me in reception.

Rhian sat stiff-backed in one of the uncomfortable plastic

chairs, hands clasped tightly in her lap, fingers wringing together in a way, even had Ben not given me the heads-up, that told me she wasn't here for a casual chat. Concern flickered across her face – pretty, but pale, drawn. Tight around the eyes. She looked like someone who hadn't slept.

I offered a thin, professional smile as I reached out a hand. 'Nice to meet you – circumstances aside, of course. If you follow me, we can find a free interview room to talk privately.'

Rhian took my hand briefly, her grip warm, and nodded, silent but composed. We walked together down the corridor, the overhead strip lighting casting harsh, artificial brightness against the white walls. The doors lining either side had small, clear glass panels, offering quick glimpses of officers hunched over desks, suspects slouched in chairs, the usual business of a working station. But I kept moving, my focus set ahead.

Within a minute, I pushed open the door to Interview Room Four. A small, boxy space – functional, impersonal. Just a table, two chairs, a dull sense of containment.

We sat, facing each other across the narrow divide.

Her eyes met mine. Wide. Searching. And that's when I knew – this wasn't just worry. It was fear.

I leaned forward slightly, keeping my tone calm, measured. 'The officer on reception told me you think Megan is missing. Can you expand on that for me?'

A flicker of anger flashed across the social worker's face, darkening her features. Her jaw tightened. 'I don't *think* my sister's missing. I *know* she's missing. That's why I'm here.'

I nodded, absorbing the weight of her words. 'Okay, I hear you. Let's start at the beginning. When did you last see or hear from Megan?'

Rhian leaned in, urgency radiating from her as she spoke, her words clipped but precise. There was no hesitation, no uncertainty – just raw, unfiltered concern. I listened intently, letting her unravel her fears, her voice taut with emotion. As she spoke, I flipped open my pocketbook, noting down every detail in the short, functional scrawl of a seasoned officer.

When Rhian finally finished, I looked up, recapping the key points. 'All right, let me make sure I've got this right. You left Megan's flat about twenty minutes ago, having arrived about ten minutes before that. Her back door wasn't just unlocked – it was open. The quilt was missing from her bed. Her mobile was left on the lounge table. That about right, yes?'

Rhian's brow furrowed. 'Oh, yes...' She hesitated, eyes widening slightly. 'That's right, And Megan's *obsessive* about security. The very idea of her leaving a door unsecured is unthinkable. And her phone? She *never* leaves the flat without it. She only goes out when she *has* to, and when she does, it's a really big deal. She's extremely risk-averse – she sees danger in *everything*.' Rhian exhaled sharply, her hands tightening into fists. 'Something's very wrong. I *know* it is. I need you to understand that.'

I held her gaze, measuring her conviction. In all honesty, I was fearing the worst. Ten years of trauma, of paranoia, of living under the weight of what had happened – maybe it had finally become too much. Maybe Megan had... ended it.

I chose my words carefully. 'I saw your sister last week. She called here at the station. Not for the first time, she thought she might have identified her attacker. She seemed... emotionally fragile. Vulnerable. I advised her to speak to her therapist.' I paused, then pressed on, all the time knowing Rhian wouldn't appreciate my words. 'I have to ask – do you think there's *any* possibility Megan may have harmed herself?'

Rhian's reaction was instant. Another flash of anger, her spine snapping straight, muscles taut beneath her skin. Her whole face changed, the contours tightening with raw emotion. '*Suicide?*' Her voice was sharp, incredulous. 'That's what you're alluding to, isn't it?' She didn't wait for a reply. 'The answer is an *emphatic no*! A cousin of ours ended her life several years ago. Severe depression. It devastated her immediate family – ripped them apart. Megan and I saw it first-hand. We've talked about it, many times. And I can tell you, without a single doubt in my mind, Megan would *never* do that.' Her eyes locked onto mine, burning with certainty. 'I hope I've made myself perfectly clear.'

I still wasn't entirely convinced. But I wasn't about to admit that – not to her. It was time to move things along. 'I wouldn't be doing my job if I hadn't asked.'

Rhian pulled a face, like I'd just wafted something rotten under her nose. 'So, what happens now?'

'Megan qualifies as a vulnerable person under the definition, which means we'll treat finding her as a high priority.' I kept my voice steady, professional, but firm. 'We'll contact all the local hospitals – see if she's had an accident, been taken ill, anything like that. And I'll need you to give me the names and addresses of any friends or family she might have visited. We'll check them today. I'll have one of my DCs go over the flat properly – see if there's anything you've missed. And we'll knock on a few neighbours' doors, see if they've seen anything useful.'

Rhian wiped at a stray tear, her movements sharp, agitated. 'Megan doesn't have friends any more. It's amazing how quickly they disappear if you hit hard times. And family-wise, there's only me and Dad. And he's away on a fishing holiday in Florida, flew yesterday, so there's zero chance Meg's at his place. He just locks up and goes. No spare key, nothing. He's always been the independent type.'

'Okay, by all means give him my name and contact details when you next speak to him. He's bound to have questions that need answering.'

Rhian nodded. 'I've got a key to Meg's flat if that helps?'

'That would be great, thanks. I was about to ask.'

She rummaged in her handbag, pulled out the key on a blue fob, then hesitated before handing it over. When she spoke, her voice was lower, edged with something close to panic. 'I can't believe I'm even saying this... but I don't think Megan's just *gone off* somewhere. Not voluntarily.' She swallowed hard. 'I think someone's taken her.'

I held her gaze, keeping my expression neutral. 'Let's take this one step at a time. And if there's *anything* to suggest a criminal offence, I promise you – it will be investigated accordingly. I know Megan. I know what she's been through. And I like her. If it makes you feel any better, I'll be supervising this personally. I'll do everything I can to find your sister safe and well. You have my word.'

Something in Rhian's posture softened, a flicker of relief crossing her face. 'Thank you. I appreciate that.'

I nodded, offering a small smile. 'Do you have a recent photo of Megan? Something that clearly shows her face?'

She took out her mobile, scrolling quickly before settling on a headshot. She turned the screen towards me. 'Will this do?'

I took a glance and nodded. 'Perfect.' I jotted down my force email and slid the paper across the table. 'Send it over now, and I'll get it circulated to all officers in the area. Also – any idea what she might have been wearing? A coat, for example? If it's missing from the flat, that might help us spot her.'

Rhian gave a fleeting smile, but it vanished almost instantly. 'She's got a knee-length grey wool coat with three buttons. If she's wearing one, it'll be that one. Oh, and her navy-blue hat. I bought it for her last Christmas – it's got a white bobble on top.'

I jotted the details down. 'Ah, yeah. I know the one. My partner's got one in red. Does Megan ever wear glasses?'

'No.'

I nodded, writing as she spoke. Then I paused, pen hovering. 'One last thing, Rhian. Before I circulate the report. And I'm sorry, but this is something else I *have* to ask.' I met her eyes. 'I know about your sister's scars from her attack. But does she have any other distinguishing marks? Tattoos? Birthmarks?'

Rhian stiffened. 'My sister's not dead,' she snapped, almost spitting her words 'She's alive. I can *feel* it.'

I exhaled slowly. 'I very much hope you're right. And I have no reason to think otherwise. But I need that answer, Rhian. Before I send the report. It's a matter of procedure.'

She looked away, her voice quieter now. 'She's got a small birthmark on her left shoulder. Crescent moon shaped. Our dad used to call her "Moony" when we were kids. Just joking around. She used to laugh. You could joke with her back then.' She hesitated, her voice catching slightly. 'Not so much now. I can't even remember the last time she smiled.'

The words settled heavy between us.

Ray Lewis, my old DS, now happily retired, often used to talk about his gut instinct. I never gave it much credence back then, always figured it was unreliable at best. But as I stood, straightening my spine, something deep in my gut twisted.

And for the first time, I felt it. A sense of something dark. Something wrong. And the alarm bells inside me wouldn't stop ringing.

19

THE SURGEON

The first few days entertaining my guest in her new concrete home have been nothing short of fascinating – both scientifically and personally. I've observed every moment, studied every reaction, watched her unravel in real time. And thanks to my state-of-the-art surveillance system, I've missed nothing. Worth every penny I've spent.

The cameras – *crystal clear*. Every twitch of muscle, every shudder of fear and cold, every humiliating attempt to shield herself in her nakedness is captured in glorious detail. There isn't a shadow for her to hide in. No moment of privacy. And, of course, no escape.

The microphones? *Perfect.* I hear *everything*. The ragged breaths. The quiet sobs. The pathetic, whispered prayers to a god that won't answer. The broken pleas that spill from her lips.

Megan is mine to study, to document, to break.

And I have to say – bringing her to the bunker was truly inspired. Any risks are insignificant – mere footnotes in comparison to the rewards.

Because I've come to learn the real power lies in possession, in the absolute control I now wield. She's mine – mind, body, and every trembling, broken breath in between. Mine to manipulate, to mould, to destroy, piece by fragile piece. For as long as I choose to let her live, she exists for *me*.

Yes, the bitch is my property. Completely. Irrevocably. And she will learn that soon enough. Her life, for what it's worth, is no longer her own.

Even I, the great Professor Sir Alexander Aitken – blessed with such truly exceptional intelligence and superior medical knowledge – have been astonished by the speed of her deterioration. Her body, mind, and spirit… all crumbling even faster than I anticipated. It's fascinating. Exhilarating. Well worthy of note.

I've long believed that hope is the cornerstone of endurance. A fundamental factor in happiness, in survival. And I've taken that from her. Stripped it away.

Since her arrival, I've given her barely enough sustenance to keep her lingering in the purgatory between life and death. The circular steel hatch in the ceiling opens only when *I* decide. And when it does, it's never to offer salvation. Just the occasional morsel of stale food, thrown down like scraps to a dog. A plastic bottle, partially filled with filthy water – contaminated, tainted.

I pissed in it once. Just to see. To watch. To witness the raw, primal desperation of a creature driven to its limits. And for a moment, she almost drank it. She raised it to her lips, trembling, shaking with need. Then the realisation hit her – like an electric shock, short-circuiting whatever pitiful survival instincts she had left. She screamed, a wild, broken wail, hurling the bottle across the bunker, bouncing it off a wall. And that made me laugh so very much I very nearly fell off my chair as I sat watching the monitor.

Well, at first I laughed. A deep, guttural sound, raw with amusement. Watching her convulse in revulsion, her face contorted in horror, had been delicious. It was a performance worth savouring.

But then – the rage came. That deep, seething, uncontrollable fury – a central part of who I am. *What* I am. It surged through me, burning, unrelenting, absolute. It always does. *Always.* And rightly so. My lab rat showed such ingratitude. And I despised her for that. I have no obligation to keep the needy bitch alive. Every breath she takes is a gift – my gift. My generosity.

And yet, despite everything, she refuses to see the truth. She is fed. She is watered. And that is more than so many are afforded. She should be grateful. She should see my acts of generosity for what they are – a privilege. Something she hasn't even earned.

But the bitch spat in the face of my benevolence.

So, I corrected her. As a good owner should. A fair and just punishment. A lesson in respect.

I left the pounding music and the blinding spotlights on for a full twenty-four hours without a moment's break. No pause. No reprieve. Just relentless, merciless torment. I turned the volume up to maximum. The walls trembled with the sheer force of it. Sound vibrating through bone. Heat prickling against clammy, malnourished skin.

And oh, how she suffered. I could see she whimpered at first. Like a pathetic baby creature in need of its mother. And then she cried. Then screamed. But no one came. No one ever will.

Yes, the bitch suffered. And all of it – every second of it – was no more than she deserved. Megan brought it all on herself. I need the world to understand that. Her agony isn't just inevitable – it's earned.

And the next time? Well, if she *dares* to disappoint me again with her lack of appreciation, her sheer insolence, I'll remind her exactly who holds the power. She will learn to respect me. To worship me in the way I deserve.

There are endless ways I could make her suffer. A limitless array of punishments at my disposal, each one more creative than the last. All it takes is a whim. A single moment of my disapproval.

If it weren't for the integrity of my academic study, she'd already be in pieces. Torn open. Sliced apart like the specimen she is. But all in good time. Soon enough, she *will* learn. And when she does? She'll *never* forget. Until she breathes her last gasping breath. There is still so much work to do.

Dispassionately looking back on the events of recent days, evaluating both my lab rat's situation and mine, I think it's fair to say I've been more than reasonable. I could have killed her the moment she arrived. If she only knew how difficult it has been for me to delay ending her life, she'd fall to her knees and thank me. She'd worship me as her master.

My scalpel lies ready. Always within reach. But no, I will keep her alive a little longer. In the name of science. And then... the moment I've craved for six long years.

The introduction of sharp blade to flesh. No anaesthetic, of course – where would be the joy in that? Until she finally bleeds out. It will be glorious. Exquisite. And sometimes, just occasionally, the anticipation alone is almost too much to bear.

I can picture it now. Make it real in my mind, big, bright and loud. I will loom over her – towering, invincible – drinking in the sheer magnificence of her suffering. The tremors of agony rippling through her flesh. The raw, unfiltered fear in her eyes as realisation dawns. That moment – *that precise moment* – when she finally understands the truth.

That she is nothing. That she never was anything.

That she exists now only to serve me. And that, for the very first time, she has value. She has finally found her vocation. The reason for her birth.

Her sobs will turn to screams, her screams to whimpers, her body convulsing, betraying her with its weakness. She will beg. She will plead. But her words will be wasted breath, empty and meaningless. I will hear them, of course. Every desperate gasp. Every pitiful prayer.

And I will savour them. Because *finally*, she will serve a purpose. And I will be satisfied. For a time. Until the next one. Because the hunger is never truly gone. It settles for a while, lulled into a brief, blissful quiet. But it always returns. A whisper at first, then a murmur, then a full-blown roar inside my skull, demanding more. Always more.

I can feel it now – the anticipation curling around me, thick and heady, pulsing through my veins. The power. The absolute, untouchable control.

Her life has taken on meaning at last.

And mine? My life has been reborn after those barren, wasted years of imprisonment. Years lost, stolen from me, wasted on the ignorant and unworthy. Locked away like some common criminal when I am so much more.

No longer confined to the cold, grey world of fantasy. No more imagining. No more dreaming of what could be. It's *real* now. *She's* real now. Her body, her mind, her suffering – all mine to shape, to manipulate, to destroy.

I am the dominator. The architect of her demise. The master of life and death. I am utterly and completely devoted to my studies. And I will never stop. Because why would I? I was born for this. And the world will never understand what it means to truly exist until they are looking up at me.

I relish my resurgence. Every calculated act, every happy detail of her torment, solidifies my dominion over chaos. The dark hunger inside me grows, fuelled by the knowledge that each scream only serves to fortify my legacy.

I sit back and let the silence of my newfound power wash over me – a silence that promises future triumphs. Soon, the world will tremble beneath the weight of my genius. It is simply inescapable.

20

THE DETECTIVE CONSTABLE

My name's Jacqueline. Or, to use my new title, Detective Constable Nicholl – a label I'm still getting used to hearing. A role I'm proud of. A job I've earned through sheer grit and determination. It wasn't handed to me. It wasn't a given. I worked for this. And now, finally, I wear my plain clothes like a second skin.

I've been a police officer for a little over seven years now, after leaving my previous life as a practice nurse. A different kind of service, but in some ways, not so different at all. Pain, suffering, damage – it finds you in both professions. The only real difference is the uniform. And I've only been out of mine for a matter of weeks, newly minted as a DC, still adjusting to life outside of first response.

Which is why, when DI Kesey asked me to take the lead on Megan Morgan's disappearance, I had to fight to keep my expression neutral. Had to stop myself from grinning like a fool. Because, honestly? I was thrilled.

But let's be real – I'm not naïve. I know full well my being assigned to this case had more to do with staffing shortages than her faith in my ability. A skeleton crew, too many officers off sick or sunning themselves on annual leave – I was in the right place at the right time. Right place for me, anyway.

Still, the DI chose me. And that means something.

I'm here now. I'm *in this*. And I'm determined to prove I belong. I'll do a good job if it's the last thing I do.

I pored over Megan's case file before heading to her flat, absorbing every grim detail on the computer screen. It didn't take long to realise she's been through hell.

Megan's life was stolen from her at age sixteen.

When I was studying for my nursing degree, worrying about coursework deadlines and job applications, Megan was lying in a hospital bed, her body torn apart by multiple stab wounds. While I was making plans for the future, she was clinging to life, her world changed forever. A cruel twist of fate. One it seemed she never really recovered from.

And now she was missing. A coincidence? I very much doubted it. The DI told me Megan had received counselling help over the years – for whatever good that's done. But I don't need a psychology qualification to know that living in fear, never knowing who tried to kill you, never getting justice... that leaves scars far deeper than the ones on her body. The fact we never caught her attacker? That has to be a factor in her vulnerability. A decade of trauma, of looking over her shoulder, of wondering if the bastard is still out there, watching, waiting. It's enough to break anyone. I'm sure it would break me.

I very much hope Megan hasn't harmed herself. I really do. But I'd be lying if I said I wasn't considering the possibility. And, in truth? If she's found dead, it wouldn't surprise me at all.

All those thoughts – and more – whirled through my mind as I drove the short distance from police headquarters to Megan's rental flat, gripping the steering wheel a little too tightly. The weight of the case pressed down on me, an unease twisting in my gut. Hoping for the best. But bracing for the worst.

The street was surprisingly quiet when I arrived, the kind of eerie stillness that made the hairs on the back of my neck stand on end. A bit dramatic perhaps, but true. I let myself in, stepping into the stale hush of Megan's home – a place seemingly abandoned mid-routine.

I moved slowly from room to room, my eyes sweeping every detail, searching for something – anything – that might help me build a picture, one piece of the jigsaw at a time. And then, in the bedroom, I found it. The grey coat DI Kesey had mentioned. Hanging neatly on a hook behind the wardrobe door. Undisturbed. Waiting.

I coughed, sniffed, sneezed, then reached for it, fingers brushing the thick fabric.

Then, inside one pocket, the navy bobble hat. The one her sister had said Megan almost always wore. My stomach sank. Whatever Megan was wearing when she left the flat, it wasn't either of those.

And that meant she'd gone out – into the cold – without them. Not planned. Not prepared. Or, at least, that's how it seemed to me. And that's what worried me the most.

I was wearing thin blue rubber gloves when I picked up Megan's phone from the table in the lounge, its smooth, lifeless screen reflecting the dim light in the flat. A slim, black rectangle – ordinary, unremarkable – but maybe crucial. Possibly even the key to understanding what happened to her. Another piece of the jigsaw?

I lowered myself onto the two-seater sofa, sinking slightly into the worn purple velour. The fabric was tired, threadbare in places, carrying the faint musty scent of charity shop.

I tried everything I could to access the phone's contents –

swiping, pressing, willing it to unlock – but it was no use. Locked tight. A digital wall I couldn't break through.

Frustration prickled, but I knew this wasn't my skillset. A job for the tech team. They were good at that sort of thing. So much better than me.

I slipped Megan's phone into a clear plastic evidence bag, sealing it with a flick of my fingers. The smooth surface of the mobile was now distorted by the crinkled plastic, its secrets locked away – for now. Maybe a silent witness to whatever had happened?

Cradling it carefully, I made my way to my car, opening the door and securing the phone inside for safekeeping. I took a quick gulp of warm coffee. I always carry a flask when I can. But I had no time to sit and relax. There was still work to be done.

Steeling myself, I turned back towards the row of flats and houses, their dull facades staring blankly. I started knocking on doors, one by one, hoping – praying – that someone had seen something. A flicker of movement. A shadow in the night. Perhaps a detail small enough to be dismissed but big enough to matter. Because Megan hadn't just vanished. Surely someone, somewhere, must have seen *something*. And if only I could be the one to secure the breakthrough evidence, my future in CID would be assured.

There was no reply at the first two doors I knocked on. But at the third, I finally heard something.

A faint shuffle. Slow and deliberate. The hesitant drag of shoed feet against worn carpet, punctuated by the rhythmic tap... tap... tap of something striking the floor.

I leaned in slightly, peering through the hazy glass pane, the distorted interior offering little more than vague shapes. Patience has never been my strong suit, but I forced myself to wait as the figure edged forward, step by painstaking step.

And then, at last, the latch clicked, the door creaking open an inch before widening further to reveal the man inside.

He looked ancient – late eighties, maybe early nineties. A frail frame, his body folded into itself with time, draped in a threadbare yellow cardigan that hung loosely over thin shoulders. His hands, knotted with age, gripped the wooden handles of two walking sticks, his knuckles pale with the effort. His breath was shallow, wheezing slightly as he lifted his head to study me, clouded eyes narrowing as they adjusted to the external light.

I waited, holding the old man's gaze, my warrant card already in hand. Because in the unlikely event he had seen something – *anything* – I needed to hear about it.

I forced an unconvincing smile as the old man squinted at me, his rheumy eyes seemingly struggling to focus. 'Hello, sir. My name is DC Nicholl from the local police. I'd like to ask you a few questions.'

A gap-toothed smile split his weathered face, and then came the line I'd already heard more times than I cared to count. 'You haven't come to arrest me, have you, darling? You don't look old enough to be a copper.'

I forced a quick laugh, biting back my impatience. 'No, sir, you're safe for now.' I noted the hearing aid nestled in his ear and raised my voice slightly. 'It's about one of your neighbours. A young woman named Megan Morgan, who lives in Flat One at the end of the terrace. I'd be grateful if you could tell me when you last saw her.'

His expression shifted, a shadow of thought crossing his face before he wobbled slightly on his thin legs and turned slowly, shuffling back down the hallway. I followed as he motioned me inside. 'Come on in,' he said over one shoulder. 'We can talk in the lounge. The old body's not what it was. I need to take the weight off.'

I stepped inside and followed him into a small lounge, where he lowered himself with effort onto a battered brown leather sofa. I took the armchair opposite, watching as he settled, adjusting his sticks beside him.

'Right, first things first,' he said, his voice thick with a nasal North Wales accent. 'I don't get many visitors these days. Just the home help twice a week. And she's gone almost as soon as she arrives. Everyone's always in a rush these days. No time for the likes of me. How about a nice cup of tea?'

I didn't have time for small talk, either, which I guess proved his point. 'No tea for me, thanks. There's things I need to be getting on with. I was asking you about Megan.'

He nodded, a flicker of disappointment passing across his face. As if he'd been hoping for company, even if it came in the form of a detective. 'Megan, oh yes, Megan. I do know her. Not well. But we say hello if our paths cross.' He hesitated, frowning slightly. 'But let me think... My memory's almost as bad as my legs. No, no, I haven't seen her for months. Such a nice, pleasant girl. I do hope she's okay.'

'She's missing,' I said, thinking I was wasting my time. 'I'm trying to find her. That's why I'm here.'

I'd just stood to leave when his next words stopped me in my tracks. 'I haven't seen Megan,' he began, scratching the side of his veined nose. 'But I *did* see something strange a few nights back.'

And just like that, my interest was piqued. I lowered myself back into my seat, fixing him with a steady look. Open-ended questions always worked best.

'Okay, I'm listening. Can you tell me what you saw?'

He smiled slightly, and I suspected he was pleased to have my attention for a little longer. 'I *will* tell you,' he said, rubbing his hands together. 'But how about that cup of tea first? You can make me one at the same time. And maybe a couple of digestives. I'm feeling peckish.'

I exhaled, accepting defeat, then pushed myself up and made my way to the kitchen. The countertops were cluttered with old newspapers and mismatched mugs, the kind that had been collected over decades. I found a kettle that looked like it had seen better days and filled it, waiting as it rumbled to life.

Two mugs of tea. His with milk and two sugars, just as he'd requested. And two biscuits on a cracked plate.

I handed him his order, watching as he blew across the tea's surface before raising it to his mouth. It left a milky moustache above his top lip as he sighed with satisfaction. And maybe now my frustration was getting to me. Perhaps I wasn't listening as well as I should have. But I asked the right question. Moving things along.

'You were going to tell me what you saw.'

'Ah, yes, yes... now, where was I?' He smacked his lips, looking up at the ceiling as if retrieving the memory from some distant corner of his mind. 'It was three or four nights ago... or perhaps a little longer. I can't be sure. I don't sleep well, you see. The tablets don't work as well as they used to. You get used to the damn things – that's the problem. And my doctor won't let me up the dose.'

I fought the urge to hurry him along, but in the end impatience got the better of me. 'What exactly did you see?'

He took another slow sip, not bothering to blow on it this time. 'One thing at a time,' he murmured. 'I was just coming to that.'

I held my patience this time, waiting as he continued.

'It was in the early hours. I'd just been to the bathroom for a pee when I decided to take a look out of the bedroom window – see if I could spot any foxes. I do that sometimes to pass the time.

I knew I wouldn't get back to sleep.' He paused. 'And this is where it gets *strange*.'

I leaned in slightly, watching the change in his expression. 'Strange how?'

'I didn't see any animals,' he continued, his voice quieter now. 'But I *did* see a man hurrying down the road past my house, carrying something over one shoulder.'

My pulse kicked up a notch. But I kept my voice level. 'Carrying what?'

He shook his head, a look of despondence clouding his features. 'Sorry, darling. I'd be guessing. I've got no idea.'

'Was it a short thing or a long thing?'

'Um, long, I think. Sort of hanging over his shoulder to front and back. They used to call it a fireman's lift. No idea if they still do these days. All that politically correct nonsense. So much has changed.'

I swallowed hard. 'Could it have been a *person*? Could it have been Megan he was carrying?'

He hesitated. A beat of silence. 'Well... I suppose it *could* have been,' he said. 'Or a rug or carpet, maybe. Something like that. Hard to say. I didn't have my glasses on. And I can't even see that well with them. Not like I used to when my wife was alive.'

I took out my pocketbook, flipping it open to a blank page. 'Please try to think very hard. Which night was it?'

He beamed. 'Do you think it's important?'

'Might be. So, which night?'

'Um...' He pursed his lips, brow furrowed in thought. 'Maybe early this week. I'm fairly sure of that. But beyond that, I can't say.'

Frustration prickled again, but I forced it down. I wasn't sure how useful his information was, if at all. But I had to push on, just in case. 'Can you describe the man for me?'

He exhaled heavily. 'Hmm... I *think* he was tall. Yes, tall.'

I paused, pen poised. 'Think, or know?'

He winced. 'Sorry. I wouldn't want to swear to it.'

There was that frustration again. 'Any idea of his build?'

He drained his mug, setting it carefully to one side. 'That's a tough one. I *think* he was strong. Not a fat bloke, I'm fairly sure of that. And I think he was wearing a hood. That stuck in my head because it wasn't raining.'

I pressed my lips together. Not much to go on. But something nagged at me. A man. Hurrying down the street. Carrying *something*. Hood up? Really?

If the old man was right – which I seriously doubted – in the unlikely event that the *something* was *Megan*, then I had to rule that out without wasting too much time.

I took a full written statement at that point, starting with the old man's name – Jack Davies – and then his Carmarthen address, neatly printing both at the top of the page in black ink. His voice wavered as he repeated what he'd seen, his frail hands trembling slightly as he watched me write, his cloudy eyes flickering between me and the page as though the weight of his words had only just settled on him.

I kept the statement as succinct as possible, cutting out the rambling as best I could while making sure the key details remained intact. When I finally slid the paper towards him, he read it slowly, lips moving silently with each word before nodding. He picked up the pen with stiff fingers, his signature scrawled in shaky, uneven strokes at the bottom of the page. A true record.

By the time I was back outside, I felt, if not entirely confident, at least satisfied that I'd found *something*. It wasn't much. It wasn't the obvious breakthrough I'd been hoping for. But it was something. And that was more than I'd got from every other door I knocked on.

I told myself that as I said my goodbyes and climbed back into my car. That the visit hadn't been a complete waste of time. That I'd walked away with a potential lead.

But that feeling of self-congratulation didn't last long.

By the time I'd driven a few streets away, doubt had started creeping in. The longer I replayed the conversation in my head, the weaker the lead began to feel.

By the time I was halfway back to police headquarters, I had a sinking feeling deep in the pit of my stomach. And by the time I pulled into the busy car park, I was in two minds about even showing the statement to DI Kesey at all. Would she thank me for following up on every angle? Or would she tear me apart for wasting her valuable time with vague, unsubstantiated claims from an elderly man with poor eyesight and an even worse memory? I really wasn't sure. But in the end, I told myself that I'd done my job. I'd collected the information. And it was her call what to do with it.

The DI wasn't in her office when I pushed open the door. Empty. I checked the time, debating whether to wait. Gave it a few minutes before deciding to try my luck elsewhere. If she wasn't at her desk, there was a possibility she'd retreated to the canteen. It had to be worth a try.

Sure enough, about five minutes later, I spotted her.

She was sitting alone at one of the Formica-topped tables, a steaming cup of black coffee in front of her, posture relaxed but eyes sharp. Even now – off duty, or as off duty as a DI ever really gets – there was a quiet alertness about her. A presence that never fully switched off.

I approached cautiously, bracing myself for irritation, but to my relief, she looked up and offered a warm smile. 'Have you got two minutes, boss? Sorry to bother you while you're taking a break.'

'Not a problem. Take a seat. And tell me how I can help.'

First hurdle cleared. Now for the next. I slid into the seat opposite, inhaled, and summarised what Jack Davies had told me, keeping my tone even, watching her closely.

The DI didn't interrupt. She just listened, nodding slightly, fingers idly tracing the rim of her coffee cup.

Then, to my relief, her response was surprisingly positive. 'This reminds me of a case Gareth Gravel – DI Gravel, long retired – once told me about,' she said, tilting her head to one side in thought. 'Long time ago now. A kidnapped seven-year-old boy, carried into a house wrapped up in a Persian rug.'

I sat forward, pulse ticking up a notch. 'Do you think this could be the same kind of thing, boss?' I asked, a little too eagerly.

She met my gaze. 'Could be. Stranger things have happened. But let's not get ahead of ourselves. It's a *potential* lead – no more than that.'

I nodded, forcing myself to slow down, to not make assumptions. Then, as I sat back and listened, DI Kesey leaned forward, eyes sharp with focus as she laid out my next steps. 'I want you to revisit all the properties you didn't get a reply at earlier. See if anyone else saw the mystery man Davies claims to have seen. You said yourself the old man's an unreliable witness at best. But let's not dismiss his statement without very good reason. As of now, it's all we've got.'

A weight lifted from my chest. She was taking this seriously. And I couldn't have been more pleased. 'Yes, boss.'

'And once you've finished knocking on doors, later today, I want you to start going through all the available CCTV from the moment Megan's sister last knew where she was to the time she was reported missing. We don't have cameras on Megan's street – but let's find out who was nearby.'

Her voice was crisp, commanding, her mind already three

steps ahead. And I have to admit I was impressed as the DI continued outlining her orders. One day, I'd like to be like her. 'Anyone with a relevant history – house breakings involving violence, kidnappings, sexual offences against women – I want to know about it. Let's get them checked out.' She paused, studying me. 'Any questions?'

I stood, shaking my head. No questions. No hesitation. It was time to get back to the job.

But as I turned to leave and head to my shared CID office, a nagging voice whispered at the back of my mind, a low murmur I couldn't ignore. An instinctive prickle of unease. This wasn't just another case. It wasn't just another missing person enquiry destined to drown in paperwork and dead ends. No, this felt different. Maybe Davies had seen something significant, as unlikely as that seemed. And perhaps it mattered more than I realised.

The uneasy weight of it all pressed down like a warning as I approached the lift one hurried step at a time. This could be the case that secured my CID posting. Every unanswered question seemed to pulse with life beneath the surface. My mind raced through every possibility, each more unsettling than the last. I knew that I'd dig deeper, attempt to peel back layers until every secret was exposed. And whether the case became my triumph or my undoing, I was determined to follow its trail to the bitter end.

21

THE SURGEON

It's been another fascinating day in Bunker World – as I've come to think of it. And, if I do say so myself, that's an inspired choice of words, worthy of my undoubted genius.

After all, what is a bunker if not a world in itself? A self-contained ecosystem. A controlled environment. A prison so perfectly designed that my lab rat's entire existence now depends on the walls that entomb her.

She exists inside a coffin of reinforced concrete – twenty feet long, twelve wide – a lifeless box without doors, without windows, without mercy. The ceiling hatch, cold and steel-clad, taunts her from above, the only exit now a cruel illusion. The folding aluminium steps once secured to the ceiling are long gone, stripped away by my hand. Without the step ladder I deliberately withhold, she's as powerless as a pinned moth, flailing in the dark, utterly mine. As helpless as an insect in a glass jar.

There is no bed. No chair. No furniture to offer comfort or rest. I have, however, allowed my research subject the use of a portable chemical toilet. But not out of kindness. I don't indulge such weakness. That would only detract from my work – limit what's possible. An abomination in itself.

No, the toilet is for my benefit, not hers.

Because I have no desire to wade through her filth.

Of course, it does mean I'll have to empty the damned thing from time to time. Lowering a strong nylon rope through the hatch and ordering my lab rat to tie it to the plastic handle before hauling it up like some menial tradesman. The very thought of it makes my skin crawl. Such a regrettable inconvenience. A task so far beneath me. Far more suited to a simpering nurse than an eminent doctor like myself.

But as of now, I have no assistant. No one I can trust to share in my work. Perhaps, in time, that will change. Maybe, at some future date, I'll find someone worthy of the role. Someone who truly understands what I'm striving to achieve. Bella, maybe, the rather attractive influencer who so adores me. Someone like that. A woman who admires me and who might see the brilliance in my research. And it does *have* to be a woman. Men revolt me. Too strong, too opinionated. I do sometimes appreciate female company. And it would be helpful if someone utterly subservient could sometimes take some of the burden. So I have to believe such things are possible. But enough of that. I need to focus. Back to the now.

I had something special reserved for today. A complex psychological experiment, studiously designed and carefully structured – a process I implemented only after a good breakfast. Sufficient nourishment to keep me performing at my very best. After all, one can't conduct truly groundbreaking research on an empty stomach.

I remember reading, somewhere in the depths of an academic textbook, that hope is a crucial factor in human resilience. A force that has the potential to carry a person through even the most extreme of circumstances. A glimmer in the darkness, keeping them fighting, pushing them forward despite all they endure.

And if you think about it – as I have, extensively – who could possibly find themselves in more extreme circumstances than my lab rat?

As I took a break from my writing, I watched the playback on my high-resolution surveillance screen, reliving the events in stunning clarity. Not just for my own enjoyment – though that is certainly a factor – but to ensure every detail is captured, every moment committed to record with absolute accuracy.

Because true academic rigour demands nothing less. Only a true scientist like myself would fully appreciate that.

The inspired premise of my experiment was deceptively simple: to give my rat hope. To allow her, just for a moment, to believe in potential salvation. To lift her spirits to new heights – and then, just as quickly, to snatch all hope away again.

A brutal lesson. A perfect demonstration of authority. Because nothing breaks a subject more effectively than hope turned to despair. That was my hypothesis. And I fully intended to prove myself correct.

I began by switching off the music, plunging the bunker into an almost unnatural silence. The kind that rings in the ears, oppressive in its weight. Next, I dimmed the previously blinding lights, reducing the harsh glare to something subtle, almost soothing – a stark contrast to the relentless torment of the past twenty-four hours.

I wanted Megan to feel the shift. To sense that something had changed. Then, precisely thirty minutes later, I slowly unlatched the steel hatch, allowing a shaft of pale morning light to spill into the void below. A sliver of hope. A taste of something outside her prison. A fleeting reminder of the world she no longer belongs to.

With calculated precision, I dropped in a sealed container –

fresh, warm porridge, sweetened with brown sugar, the gentlest touch of feigned kindness woven into an act of complete dominance. A clear plastic bottle of chilled spring water followed, condensation clinging to the sides – a clever temptation after days of filth and deprivation.

And finally, I allowed her a small indulgence she certainly didn't deserve. A spoon. A simple metal utensil, deliberately chosen after a brief deliberation. *Would she use it to harm herself?* Unlikely. And even if she tried, what difference would it make? How much damage could she do?

A knife or fork would be out of the question. Because her suffering is mine to dictate. I decide when she hurts. I decide when she begs. And when she dies.

I decide *everything*. That's as it should be. No more and no less.

With my part complete, I returned to the house, settling into my chair before the high-definition surveillance feed, fingers poised over the controls, eyes locked onto the screen. The anticipation glorious.

My lab rat didn't move at first. Not for almost five full minutes. She just sat there, hunched in a far corner, her thin, naked body curled in on itself, knees pulled tight to her chest in some pathetic, instinctive attempt at modesty. A useless act, given that I see everything.

And then, all of a sudden, just as I'd anticipated, her hunger *and* thirst got the better of her. Her body betrayed her as I knew it would.

Slowly, painfully, my lab rat crawled forward on all fours, her movements sluggish, weakened by starvation and exhaustion. A broken thing scrambling for scraps.

And then – fascinating. She scuttled back to the wall, clutching the containers, and devoured the items in what I can only describe as a feeding frenzy. Hands scooping, no spoon, shovelling, barely chewing – pure, animalistic desperation on display. It was quite the spectacle. Both entertaining and informative.

I allowed myself a small chuckle, purely out of amusement, of course. But this isn't about humour.

This is science. And then, the moment I'd been waiting for. The climax of my experiment. The part where I took all that hope – that fleeting sense of reprieve – and tore it apart.

I waited two full hours before I finally spoke through the sound system. I let the silence stretch, unbearably long, allowing her to settle into the illusion that the worst had passed. That the food had been some kind of turning point. That the shift in atmosphere signified a thread of humanity, some reluctant mercy.

And then, when I judged the moment precisely right, I broke the silence. I kept my tone soft at first. Calm. Measured. The kind of voice a master might use to praise a loyal dog. And most crucially – I used her name. *'Megan.'* I let it roll off my tongue with deliberate ease. As if she mattered. As if she were a real person, someone with worth, someone of value in this world. Someone like *me*.

But of course, she is none of those things. That seems obvious. But it was an inspired touch, another stroke of psychological brilliance, if I do say so myself. Because when the verbal blows *did* come – when the reassurance curdled into something sharp, cruel, devastating – the impact was so much greater. A well-executed illusion is only as good as its collapse.

'Well, hello, my dear Megan, it's a delight to see you again.'

I let my voice drip with mock warmth, the kind of tone a doting father might use to greet his needy child. Soft. Reassuring. A far cry from what was soon to come. 'I do hope you enjoyed your meal. I made it for you specially with my own fair hands.

Perhaps a round of applause and an expression of verbal gratitude would be appropriate at this point?'

I paused, watching her reaction on the high-definition screen, drinking in every tremor of her wasted, hollow-eyed face. She was painfully thin when she arrived. And had lost weight very quickly.

'I could see how much you enjoyed my offering,' I continued. 'Best show your appreciation, don't you think? After all, I have no obligation to keep you alive.'

For the briefest second – just a flicker – a look passed across her face. Recognition? A flash of memory. Perhaps. But it was gone almost as quickly as it appeared.

And then, like a trained seal, she began to perform.

Clap. Clap. Clap. Exactly as she was told. But there was no genuine gratitude. Instead, she tried – laughably – to appeal to something in me that doesn't exist. To plead to a sympathy that simply isn't there. For myself, yes, but not for a worthless creature like her.

'Please, I'm b-begging you, please l-let me go,' she stuttered, her voice cracked, raw with desperation. 'I wouldn't go to the p-police. I have no idea where I am or who y-you are. You c-could blindfold me and take me home. P-please take me home.'

I let out a soft chuckle. Such entertainment. I couldn't tear my eyes away from the screen. It was time to up the pressure, turn the screw. 'Ah, so you claim you don't know who I am? And I could set you free without fear of consequences. That's what you're claiming, isn't it? I'm not mistaken, am I?'

She froze, her gaunt face pinched with confusion. Her mouth opened slightly, but no words came. Instead, she nodded – frantic, desperate, as if her very survival depended on convincing me.

And that was it. The glorious moment I'd been waiting for.

The big reveal. The very moment I would take that tiny, fragile ember of hope she was clutching on to and crush it into dust.

I inhaled slowly, deliberately, shifting my chair a few inches closer to the screen, my pulse thick and pounding in my ears. My penis throbbed inside my trousers, the pure exhilaration of absolute control electrifying every inch of me. And then, I delivered the final blow.

'You may be surprised to hear that you're wrong in what you said.' I let the words hang, let her drown in the weight of them before continuing. 'We have met before. It was some ten years ago, in the lovely town of Tenby. Surely that's something you must recall.'

She didn't move. Didn't even breathe. And I drove home my advantage, never more powerful, never more aroused as I ejaculated without the need to touch myself. 'Do you remember, Megan?' I tilted my head, my voice a whisper now, intimate. Deliciously cruel. 'The man who stabbed you? Left you for dead?'

Her whole body tensed, her fingers curling into trembling fists against the floor. And I smiled so broadly my face ached. 'I feel a trumpet fanfare might be appropriate at this point. Try to imagine it in your head.' Another pause. Letting her anticipate the horror before I finally ripped it open. 'Are you ready? Yes? Well, here goes. I'm certain you've already reached the logical conclusion. But I'll say it anyway in the interests of openness. Your attacker was me. And there'll be no need for my mask any more. Not now that we're so well acquainted. My name's Professor Aitken.'

And just like that, I watched the last scrap of hope die in her eyes. She crumpled, reminding me of a slowly deflating beach toy as her head hung towards the floor.

I was about to switch off my monitor, stretch my legs, and lift a well-earned glass of French claret – a quiet moment of celebration for a job well done before making my notes.

But then – a sudden flash of genius stopped me in my tracks. A bolt of inspiration, so sharp, so utterly perfect, that I felt a surge of exhilaration course through me.

Because that's the thing about high achievers like myself. We are rarely, if ever, satisfied for long, no matter how much we accomplish. We are driven by something greater. A relentless pursuit of excellence. It's what separates men like me from the weak, the feeble, the ordinary, the majority.

And so, without hesitation, I decided to hammer home one last metaphorical nail into my lab rat's coffin. Not out of necessity. Not out of science. But simply for the joy of it. Because I deserved a treat after all my hard work. No reasonable person could think otherwise.

I cleared my throat, coughed lightly, then leaned forward, my fingers hovering over the microphone control. And then, I began. 'Listen up, Megan. Look at the camera lens. Now. Do as you're told.'

She didn't move at first, but I could see her shoulders tensing, could hear the ragged, uneven breaths rattling from her chest.

'Stop your pathetic snivelling, girl. You're starting to anger me. And that's *never* a good idea.' A pause. Just long enough for the tension to curl, to tighten like a noose. 'It's important that you accept something. This' – I gestured towards the screen, to the filthy concrete cell that now defined her existence – 'is your home now. So don't ever ask to leave again. Because if you do, even once, I'll have no choice but to punish you.'

I let that settle for a few seconds. Let her stew in it. And then, smoothly, precisely, I twisted the knife.

'The music can always be louder. The lights brighter. And there's so much worse than that if you fail to please me.' I smiled to myself, watching her body curl in on itself, like a wounded animal expecting another blow. 'Horrors you could never even imagine in your worst nightmares.'

A quiet, choked sob escaped her lips. Perfect. But she didn't utter a single word.

'And don't waste your energy hoping someone will come for you. No one ever will. No one even knows you're here. Or that your new home even exists. You escaped me once... but not this time, my dear girl. Not this time.'

I shifted in my chair, getting comfortable, savouring the moment. 'You see, Megan, I live in a large, detached country house. Comfortable. Private. Isolated. And your little burrow? Perfectly hidden, nestled beneath a two-acre lawn at the back of the property. No prying eyes. No unwanted visitors. Nothing but grass, trees, and shrubs.'

I chuckled, shaking my head at my sheer brilliance.

'And the best part of all? The delicious irony? The bunker was built during the Cold War, a relic of paranoia. And – now, this is where it gets funny, so do try to see the humour – I was only told about it by the seller after I'd purchased the house.' I grinned, my amusement genuine. 'No planning permission. Completely off the record. Isn't that wonderful? Isn't that just... perfect? It's as if this was always meant to be. Had the police found the bunker when I was arrested six years ago, none of this would be possible. But they didn't find a thing!'

I waited. For something. A response. A cry. A broken plea. But there was nothing. Just weeping. Deep, guttural sobs. Her frail body shuddering, gasping for breath, her shoulders convulsing with the force of it.

A little disappointing, if I'm honest. But no matter. I'd make up for it next time.

Now, it was time for that wine. A large glass of deep, velvety

Bordeaux, rich and full-bodied, the kind that lingers on the tongue. And some Swiss chocolate to go with it, smooth, decadent, the perfect contrast of bitter and sweet.

Because why not? If *I* didn't deserve such small indulgences, then who on earth does? It has taken every ounce of my remarkable self-discipline not to have killed the needy bitch already. Every instinct in me screams to cut her open, to feel what I have waited so long to feel, but I have resisted. Controlled myself.

Because I am a man of science. A man of extraordinary willpower. And those virtues alone earn me a metaphorical pat on the back. And, who knows? Maybe at some future date, a Nobel Prize? Well-deserved, I'd say. I'm at the very top of my game. And there is so much more to come.

I sipped my wine, rolled it over my tongue, savouring the way it tasted, the way it lingered. Like triumph. Like destiny. The bunker's surveillance feed glowed, and I watched as my lab rat dissolved into something close to silence.

But I knew better. It wasn't silence. It was surrender. The first crack in the foundation of who she was. And soon, she won't just ask for freedom – she'll plead for my approval, for my kindness. She'll beg to exist on my terms. And that, I think, is when my real work will begin.

22

THE DETECTIVE CONSTABLE

DC Nicholl. I still haven't got used to the new title. My investigation of Megan's case has moved on a little.

I followed DI Kesey's orders to the letter, heading back to Megan's street at a time most residents were home from work. The place had a different feel after dark – curtains drawn tight, windows glowing with artificial light, the occasional flicker of a TV screen breaking the monotony. A quiet street that shouldn't feel ominous, but did.

Only one resident was out – a shift worker from the local hospital – but I managed to speak to her by phone, so no issues there. That's the good news. My enquiries went smoothly enough. No hostility. No resistance. But then, the downside. No one else I spoke to had seen the man Jack Davies described. Not at the time, not before, and not after. No figures moving in the night, no one carrying anything suspicious. Nothing.

And I'll be honest – I'm still not entirely sure if our mystery man even exists. Maybe the old man dreamt him up. Maybe he saw someone who just wasn't there. Davies is forgetful, that much is obvious. But am I ready to throw his statement out? Not quite yet. Because, as DI Kesey said, we don't have much else to go on. If anything at all.

And then, the worst news of all – there's still no sign of Megan. No sightings. No bank activity. I've checked. Twice. And to be honest, I can't say I'm hopeful of finding her alive and well.

I wish I felt differently. And I want to be wrong. But something about this case... something about the way she's vanished without a trace... it doesn't sit right.

Still, I'll keep pushing. Keep digging. Not just because it's my job. But because Megan matters.

So, fingers crossed. If there's anything to be found – I'll find it.

I've spent the best part of the day trawling through hours of grainy, low-resolution CCTV footage, my eyes burning from the relentless glare of the screen. The monotony was suffocating, the endless parade of cars and shadowed figures blurring together in a maddening loop. It was a soul-crushing task, made bearable only by a steady intake of strong, syrupy coffee that did little to keep the fatigue at bay.

There's still more to do – double-checking, rewinding, scrutinising frames I sped through in desperation to cover ground. But even so, I've found something. Twelve known offenders, each with a past worth noting, passing through Carmarthen between the relevant times. A potential lead, but hardly a breakthrough. The footage doesn't stretch far enough, doesn't show whether any of them ventured into Megan's street, let alone her flat. The system is flawed, riddled with blind spots – frustrating gaps where answers might be hiding out of reach.

And the forensics team? No help there. Not a single significant print in the flat. No red flags. Just a dead end wrapped in the stale scent of failure. If Megan was abducted, maybe the offender wore gloves.

With my sergeant's help, I've ranked my list of offenders in priority order. Every last one of them will have to be tracked down and interviewed, a daunting task given our skeletal staffing levels. Now I need to report my findings to DI Kesey. I can only hope my efforts make her job a little easier.

There was one name I considered adding to the list, but didn't. Not because I overlooked it, but because it didn't belong. I recognised a particular vehicle on the CCTV, cruising through town in the early hours of Monday morning. A black Mercedes. Familiar. The man behind the wheel – Alexander Aitken. A once-respected hospital consultant, and now a free man. Cleared of all wrongdoing. The law said he was innocent. But some stains never truly fade, do they?

I hadn't added his name to the list. Why would I? There was no legal reason to: I could only list known offenders and Aitken didn't fit that description. And yet, something ate away at me. The timing. The history. The way his name still sent ripples through the station. After too much deliberation, I finally made my decision. If I were Laura Kesey, I'd want to know.

I found the DI in her office, weighed down with paperwork. She barely looked up as I stepped inside. 'Got time to talk, boss? I've done the run-through of the CCTV and put together a list of offenders for your consideration.'

She took the sheet of paper from my outstretched hand, her glasses slipping to the tip of her nose as she skimmed through it. A faint nod. 'Yeah, thanks. Helpful. Some of the usual suspects. I'll decide the best approach and let you know. It's late. You've done enough for today. We'll make a start in the morning. Be here for eight.'

I hesitated. The weight in my chest told me to leave it, to walk away. But I couldn't. 'There's... err... one other thing, boss.'

She finally met my eyes. 'Okay, I'm listening.'

I forced the words out, wanting to be done with them. 'I know he's not a criminal. I realise all that's over with. But I thought you should be aware that Professor Aitken's Mercedes was recorded during the relevant period. I've noted the exact time and date, if that helps?'

A muscle in Kesey's jaw twitched. Her fingers drummed against the desk. 'What's the relevance?'

I swallowed hard. 'Word around the station is that his search history was... disturbing.'

The DI let out a slow, measured breath, her expression darkening. 'Oh, it was. Horrendous. The man's a creep. Thank God he hasn't gone back to work. I wouldn't want him near anyone with a scalpel. But that doesn't make him a suspect. And I want that crystal clear.' Her voice dropped, each word laced with warning. 'Aitken's already alleging harassment. His case was ruled a miscarriage of justice, and he's got the press on his side. The last thing the chief super needs is us giving Aitken another reason to throw more shit at the force. He's got more than enough already. So you stay well clear of him. And that's an order.'

Her reaction caught me off guard. It was sharper than I'd expected, laced with something I couldn't quite place. I never intended to interview Aitken – hadn't even considered it – but now, standing there under the weight of her scrutiny, I wished I'd kept my mouth shut. I cleared my throat. 'Yeah. Sorry, boss. I understand.'

The DI barely acknowledged me, her gaze already back on the open file in front of her. The faintest rise and fall of her shoulders betrayed the effort to keep her composure. 'I'll see you in the morning, Jacqueline. And don't be late.'

Dismissing me. Not a great start to my time in CID.

I felt my stomach churn, that uneasy feeling growing with every step as I left the room.

I exhaled slowly, trying to shake off the nagging feeling

coiling in my gut. Kesey's reaction had been too sharp, too final – almost defensive. I'd only flagged Aitken as a point of interest, not accused him of anything. But the way she shut me down so quickly... it didn't sit right. Was it just politics? The force covering its back? Or was there something else – something she wasn't saying?

I pushed the thought away, but it lingered, unwelcome. If I'd already learned one thing in this job, it was this – instincts mattered. And mine were screaming.

23

THE DETECTIVE INSPECTOR

Jan and Ed were huddled up together on the sofa when I stepped through the door at just after six this evening, the glow of the laptop screen flickering across their faces. The repeated sounds of digital gunfire filled the lounge, punctuated by Ed's excited chatter. He was the first to notice me, springing to his feet with a grin, his arms wrapping around me in a warm hug.

'Mum! Guess what? I made the school football team!' His eyes shone with unfiltered pride, his energy infectious.

'Nice one. That's brilliant, Ed. It'll be a Welsh cap next. You and Gareth Bale knocking in the goals in the World Cup final.'

He laughed, just as I'd intended, before diving straight back into his game, the controller back in his grip within seconds.

Jan smiled too, but it didn't reach her eyes. Forced. Tight. A poor disguise for whatever was bothering her beneath the surface. I knew her too well to be fooled. I could read her like a large-print book – every crease in her forehead, every flicker of hesitation, communicating that something was wrong.

And yet, she said nothing. Not with Ed in the room, his attention again fixed on the flashing screen, oblivious to the undercurrent of tension thickening the air. But Jan would share whatever was worrying her. I knew she would. It was only a matter of time. That's how these things always play out between us – the same unspoken pattern, the same inevitable reckoning. And tonight would be no different.

The game ended with a final loud explosion, pixels scattering in digital destruction. Jan stood, smoothing down her top, her movements deliberate, measured. She flicked a glance towards the kitchen – a silent signal. Message received.

The rich aroma of tasty food curled through the house, something slow-cooked, spiced just right. My stomach grumbled in anticipation as I pulled out a chair at the kitchen table. But Jan wasn't thinking about food. Not yet. I could see it on her face. Her mind was elsewhere. And whatever it was, it wouldn't stay unsaid for long.

'Glass of wine?' Jan asked, already reaching into the fridge, the chilled bottle of white clinking against the shelf as she pulled it free.

I nodded, forcing a reluctant smile as she poured. It had already been a long, punishing day, and I'd been hoping for a quiet, convivial evening – some brief reprieve from the weight pressing down on me. But the set of her shoulders, the tightness around her mouth, told me that wasn't going to happen.

I accepted the glass, lifted it to my lips, and took a slow sip, letting the crisp liquid settle on my tongue. 'Anything we need to talk about?' I asked, already knowing the answer, already feeling the tension creeping in.

Jan checked the timer on the cooker, turning the temperature up a notch before joining me at the table. Her face was drawn, her expression sullen. When she finally spoke, her voice was lower than before, edged with something brittle. 'I saw *that man* again today. Aitken. The surgeon.'

I kept my face neutral, or at least I tried to. But I knew my body betrayed me – the tightness of my jaw, the slight shift in my posture. 'Oh, really? Where?'

Jan exhaled sharply, irritation laced through her breath. 'Outside the school again. When I picked up Ed. Sitting there in his big posh car, just like before. It's a public place, I get that. He's not breaking any laws. But the man gives me the creeps. He was staring at me with this... this really weird expression. As if he *hated* me. Like I was something vile. Something beneath him. A shit stain on his shoe.'

Jan's fingers tightened around the stem of her glass. 'I was this close to marching straight up to his car window and asking him what the hell his problem was. First, he turns up near the house, and now twice at the school. It's starting to feel deliberate. Almost as if he's following me.'

I leaned forward, my pulse kicking up a notch. 'He didn't try to speak to you, did he? Or Ed?'

Jan shook her head, then drained the remainder of her wine. 'No. He just sat there. Watching. It felt like... like I was under surveillance. Or like he *wanted* me to know he was there, that he could make me feel uncomfortable if he wanted to. He had this sick grin on his face when I glared at him. He looked, well, almost evil.'

She set the empty glass down with a soft click. 'I was relieved to get back in the car and drive away.'

I shrugged, gave a sympathetic look, unsure of what to do or say. 'I get what you're saying, Jan. But like you said, he's not breaking any laws. And it's only the three times you've seen him. Maybe him being there was just a coincidence.'

Jan pulled her head back, looking far from persuaded. 'You wouldn't be saying that if you'd been there. What if it's personal? He made his opinion of you pretty damned clear when he was all over the news. He blames you for his time in prison. Maybe this is about that. Maybe it's about *you*.'

I made a face. 'I guess I have to accept that's a possibility.'

She met my gaze now, her eyes searching. 'You couldn't have a quiet word with him, could you? Warn him off? Tell him to stay away? Tell him he's freaking me out?'

The request hung in the air between us, heavy, unspoken implications rippling beneath the surface.

I wasn't sure what unsettled me more – Aitken's repeated presence or the insistent feeling that this was only the beginning.

I shook my head, exhaling a slow, resigned sigh. And I already knew she wouldn't appreciate my reply. 'Sorry, Jan. Halliday's made it clear – I'm to stay well clear. You know what the chief super's like. Always got one eye on the force's reputation, the other on his next promotion. Aitken lodging another complaint could end my career. Demotion at the very least. A hefty pay cut. And we're already struggling to cover the bills as it is.'

Jan's frustration simmered just beneath the surface, barely contained. 'Well then, what the *hell* do I do if Aitken keeps turning up? I can't just ignore him. I've got to do something.'

I forced myself to stay calm, to offer something – anything – that might reassure her, even if I knew deep down that my words were inadequate. This was one of those situations where nothing I said would be of much use. The law didn't help. Hard won experience had taught me that. Not unless things escalated. Not unless it got a whole lot worse. 'Keep a note of every time you see Aitken. Where it happens, the time of day, the date. And if you can, get a photo on your phone. Hopefully, we're both worrying about nothing. But if it becomes a clear pattern, we'll speak to our solicitor, look into a potential injunction. If we really have to.'

Jan's lips pressed into a thin line.

'And, naturally, if he ever makes a direct threat of any kind, that changes everything,' I added, my voice firm. 'I'd have him arrested and charged before he can blink, complaints or not. That's a promise. You and Ed come first.'

My words lingered between us, thick with unspoken weight. A pledge. A warning. Or maybe both. Did Aitken pose a real threat, beyond his relentless efforts to drag my good name through the mud? Was this personal, something darker than a grudge, or was I letting paranoia creep in? I didn't know. Not yet.

But there was something about him – something in the way he kept appearing, always just close enough to be noticed but never quite stepping over the line. A calculated game. A subtle kind of intimidation.

Every instinct told me to tread carefully. How carefully? Only time would tell.

Jan exhaled sharply, rubbing her temple, frustration still etched across her face. 'I just hate feeling so powerless, you know? Like he's got the upper hand, and I'm just supposed to accept it.'

I reached for her hand, giving it a gentle squeeze. 'You're not powerless. We'll handle this together.'

But even as I said it, my mind was whirling. Aitken wasn't just lurking – he was making sure we saw him. And that meant something. If he was playing a game, the question wasn't just why. It was how far he was willing to go to win.

24

THE SURGEON

My primary focus in recent days, by fortunate necessity, has been my lab rat – every detail, every reaction, every gratifying discovery my research provides. The depth of knowledge, the thrill of authority. A gift that keeps on giving.

But I am not a man of singular purpose. Multitasking comes as naturally to me as breathing, a skill I wield with precision far beyond the average, far beyond the mundane minds that stumble through life unaware.

And so, in perfect alignment with my goals, I've been watching. Observing. Calculating.

The pig. Kesey's partner. Their unsuspecting child. Still deciding how. Still deciding where. But when the moment comes, I'll be ready.

I have no interest in children. Not in the slightest. They mean nothing to me. But if the brat gets caught in the crossfire, then so be it. Collateral damage. Kesey brought everything on herself. She lit the match – and I'll be the one to watch it burn.

I cannot wait. The anticipation is almost too much to deal with. I'll tear Kesey's world apart, rip it to shreds piece by agonising piece. My plans are in place. And when the truth finally crashes down on her, when the full horror of what I've done finally sinks in, she'll think she's cursed for her misdeeds. For crossing me. For sending me to rot in a prison cell for a crime I didn't commit. And that knowledge fuels me. It drives me forward like a raging furnace in my veins, feeding my loathing, sharpening my resolve. And when the time is right, when every detail is in place, I'll unleash a storm so devastating she won't see it coming till it's far too late. A tsunami of suffering. She'll choke on it. Yes, she'll never know what hit her.

I despised every second of my time in prison – six endless years entombed in filth, surrounded by society's human waste. The stench of sweat and desperation thick in the air, the walls closing in like the jaws of a steel trap. Days bled into nights, months into years, each moment a reminder of what had been stolen from me. No textbooks, no research material, no stimulation beyond the mindless prattle of the damned. Wasted time. Stagnation.

And yet, with distance comes perspective. I've come to realise that even the darkest cell has its cracks, and through those cracks, opportunity seeps. Some say prison is a university for the criminal class. A tired, overused cliché – but one rooted in truth. I observed, I listened, and I learned. I made connections. Useful men with useful skills. Tools, waiting to be wielded.

And wield them I will. The next stage of my initiative is in motion, and I intend to use every advantage at my disposal. This time, nothing will stand in my way.

Megan has started to bore me. There's only so much one can extract from a single lab rat before the experiment becomes redundant. Information, pleasure, power – all finite resources when drained from the same source. I've toyed with her long enough. Stretched out the game, wrung every last drop of usefulness from her trembling frame. And if I'm honest, my patience is wearing thin.

Watching her slow, inevitable decline on the screen is one thing – her body shrinking, her spirit withering, the spark in her eyes flickering with each passing day. The way she paces in that concrete room, dragging herself from corner to corner like a wounded animal, knowing there's no escape, no salvation. The occasional outburst of defiance, the desperate, pleading eyes when she thinks I might listen, that I might care. It's almost amusing. Almost.

But witnessing it up close and personal? That's something else entirely. Feeling the fragility of her bones beneath my fingers, the hammering pulse against her throat, the warmth of her breath as she stifles a sob? That is the real thrill. The moment of true power.

And that's the problem, isn't it? She's here, ripe for the taking, and yet I've kept my distance, watching through the cold, detached lens of a screen. The anticipation, the restraint, it once heightened my pleasure. The build-up, the patience, the control. But now, it irritates me. I want more. I need more. And I must have it.

Megan's worth is dwindling, her fear turning stale. There's nothing left to learn, nothing new to take from her. Except, perhaps, that final moment – that delicious instant when she realises it's finally over, when the last embers of hope fade out, leaving nothing but pure, unfiltered terror. Yes. I think it's time. Time to stop watching. Time to feel. Time to end this. I do like to be personal.

And then, once I'm done – once my little lab rat is nothing more than a memory, a mess of severed flesh and silence – I'll move on. My work must continue. The game must go on.

Kesey's partner will be next. Carefully selected, perfectly

executed. She'll be introduced to her new subterranean home, a world of cold concrete and whispered screams. The last place she'll ever see. The last place she'll beg for mercy. And oh, how she will beg. Just like Megan. At first, anyway. Until exhaustion takes over, until she understands there is no mercy here.

There is still so much more fun to be had, so many delightful experiments yet to conduct. Every yelp, every whimper, every fractured plea is a lesson. A delicate balance of hope and despair. How much can Janet endure before she finally breaks? How far can I push before she shatters completely?

I intend to find out. And when it's done, I'll post a recording to Kesey. Nothing that risks identifying me, of course. I'll wear a suitable disguise as I slice her soulmate apart.

I can already picture it as clear as day – Kesey's face as she watches. The helpless rage, the gut-wrenching horror as she realises she was powerless to stop it.

She will no doubt dissect every frame with her detective ways, searching for clues that don't exist, analysing every sound, every shadow, desperate for a thread to pull. But there will be nothing. Just suffering. Just pain. Just the absolute certainty that she failed.

And that knowledge – knowing I've left her hollowed out, drowning in grief and fury – will be even more satisfying than the act itself. Oh yes, Kesey. I will make you bleed. There is a raging storm heading your way.

25

THE DETECTIVE INSPECTOR

It's been one hell of a week. The kind that grinds you down, body and soul. Staffing levels are still an absolute joke – stretched so thin it's a wonder we get anything done at all. Crime reports stack up faster than I can process them, a relentless tide of misery and violence, each file another grim reminder of the world we live in.

Halliday's in a foul mood as usual, not that I can entirely blame him this time. Aitken's lawyer has sent yet another letter, another tiresome attempt to twist the system in his client's favour. The creep should be waiting patiently for his compensation, not clogging up our inboxes with legal posturing. But the wheels of justice turn slowly, and some days, they barely turn at all.

And then there's my frigging cold. A nasty little virus that's been making the rounds, leaving me sniffling, aching, and running on fumes. Jan's noticed, of course. She's got that look in her eye again – the one that means she's worried. She even suggested I take a few days off, rest up, maybe even book that next holiday she keeps going on about.

But we both know that's not happening anytime soon. I haven't got time for rest. Haven't got time for holidays, for sick days, for anything beyond the relentless pull of this job. There's too much to do. Too much that won't wait. And whether I like it or not, the world keeps turning, the cases keep coming, and I'm the one left to pick up the pieces. I sometimes wonder why I applied for promotion at all. The responsibilities of rank can be a burden as well as a reward.

The Megan Morgan case is moving forward, but I'd be lying if I said it was going well. There's still no trace of her. Not a single confirmed sighting. No activity on her bank cards, no digital footprint, nothing. It's as if she vanished into thin air, swallowed whole by the darkness. And interviews with those men on the list of potential suspects have come to nothing. Not that I'm even certain there's been a crime at all. Yet, despite everything, I still cling to the hope that she's alive. That we're not just chasing a ghost. I like the woman. It feels personal. I know what she's been through better than most.

Yesterday morning, I held a press conference here at headquarters at ten sharp. Megan's sister sat beside me, pale and drawn, her fingers twisting in her lap, her eyes darting around the room like a cornered animal. A large photo of Megan dominated the space – a smiling girl frozen in time, oblivious to the events that would steal her away. I laid out the known facts, every frustrating detail of her disappearance. And then I made my appeal, the same one I've made too many times before. 'Someone must have seen something. Someone out there holds the key. And if they do, they need to come forward. Before it's too late.'

After the conference wrapped up, I called Steve Donovan – a DI over in Pembrokeshire. Just ten minutes on the phone. I needed to hear a familiar voice. Needed to speak the words out loud in an attempt to make sense of my thoughts.

'Hi, Steve, got time for a chat? It's Laura.'

'Yeah, no probs, anything specific?'

I sighed, blew out air. 'I've just sat through a press conference on the Megan Morgan case. It was a throw of the dice. There's still no sign of her. And I meant well. It's something that's worked with other cases and I thought it might this time. But in truth, the journalists weren't there for Megan. Not really. The moment the floor opened for questions, it was Aitken's name on their lips, their voices sharp and accusing. They didn't care about a missing girl, not when there was a bigger headline to chase. The barrage came fast and relentless. Why had the Aitken case gone so horribly wrong? Why was I still in charge? The room was a firing squad, and I was the target. Not a comfortable place to be.'

'Sounds like a right shit show.'

'Yeah, and, in part, I blame myself. I should have seen it coming. Of course I should have. It was inevitable, predictable. But sitting there, taking the hits, feeling the weight of their scrutiny pressing down, I found myself thinking the unthinkable. I wished I hadn't held the press conference at all. I'm not proud of myself for that. But then, I'm only human.'

Steve hesitated before responding. 'You did the right thing, Laura. And fingers crossed the publicity will pay off now it's over. Maybe someone out there will pick up the phone and hand you the break you need. A name. A sighting. A sliver of information that finally cracks this case wide open.'

I let out a laugh that had nothing to do with humour. 'I won't hold my breath. Not after the way things have been going lately. Right now, I feel as if I'm drowning. It's not just Megan. It's not just the potential fallout from Aitken's release, the looming threat of his legal action hanging over my career like a guillotine. It's more than that. It's *him*.'

'Him? What are you talking about?'

I hadn't meant to say as much as I did. Not about Aitken. Not about how he was affecting me and my family. But once I started, it was as if a floodgate opened. The words poured out of me in a torrent I couldn't stop.

'It's the way Aitken operates,' I began, feeling my chest tighten. 'The way he loiters on the periphery, poisoning the air without ever laying a finger. Because the longer it all drags on, the more certain I am – it's deliberate. Every move, every shadow he casts, every whisper of his presence, it's all calculated. A game of power. He wants me to feel it. The slow, creeping sense of unease. The subtle intimidation slithering under my skin.

'And I have to admit – it's working. The bastard is really getting to me. Needling his way into my thoughts, poisoning every decision I make. And the worst part? There's not a damn thing I can do about it.'

'Why the hell not?'

I shifted in my seat. 'Because if I go anywhere near Aitken, if I so much as breathe in the bastard's direction, he'll twist it. Turn it into another complaint, another mark against my name. And this time, I'll be the one who pays the price. Halliday's made that crystal clear.'

Another hesitation, two seconds' silence. 'Okay, I get what you're saying. But don't you think you're giving Aitken more power than he's actually got?'

I shook my head. 'No, not at all. Not even slightly. I'm acutely aware that on paper, to anyone on the outside looking in, Aitken's done nothing wrong. A victim of the justice system and a vindictive police officer who just won't let go. That's how he's playing it. That's how they'll see it. And no matter how much I know the truth, how much I want to scream it from the rooftops, it won't make a damn bit of difference. That's the real kicker. The worst part of all. Because Aitken isn't innocent. Not even close.'

'What are you saying?'

I took a breath. 'He's watching Jan. He's watching Ed. And for what? I don't know. Is the watching enough for him, or is it just the beginning? A prelude to something worse? A slow, calculated tightening of the noose? I can't answer that. And that uncertainty, that inescapable doubt, it's making my life a living hell.'

'Really? That bad?'

'Fine, so Aitken didn't kill Holly Larkin. That much is true. I have to accept that. But that doesn't make him guiltless. Not by a long shot. I saw his search history. I know the kind of sick filth that twisted mind of his obsesses over. And I don't believe, not for a single second, that he was trying to *revive* Holly, like he claimed at trial. She had his tooth marks on her neck. On her breast, for God's sake. And her blood. He was plastered in the stuff. Almost as if he'd tried to drink it.'

'Yeah, terrible. I remember you saying at the time.'

'Aitken's evil. And yet here we are. He's the one walking free, a so-called victim of a justice system that failed him. And me? I'm the one under scrutiny. The one they say is obsessed, incapable of letting go. The one with something to prove. That's what makes the deviant bastard more dangerous than ever. And I've never been more certain of anything in my life.

'Yesterday afternoon, I made a decision. No more second-guessing, no more waiting for proof to fall into my lap. I needed to see it for myself. So I parked near Ed's school in an unmarked car, blending into the background, just another vehicle in the sea of parents and commuters.'

'What happened?'

'I slouched low in the driver's seat, my eyes locked on the road ahead. And then, right on schedule – 3.30 to the second – he appeared. Aitken. Creeping along the street in his black Merc, moving at a deliberate crawl, eyes scanning, calculating. He drove past once, slow enough to take in every detail, then eased into a parking spot like he belonged there. Like it was normal. Like he wasn't a predator circling the outskirts of his prey's world.

'And that's the conclusion I reached. He's dangerous. A potential risk to my family. But what can I do about it? I've never felt so powerless. It seems I can do nothing at all.'

'Oh, for fuck's sake. Not an easy situation. Maybe things aren't as bad as you think.'

'My head's so full of questions. What the hell does he want? Is this the end or only the start? And what, if anything, should I do next? I'm really not sure.

'Every instinct in me screamed to drag the bastard from his car, to make him answer for the way he was circling my family like a vulture. But I couldn't.

'Because one thing is sure: Aitken would love me to crack, to lash out, to give him exactly what he needs to paint himself as the wronged party once again. And that's what scares me most – I'm not sure how much longer I can hold back.'

26

THE BULLY

No names. No faces. No trace. There's not a chance in hell I'm giving anyone my details. And I'm no grass. Never have been, never will be. I want to make that clear. That's not how I operate.

I've done my share of jobs over the years – burglary mostly, in and around Carmarthen and further afield when the opportunity was right. Nothing too flashy, nothing that draws heat. But even so, I know better than to invite trouble. And the last thing I need is to get tangled up with the pigs, even as a witness.

They say doing the right thing matters. That people should step up, speak out. But those people don't live my life. They don't understand the rules of the street. You keep your head down, your mouth shut, and your business your own. Anything else, and you're asking for trouble. And trouble? I don't need it.

I don't usually bother with the news. It's the same old depressing shit, day in, day out – politicians lying, people moaning, the world going to hell in a handcart. None of it interests me. But that night – the one I'm talking about – I made an exception.

The Welsh rugby manager was on, squirming under the studio lights, trying to justify fourteen losses in a row. It had all gone to shit, and I wanted to know what the fuck he was thinking to do about it. Sackings? Rebuild? Or just empty excuses?

I'd just cracked open my third can of lager, letting the cold bitterness wash down my throat, when the screen flickered – and there she was. Laura Kesey. The pig bitch who'd interviewed me the last time I got nicked, sitting there all smug and self-righteous, like she was better than me. Like she hadn't played a part in screwing up my life. Six months I got, because of her. And as I sat there, lager can gripped tight, jaw clenched, I felt that old anger simmer to the surface. But that's another story.

The pig was banging on about some needy tart named Megan – some girl who'd gone missing. The name meant fuck all to me. Just another face, another story, another problem that wasn't mine.

But my missus? She perked right up the second this Megan was mentioned. Said they'd been in the same class at school. Like I should give a shit. I didn't. Why would I?

The pig was asking if anyone had seen this Megan sort. Or if anyone had noticed anything suspicious or unusual on the street where she lives. And, truth be told, I had. I'd seen some tall bloke with a short beard legging it down the road, something big and long slung over his shoulder, moving fast, like he didn't want to be seen. Could've been a bag, could've been a rug, could've been the girl for all I know. But so what? Not my problem. People go missing all the time. Some turn up, and some don't. Either way, it's got fuck all to do with me.

The missus disagreed, of course. No surprise there. She started droning on about it, voice shrill, getting herself all worked up like she was some kind of saint. She wouldn't let it drop, kept going on and on, her face all pinched and righteous. So I gave her a slap.

Just a quick one to shut her up. And she did. I know what

works. No more nagging. My old dad was the same with my mum and he taught me well.

This morning, when I'd sobered up, I muttered a half-hearted apology, same as I always do. She gave me that look, all wounded pride and silent resentment, but she'll get over it. She always does. I'll grab her a small box of chocs later at the petrol station. A peace offering. If I don't, she'll be moaning for days.

Oh, and I told her – if she wants to ring the pigs herself, she can. Makes no difference to me. As long as my name stays well out of it, she can do whatever the fuck she likes.

She seemed pleased with that. Like I'd given her some great moral choice, like it made her special. Deluded cow. Not that it matters. The pigs won't take her seriously, not with her track record. I've told her that. Spelled it out nice and clear. 'They won't listen to a fucking word you say, you stupid bitch. Not with your drug history, and being on the game. Waste of time.'

But she never listens. And at the end of the day, it's up to her. The silly cow. I'm nothing if not reasonable. That's the kind of bloke I am.

I lit up a fag after the missus stormed off, watching the grey smoke curl towards the ceiling, and thought it all over. But I soon caught up with her. 'If you do ring the pigs, you *do not* mention my name, right? 'Cause I know what you're like. You get in one of your moods, and suddenly, you've got a big mouth. Yap, yap, fucking yap. You talk too much, forget yourself. And if you do? If you let something slip, even by accident? Well, then we'd have a big problem. One *I'd* have to sort. I'd have to give you a good hiding. No change there.'

27

THE SOULMATE

I'm so terribly stressed I can feel it in my bones, a constant tension that won't let up. Sleep doesn't help. A few glasses of wine doesn't take the edge off. Not even my yoga, which I love. The strain is just *there*, pressing down on me like a weight I can't shift.

Laura's the same. Busy, always busy, burying herself in work like it's the only thing keeping her upright. But I can see it, clear as day – this business with Aitken is really getting to her. She won't admit it, tries not to let it show, but it's eating away at her. It's in the way her jaw tightens when she thinks no one's looking, in the way she grips things a little too hard, in the restless way she moves when she's pretending to relax. And we haven't made love in *ages*. That alone speaks volumes.

It's not like us. Never has been. We've always been close, always had that connection – something deeper than words, something unshakable. Touch, warmth, intimacy – it's always been there, like second nature. But now?

Now there's a distance. A cold, silent space between us that wasn't there before. I miss sex. I miss *her*. The way she used to melt into me, the way her body responded, the way we fit together so effortlessly. I miss the heat of her skin against mine, the quiet reassurance of her breath in the dark, the unspoken comfort of simply *being*.

But that's gone. Replaced by the weight of everything she refuses to talk about. And I don't know how to get it back.

Laura acts like she's absolutely fine, like she's in control. But I see the cracks, the little giveaways she thinks she's hiding. The way her eyes flick to the window without meaning to, the restless energy in her hands. She's not fine. Not even close.

I've seen Aitken. Lurking. Watching. And now she has too. She tries to play it down, makes excuses, shrugs it off like it's nothing. Just coincidence. Just paranoia. But I know better. I see the way her expression tightens when his name is mentioned, the way she hesitates before answering. She's minimising her concerns, locking them away, trying to keep me in the dark.

And I wish she wouldn't. I wish she'd just be honest with me, let me in, and trust me the way she used to. Because I can handle more than she thinks. I'm not blind. I see what's happening, feel it in the air, the unspoken weight pressing down on both of us.

And I know – *I know* – it's not just Laura's career she's worried about. It's me. And it's Ed. If anyone puts my baby at risk, even though he's hardly a baby any more, I'll totally lose it. Completely. God help the bastard who puts him in harm's way. A case from years back put us in the firing line, dragged danger right to our door. I remember the feeling – the slow, creeping dread, the sense of something lurking just out of sight, waiting to strike. And now, this?

This feels *horribly* familiar. It has that same sickening weight, that same unshakable feeling curling in my gut. The same dark undercurrent running beneath everything, pulling tighter with each passing day.

There's menace in the air. A presence. Unspoken but undeniable. And if I've learned anything, it's that when you sense something like this – when you *know* it's coming – you don't just ignore it. You brace yourself. Because the worst is never far behind.

Laura's trying to carry the weight herself, but she doesn't have to. Because whatever's coming, whatever else Aitken's planning – I'm not going to let her face it alone.

I really need to make Laura see that. Need to break through the wall she's built around herself before it's too late. Because this isn't just about stress. It's not just another case biting at the edges of our lives. It feels like something more. Something dangerous.

And I can feel that danger creeping closer, wrapping around us like a noose. And yet, Laura won't acknowledge it – not fully. She's always been the strong one, the fighter, the protector. But even the strongest people can break. I just hope she lets me in before that happens. Because I'm not sure how much more either of us can take.

28

THE ADDICT

I'm not looking for sympathy. That's not what this is about. I'm just telling it like it is. Straight up. No bullshit.

My life hasn't been easy. Not from the start. No silver spoon in my mouth, no doting parents to tuck me in at night or give me a hug. I came into this world at a disadvantage and never caught a break. My stepfather made sure of that – an abusive bastard with filthy hands and dead eyes, a man who saw me as nothing more than something to use. An object. And my mother? Not much better. She didn't give a toss. Turned a blind eye. Pretended not to hear, not to see. I've never forgiven her for that.

I was taken into care when I was only seven years old. Not that it was much of an escape. Just a different kind of hell. First, the children's home – cold beds and even colder stares, the constant feeling that I was just another number, another case file nobody really gave a shit about. Then came the foster homes, one after another, each one promising a fresh start that never came. That's how I ended up in Carmarthen. And that's where I met Megan.

We weren't close friends, not besties or anything like that, but

I liked her. She was in my class in secondary school, and unlike the other kids, she didn't take the piss. She never called me names, never made fun of my cheap clothes, the scuffed shoes, the tired bruises under my eyes. And I appreciated that. More than she probably realised. I'll tell her one day if I ever get the chance.

Megan stayed on at school after I was expelled. Went on to finish her studies while I walked straight out of those school gates into a life that went downhill fast. I was meant to do a hairdressing course at college. Enrolled and everything. But that didn't last. Three or four weeks and I was out of there. Because by then, the drugs had already taken hold.

It started off small, just a bit of weed now and then. Then cocaine. And finally, heroin. The one that sunk its fangs in deep and never let go. I don't get high any more, just inject the brown poison into my veins to feel normal. Just to get through each depressing day. And once you're in that world, you do what you have to do to survive.

I sold sex to feed my habit. Still do, if I'm being honest. When I'm desperate. Which is often.

So, as you can imagine, the local police know me *very* well.

I live with Dave now. In a damp, stinking little bedsit we rent by the week, the kind of place that never quite feels clean, no matter how much you scrub. Peeling wallpaper, a mattress that stinks of old sweat and cheap vodka, neighbours who scream through the walls at all hours. But it's a roof. A place to sleep.

Dave's all right sometimes. When he's sober, he can be half-decent – quiet, almost thoughtful in his own way. He even buys me chocolates now and then, or flowers. But when he's pissed, well... that's another story entirely.

He slapped me hard the other night when we were watching TV. Out of nowhere, backhanded me right across the face with enough force to send me reeling. My cheekbone caught the worst of it, and now there's a deep purple bruise forming under my eye. But it's not so bad. I've had worse. And at least he was done after that. Sometimes he's not.

DI Laura Kesey, a plainclothes copper we both know to our cost, was on the Welsh news. Her face was tight, serious, the kind of look that tells you things aren't going well. And she was talking about Megan, saying she's missing, asking the public to come forward with information.

Dave barely looked up from his beer, but then he said something that made my stomach twist. He'd seen something. Some bloke, middle of the night, hurrying down the street, carrying something slung over his shoulder. Could've been anything. Could've been *Megan*.

I told him he should ring it in. Anonymously, if he had to. No names, blocked number. Just say what he saw and be done with it. Megan was good to me. One of the few. She never laughed, never sneered, never treated me like shit just because she could. She was kind. That might not mean much to some people, but to me? It meant *everything*. And if there's even a chance she's still out there, if there's even the slightest hope of finding her alive, then she deserves that much.

But Dave wasn't having any of it. Wouldn't even share the full details with me, like it was some big secret. The bastard just popped open another can, took a long swig, then turned to me with that look – the one that shut down the conversation before it even started. 'Shut your fucking mouth,' he said. Flat. Cold.

But I couldn't. I should have known better than to push. I've got enough bruises without asking for more. But that's what I got. After that, I waited. Let him drink himself into a stupor, let the worst of it pass.

And when he sobered up a bit, I tried again. Because this

time, I wasn't letting it go. Megan had been a friend to me. Now it was my turn to be one to her.

To my amazement, Dave actually told me to ring the police myself if I really had to. Shrugged it off like he couldn't care less. Just as long as his name stayed well out of it.

That part did surprise me. But what came next? That was *far* more predictable. He leaned in close, breath stinking of last night's lager and stale cigarettes, his voice low, deliberate. 'If the pigs come knocking, I'll beat the fucking crap out of you. Don't ever forget that.'

And I knew he meant it, every single word. 'Cause he's got stolen gear stashed in the bedroom – watches, phones, shit that isn't his and never will be. And then there's the drugs, tucked away in places the police would find if they looked hard enough. The kind of things that would see him banged up for longer than he could stomach.

So yeah, I get why he's on edge. I understand his logic. And I don't much fancy getting nicked again either. Prison is even worse than life on the outside. And that's saying something.

It took time to build up the nerve. Days of second-guessing, of running every possible outcome through my head, of weighing up the risks against the nagging feeling that I *had* to do the right thing.

When I finally made the call, my hands were clammy, and my pulse was banging in my ears. I locked myself in one of the downstairs toilets at the King Street library, bolted the door, and perched on the edge of the seat, knees bouncing, breath coming too fast.

That was the safest place I could think of. I love books. Always have. They don't judge, don't sneer, and they don't throw punches when you say the wrong thing. And the library? It's nice and quiet. A place to disappear, even if just for a little while. My happy place.

But not today. Today, I wasn't there for peace. I was there to do something for somebody else. Someone who might need my help. And I wasn't sure if that scared me or made me feel just the tiniest bit alive.

I dialled, heart hammering, fingers gripping the phone so tight my knuckles ached. A receptionist answered, clipped and businesslike. And I asked for Laura Kesey. Even gave her title, thinking that might help. She's one of the better ones, as far as coppers go. Less condescending, not so quick to smirk like the rest of them. And she's female, which helps. Makes it easier to talk, easier to be heard. Even when she's talking to you as a suspect, not a witness.

But to my disappointment, Kesey wasn't available. Or at least that's what I was told. And the words hit me like a punch to the gut. All that effort, all that mental build-up, and for what? To be palmed off onto some faceless duty officer who probably didn't give a shit? That pissed me right off.

For a moment, I nearly hung up, my throat dry, my eyes burning with angry, useless tears. What was the point? Why had I even bothered?

But then I thought of Megan. About what might have happened to her. About what still *could* happen if no one stepped in. I've met some right psychos over the years. Men who offer nothing but pain. Maybe Megan had, too. And that was enough to keep me talking.

I swallowed down my frustration, steadied my voice, and forced myself to continue. And you know what? I'm proud of myself for that. But that said, the call didn't go as well as I'd hoped.

I recognised the copper's voice the second he spoke, that

grating accent ringing through the line – nasal, a weird mix of Liverpudlian twang and Welsh. And to be honest, I don't like the bloke. Not one little bit.

He's young – twenties, I'd guess – and full of himself. The type that thinks he's a cut above, like he's got something special about him. But he hasn't. He's just another jumped-up uniform with a badge and a big ego.

The pompous twat's only been based in Carmarthen a few months as far as I know, and he's already nicked me *twice*. Petty shit, both times. A couple of fines when it got to the Magistrates Court. A complete waste of my time and his. So, yeah, I'd bet good money he doesn't like me any more than I like him. I wish he'd fuck right off and leave me alone.

I knew exactly what PC Grant's attitude would be before I even spoke. Could feel it through the phone. That air of superiority, the casual indifference. Like he was already bracing himself for a waste of time.

And I was right. *Spot on*. Dismissive. Cold. That sums it up. Like I was nothing. Less than nothing. Like he was speaking to something ugly and insignificant, dirt on his shoe he couldn't wait to scrape off.

'I'm ringing to help,' I said, wiping away a tear with my free hand.

His response came slow, drawn out, thick with sarcasm. Just as it always does. No surprises there. 'Are you now? Is that so? So, come on, let's hear what you've got to say for yourself. I'm all ears.'

Smug prick. For a second, I almost hung up. My thumb hovered over the button, anger burning hot in my chest. Why the fuck was I even bothering? The pig didn't give a toss. No one ever did.

But then, *Megan*. I pictured her face, small and smiling, a memory so distant it felt like it belonged to someone else. Just a hint from the past, something almost lost. Almost forgotten.

And it was *that* – not Grant's attitude, not my own pride – that kept me on the line. I swallowed down my frustration and steadied my voice. 'I saw Laura Kesey on the Welsh evening news. She was talking about Megan Morgan, the missing girl... I think I might have seen something.'

The twat fired back without missing a beat, his tone dripping with condescension. '*Laura Kesey*? It's *Detective Inspector Kesey* to the likes of you. Who the hell do you think you are?'

Arrogant little shit. I blew out a long breath, biting down my irritation, more determined than ever. He wasn't going to shake me off that easily. There was a hard edge to my voice when I spoke back. 'Do you want to know what I saw or not?'

And then, unbelievably, the scrote actually sighed. A long, exaggerated exhale, like listening to me was some massive inconvenience. Like he had better things to do. But then, finally – 'Okay, come on, let's hear it. Spit it out. I haven't got all day.'

I didn't waste a second. I took my chance, my one opportunity, and I told him everything Dave had told me. Every last detail. Only I didn't mention Dave. No way. That would be asking for trouble.

I made myself the witness instead. Because if this was going to make any difference, if Megan was still out there somewhere, I sure as hell wasn't going to let some jumped-up pig's attitude stop me from helping her. But for all my efforts, I'm not sure I helped her at all.

Because Grant's reaction? It wasn't exactly encouraging. If anything, it was the opposite. He let out another one of those *I can't believe I have to deal with this shit* sighs before launching in. 'So, let me see if I've got this right,' he said, his tone thick with scepticism. Dripping with it. 'You *claim* you were out walking in the middle of the night because of a *headache*' – a slight pause, a snide little emphasis on the word *headache*, like I'd said I was out rescuing puppies or some other fairy tale bullshit – 'when you saw a tall man in a hood carrying something that *could* have been a woman.'

'Yeah, yeah, that's right. That's exactly what I saw.'

Another pause. Longer this time. And then what sounded like a laugh. 'But you *can't* give me a proper description of him. You *can't* even tell me the exact time or date you *claim* to have seen him. And that's really the best you've got?'

I could picture the patronising expression plastered across the pig's smug face. Then came the kicker. 'You weren't out of your head on crack, were you? Are you sure you didn't just *imagine* all this? Because the *last* thing you want to do is give me false information. I'd have to nick you for wasting police time.'

And there it was. The real message buried beneath the words. *Lying little junkie*. I'd heard it so many times. Different voices, same sneer. The same tired assumptions, the same dismissive tone. It didn't matter what I said, or how I said it – Grant had already made up his mind before I even opened my mouth.

And in that moment, I *knew*. No matter what I said. No matter what Dave had seen. None of it mattered.

Grant wasn't going to take me seriously. Not for a single second. He'd already written me off, slotted me neatly into whatever category fits best in his tiny copper's brain. The time-waster. The bullshitter. The tart. The crackhead making up stories.

I'd tried my best. And I'd failed. The frustration burned hot in my chest, my fingers curling tight around the phone. I could have argued, pushed harder – but what was the point? I knew how this went. I'd been there before.

And right then? I needed my next hit. All of a sudden nothing else mattered. Time to end the call. I swallowed back the lump in my throat, forcing my voice to stay steady. 'Okay. Fine. Forget it.'

Grant didn't even bother trying to stop me. Just let out another short, dismissive laugh. 'Yeah, that's what I thought. If you think I'm bothering the brass with your shit, you've very sadly mistaken. We'll talk again the next time I nick you.'

I hung up, staring at the phone in my shaking hand, anger and frustration twisting in my gut. I'd done the right thing – hadn't I? Tried to help, tried to make a difference. But what did it matter? No one listens to people like me. No one ever did. And Megan? If she was still out there, I wasn't sure the pigs would ever find her alive.

29

THE CHIEF SUPERINTENDENT

It's DCS Nigel Halliday, OBE, QPM here – Head of the West Wales Police Criminal Investigation Department.

And I'll keep this brief. It's a matter of priorities. The average person has no concept of the sheer weight of responsibility a role like mine carries. The demands, the pressures, the constant balancing act of high-stakes decision-making. Suffice it to say, I'm a *very* busy man.

But enough of all that. Time's passing, so I'll get straight to the point. The Professor Aitken case has placed significant strain – undue strain – both on me as a senior manager and on the force as a whole. And I don't appreciate it. Not one little bit.

Since his release, the media interest has been unprecedented, relentless, a circus of scrutiny that shows no sign of abating. The questions, the insinuations, the demand for answers – from the press, from the chief constable, from other powerful figures, including the local MP. None of it convenient. And given the facts, the criticisms are hardly surprising.

I met Aitken more than once before his conviction – on local committees, at social functions. And I always found him professional, charming, a man of intellect and poise. And, if I'm entirely honest, I had my doubts about his case from the very beginning. If not for DI Laura Kesey's unwavering determination – her absolute, borderline obsessive certainty in his guilt – I very much doubt a prosecution would have gone ahead at all.

And let me be *crystal* clear on another point – I knew *nothing* about the missing murder weapon until it was too late. Had I been aware sooner, had I known that *crucial* piece of evidence was unaccounted for, things would have played out *very* differently.

A wrongful conviction is always unfortunate. But an eminent surgeon – one of the most respected in his field – spending years in prison for a crime he *clearly* didn't commit? That is beyond regrettable.

I have personally apologised to Professor Aitken on behalf of the force. And I sincerely hope he can now move forward and rebuild his life.

DI Kesey, in stark contrast, seems completely incapable of grasping the gravity of the situation.

It is frankly ludicrous. And beyond that, embarrassing.

Kesey was in my office at nine sharp this morning, standing there with that self-righteous determination of hers. Arms folded, chin high, like she had something urgent – something vital – to say. I barely had time for her nonsense, but I waved her in anyway. Our conversation speaks for itself.

'What is it now?' I asked, keeping my tone clipped. 'You can see I'm busy. So make it quick.'

When she replied after a slight hesitation I could hardly believe my ears. 'I have reason to believe Professor Aitken is watching me. Watching my family.'

I almost laughed. It was that ridiculous. It would have been funny if not so pathetic. '*Watching*? Like some kind of spy? What the hell, Laura? Do you even hear yourself? You helped send the man to prison for six years for a crime he didn't commit. And now you're standing there suggesting he's *stalking you*?'

She looked away. 'I know how it sounds, sir, but—'

'Oh, you do, do you? Because if you did, you wouldn't be wasting my time with this drivel. Do you have even the slightest idea of the damage the Aitken case has already caused? To this force? To your career? To me? And now you want to stir it all up again? What on earth is wrong with you? Not a chance in hell.'

Even after all that, she still had the audacity to push on. 'I just need someone to interview him, sir. A brief conversation, that's all. I'm worried for my family. I can feel it. Something isn't right.'

I exhaled sharply, pinching the bridge of my nose. '*Feel it*? Since when do we run investigations on the basis of feelings? We deal in facts, evidence – neither of which you seem to have. I have to say, I'm starting to worry about your mental wellbeing.'

She still didn't back down. 'He keeps turning up places he has no business being. My wife has seen him parked outside the house multiple times. My family—'

I didn't let her finish. My patience was gone. And I know paranoia when I see it. 'Enough! You will *not* pursue this, and you will certainly not drag Aitken's name into another baseless witch hunt. And that's an order. Is that understood?'

Silence. A long, tense silence. 'Sir—'

'Is that understood?' I kept my voice low, even, but there was no mistaking the warning.

Her lips pressed into a thin line. 'But, sir—'

I shook my head, blew out air. She'd wasted more than enough of my time. 'Not another word, Laura. I've thought for some time that you're struggling. And today has only served to reinforce that opinion. I'm referring you to the force psychiatrist for assessment. You have to agree you've been under a lot of pressure. I need to be sure you're capable of fulfilling your supervisory role. Because as of now, I have my doubts.'

She pulled her head back as if I'd said something ridiculous. 'You can't be serious?'

'Oh, I'm deadly serious. Your obsession with Aitken is clouding your judgement, and I won't have this force dragged through another scandal.' My voice was cold, final. 'I strongly suggest you take a step back before you don't have a career left to salvage.'

She just stared back at me. Not saying a word as I sat back in my chair, reaching for the stack of paperwork on my desk. 'This meeting is at an end. Close the door on your way out.'

For a moment, she didn't move. Then, jaw clenched, she turned on her heels and strode from the room, slamming the door behind her.

I let out a slow breath, rubbing my temples. Not everyone is cut out for senior rank, and DI Kesey is dangerously close to proving precisely that. Perhaps her promotion was a mistake. I'm not even sure she's right for the police force at all.

I'll be keeping a very close eye on Laura Kesey from now on. And if she continues down her current path – if she keeps pushing her delusions, keeps embarrassing this force – then I'll have no choice but to act.

A transfer, a demotion, maybe even a forced resignation. Each would be somewhat unfortunate, but wholly necessary. If she steps out of line again, I'll make sure she falls. Because it's not going to be me with a ruined career.

30

THE SURGEON

I toyed with the idea of keeping Megan alive a little longer. The notion had a certain twisted appeal. After all, wouldn't it be fascinating to observe her and Janet together? Two lab rats, trapped in the same concrete cage, both desperate, both broken. What lengths might they go to for even the slightest hope of freedom? What horrors might they inflict on each other with the right provocation, the right incentives, the right... encouragement from me?

It was tempting – seriously tempting. The thought of watching them both unravel together, the slow erosion of their humanity, the inevitable turning of prey against prey. A psychological experiment ripe with potential.

But in the end, with some regret, I set the idea aside. There will be others. Future test subjects. Fresh opportunities. So, what's the rush?

And besides, I have a far more fascinating idea in mind. One that sends a delicious shiver of anticipation down my spine.

I'll drop Kesey's helpless soulmate into my underground kingdom of suffering, where she'll experience something far worse than mere captivity. She won't find Megan waiting for her, trembling in the dark, clinging to the last shreds of hope. No. That would be far too easy. Too merciful. Instead, she'll find what's left of her. Rotting. The air thick with the putrid stench of decay, a sickly, cloying presence that will coat her throat and lungs, make her gag, make her retch.

And I'll watch. I'll study. The moment the realisation sets in. That her only companion is no longer a person, but a corpse. That she has been thrown into a tomb, not a cell. She'll be living in a grave.

I laugh as I picture it. The horror. The sheer, unrelenting fear. She'll recoil, heart hammering, fingers twitching with revulsion. Maybe she'll scream – short, sharp, strangled. Or perhaps the fear will steal away her voice altogether, leave her panting in the dark like a drowning woman gasping for air.

Either way, it won't matter. Not one little bit.

Because there will be no escape. No salvation. Only the nightmare I've carefully crafted for her. The thought of it fascinates me. Excites me. And so I have to make it real.

But that was for the future. Time to focus on Megan. And all the stimulation she could offer. My lab rat was waiting. Far too good an opportunity to miss.

I entertained myself for the better part of an hour earlier today after ordering my rat to the back of the bunker and climbing down my portable ladder, descending into the concrete space where she had long since abandoned hope. The air was thick down there, heavy with sweat and the stench of desperation. I breathed it in, savouring it like French perfume. The essence of captivity. The scent of power.

The lights were dimmed across the windowless walls. The soft strains of music drifted through the space, low and hypnotic, a carefully chosen lullaby to mask the horror. Nothing too jarring, nothing that might overstimulate or unsettle me. This was my moment, after all. And I wanted to be at my very best, to lose myself entirely in the indulgence of my desires. And I did. Oh, I really did.

All the waiting had sharpened my hunger to a razor's edge, had stoked the embers into a roaring flame. The anticipation, the build-up – it had only served to whet my appetite until restraint was no longer an option. My sad little lab rat had no idea what she was in for. She cowered, trembling, her breath hitching in uneven gasps as she sensed me nearby. The way she shrank from my presence, the way her body instinctively recoiled before I had even laid a hand on her – it was utterly intoxicating.

Fear makes my victims weak. Terror makes them pliable. And Megan, poor, pathetic little Megan, had been marinating in it for so long she barely had anything left to give. But today, she had one final purpose. One last offering. And what a feast she made.

Megan had stayed positioned against the furthest wall, as if the distance alone might save her. As if pressing herself into the cold, unyielding concrete could somehow make her invisible, erase her from my sight, make me forget she was there.

She slid to the floor, curling in on herself, knees drawn up, arms wrapped tight – a feeble, animalistic instinct to make herself smaller, to disappear. But there was no disappearing, no escape. She knew that. And yet still, the pleading came. The same pitiful, snivelling nonsense I'd heard so many times before.

'Please... please don't hurt me. Please I-let me go.'

Ridiculous! As if I'd ever entertain the thought.

The sheer desperation in her voice might have been amusing had it not been so predictable. I let her words hang between us for a moment, savouring them, feeling their weight dissolve into nothing. And then I laughed. A deep, guttural sound, raw and unrestrained. My head tipped back. A sound of pure, unadulterated delight.

And that was when the screaming started. It tore from her throat, jagged and wild, her last pathetic act of defiance before the inevitable. Music to my ears. But it was nothing – nothing – compared to what came next.

The first cut is always the most satisfying. The way the scalpel kissed her skin, the way the blade slid through thin flesh like butter, so smooth, so effortless. And then, oh, the colour. Such utter beauty.

Deep, rich crimson blood bloomed against her pale, white skin, seeping, trickling, running in delicate rivulets down her trembling limbs. A stark contrast. A work of art. My art. My creative genius.

My lab rat's emaciated body spasmed, her scream turning ragged, fractured by sobs, but I barely noticed. I was too caught up in the moment, too lost in the intoxicating sensation of flesh parting beneath my hand. Such things make me feel more alive than anything else on earth.

And that was just the beginning. There was more fun to be had, more pleasure to extract, more delicious distress to savour. I cut her again after that. And again. And again. And again. A slow, methodical ritual. A death of a thousand cuts. Each stroke of the blade carefully measured – not too deep, not too shallow. Just enough to wound her, to keep her balanced on the knife's edge of agony, but never enough to bring it all to a premature end. No, that part had to be savoured. Drawn out. Perfected.

The rivulets turned to streams, dark and glistening, trickling over her trembling flesh, each new wound birthing fresh waves of sobs, each spasm of pain a symphony to my ears. Her voice cracked and broke, first more pleading, then more screaming, then little more than rasping whimpers as the life drained slowly, inevitably, from her body. But I wasn't finished. Not yet.

I let it build. Let the anticipation swell inside me like a fever. And when the moment was exactly right – when I could bear to wait no longer – I finally took her throat in my hands, tilted her head back, and pressed the blade against her skin. A single, glorious stroke. From ear to ear. The ultimate crescendo.

Her body convulsed, a final, desperate struggle, and then she was gone, reduced to nothing but a lifeless, bloodied carcass at my feet. And in that moment, as the blade finished its work, I reached my own peak – more intense, more all-consuming than ever before. A climax of perfect brutality.

And then, just like that, all too soon, it was over. Poor little Megan was completely useless to me now. She was spent. Just a discarded husk. She had served her purpose, given me everything she had to give. Only the memory remained, and even that would fade in time, dulled by the inevitability of needing more. If only I could turn back the clock, live it all again, relive every orgasmic second. Not possible in this life. Not in this world. But there will always be another lab rat. Of that I'm certain. And I consoled myself with that.

Utterly drained, I collapsed beside her lifeless corpse, my breath slowing, my body heavy with the delicious exhaustion of satisfaction. I lay there, stretched out on the blood-soaked floor, staring up at the ceiling, basking in the afterglow of destruction for twenty minutes, or maybe more. Until my full strength returned.

And then I left her there, alone, entombed in the unfeeling silence of her concrete grave. I left the bunker with a glow of contentment on my face. A reaction to a job well done. Megan had been nothing before me. Just another forgettable existence, another wasted life drifting towards insignificance. But I had changed that. I had given her purpose, reshaped her from something meaningless into something of true value. In death, for the first time, she mattered. No longer worthless. No longer irrelevant.

I like to think she'd be grateful for that. That, in her final moments – when the pain had blurred into something almost transcendent – she understood. Understood that I had elevated her, made her part of something greater than herself. And she would remain, for a time, preserved in her finest moment. A masterpiece in blood and gore.

But my work wasn't finished – not yet. There was still the matter of presentation. That final flourish. I returned hours later. And with the utmost care, I arranged my lab rat's remains exactly as I wanted them – thin legs splayed wide apart, arms positioned just so, her dead eyes staring into the void. Art should always be appreciated, after all.

I stepped back, admiring my new creation with a deep sense of pride. A tableau of suffering. A testament to my brilliance. My greatest masterpiece yet.

And then I left my poor lab rat to rot, her flesh softening, breaking down, surrendering to the slow, relentless creep of decay. The stench will quickly thicken, saturating every inch of Megan's underground tomb, seeping into the walls, clinging to the very air itself. And when Kesey's love interest joins her in her bunker home oh so very soon, the place will be ripe with death.

And that's the beauty of it. Timing is everything. To truly maximise the impact, I'll need to introduce Janet at exactly the right moment – when the rot is at its peak, when the sight is at its most grotesque, when the horror will *consume* her the second she opens her eyes. I want her to feel it. The heat. The stench. The sticky, cloying presence of the corpse beside her.

I want her to know – from the very first breath – that she's already in hell. Because that's what the bunker is – hell for my lab rats, and heaven for me. A perfect balance of suffering and satisfaction, terror and control.

You've just got to be on the right side. Which, of course, I so rightly am. A living god with the power of life and death. The natural way of things. Predator and prey. Survival of the fittest. And there's nothing wrong with that.

My preparations to welcome my next involuntary guest are coming together very nicely, each detail ready, each precaution firmly in place. Execution must be flawless. I have no interest in getting caught.

It's truly astonishing what can be acquired from the dark web if you know where to look. If you know who to ask. An old prison contact pointed me in the right direction, a pitiful lesser man with limited intelligence but just enough usefulness to make him worth keeping around at the time. The fool had no idea what I'd do with the knowledge he shared, no inkling of the doors he'd opened for me. But he served a purpose well.

And online? I am untouchable! Every action masked, every footprint erased beneath layers of security. Prison gave me time – *ample* time – to study, to learn. And I did. With the unshakable certainty that one day, I'd put my new skills to exceptional use. And now that day has come.

I've obtained a police uniform – authentic down to the last stitch. The craftsmanship first class, the fit better than I could ever have hoped. With it, I am authority. I am law.

And that's not all. I've also acquired a set of false number plates for my car. A simple yet highly effective touch. I'll secure them over my own with strong two-sided tape – quick to attach, and just as easy to remove. Once I'm done, I'll destroy them. And in the highly unlikely event the pigs run the index number, they'll find themselves tracing another black Mercedes, one registered to some unfortunate soul named Ron Smith, living somewhere in the south of England. How deliciously perfect is that?

So now, almost everything is in place. *Almost.*

But not quite. There's just the small matter of my appearance. A minor inconvenience, but a necessary one. With some reluctance, I'll shave off my beard – facial hair is a recognisable trait, after all. A slight alteration, yet enough to throw off any casual observer. I'll bleach my hair, too. A fresh colour, a different shade, a subtle shift that will make all the difference. And I'll wear tinted glasses, of course. The ones with the gunmetal frames I usually reserve for holidays in sunnier climes. They'll serve my purpose well, hiding my blue eyes to good effect.

Yes, my plan is set. Tuesday morning. Nine days from now. I'll wait until Janet returns home, after she's dropped the brat off at school. And then, as long as Kesey's car isn't in the drive, I'll knock on the door.

And that will be the moment her life shatters – splintering into something unrecognisable, something from which there is no return.

And *I* will be a god again. Untouchable. Transcendent. And when I close the hatch, sealing her fate? Oh, the thrill will be wonderful.

Very soon, Janet will witness my mastery. My second lab rat will take in the horror, forced to confront what I have done. What she will be a part of and can never escape. And then? Oh, then the real fun will begin.

31

THE DETECTIVE INSPECTOR

I miss Raymond Lewis at times like this. *I miss him badly.* Ray wasn't just my detective sergeant, my second-in-command – he was my anchor. The one man I could rely on when everything else felt like it was crumbling. A good officer and an even better friend. The kind of man who had your back, no questions asked.

Ray was an old-school copper. No-nonsense. He played it straight when he could, bent the rules when he had to. And he never lost sleep over it, because he knew the difference between right and wrong – *real* right and wrong, not the sanitised version written in a rulebook. The standing orders I stick to far more than he ever did.

Policing was never just a job to Ray. It mattered. People mattered. And especially women and children – the ones who needed someone to fight for them, to stand in the gap when no one else would. And Ray? He'd go above and beyond, whatever it took.

There are plenty of people walking around today – people who've got a second chance at life – because of Ray Lewis. And I'm one of them. That's not an exaggeration. That's the truth.

People often took him at face value – gruff, blunt, a bit rough around the edges. But he had a hell of a lot more depth than most gave him credit for. There was real sensitivity under that tough exterior. You just had to know where to look. It took me some time, but I got there in the end.

And I'm delighted to see him thriving in retirement, especially since he dreaded it. Thought he'd be lost without the job, convinced he'd drink himself into an early grave. But then he met Tanya.

And she changed everything. She was the making of him, plain and simple. Got him off the booze, cleaned up his act, even got him eating properly – something I never managed, no matter how many times I told him to lay off the fried breakfasts. He lost a couple of stone, got healthier than he's been in years. So, no more heart attacks, thank God. Tanya worked miracles where I failed.

And I couldn't be happier for him. But I'd be lying if I said I didn't sometimes wish he was still here. Because on days like this, when the weight of the job presses down harder than ever, I could *really* use a man like Ray at my side.

Should I ring him? After all this time? Would it seem strange, out of the blue? But then again, why on earth not? Ray wouldn't mind. He was always ready to help if he could. That's the sort of bloke he is.

And in truth, I knew I could do with hearing a friendly voice. Someone who really *got it*. Someone who wouldn't dance around the truth or drown everything in meaningless bullshit. Yeah. A catch-up would be good.

I'd been through another soul-destroying, morale-sapping meeting with Nigel Halliday earlier, and my patience was wearing thin. The man has a way of getting under my skin – his tone, his never-ending arrogance, the way he talks in circles. Every time I leave his office, I feel like I've been beaten over the head with bureaucracy. And today was no different.

I downed a second mug of strong black coffee, swallowed a couple of non-prescription painkillers, and rubbed at the dull throb behind my eyes. Halliday always gives me a headache. Always. And I knew exactly who I needed to talk to. So why not get on with it? The decision was made.

I recognised Ray's gruff West Wales tones the second he answered. That familiar no-nonsense voice, roughened by years on the job, instantly took the edge off my tension. A voice that had talked me through more problems than I could count.

'Hi, Ray, it's Laura. Got time to talk?'

His reply came without hesitation, warm and unwavering. 'All the time in the world for you, love. It's been a while. I haven't seen you since my wedding. How's things? Have you had that promotion you were hoping for?'

I laughed, but there wasn't a shred of humour in it. 'The way things are going, I'll be lucky to keep my job at all. You must've seen all that shit about Aitken on the news.'

'Yeah, I did. Bet Halliday's loving every second of it.'

Just hearing the chief super's name made my stomach turn. The stress, the politics, the never-ending scrutiny – it was enough to make anyone sick. I let out a heavy sigh, rubbing at the tension coiled in my neck. 'I wouldn't even know where to start.'

'That bad, eh?'

'*Worse.*' There was a pause. A silence filled with unspoken things. And then, because I needed this – because I needed *him* – I forced the words out. 'Um, I hope you don't mind me asking, but I could really do with meeting up. For a proper chat. How about lunch at the rugby club? My treat. I know how much you like the place – it used to be your second home when you were in the job.'

'How would one o'clock do you? Tanya's got me booked in for a Pilates class at the library till twelve.'

That caught me off guard. I laughed – a real, genuine laugh, the first in what felt like forever. '*Pilates? You?* Are you winding me up?'

'No one's more surprised than me, love. I've even got the headband. It'll be Lycra next.'

I smiled, shaking my head. 'I'll see you at one. And thank you, Ray. I really need this. It's appreciated.'

When I walked into the quiet rugby club bar, there he was. Already seated near the worn-out pool table, a blue bottle of Welsh sparkling water in front of him, looking far healthier than he ever had when in the force. Back then it was beer and crisps. So much had changed. And for the first time in days, I felt like I could breathe.

I caught his eye across the room, waved with a grin, and made my way to the bar to order a coffee before heading over to join him. Ray looked good – *really* good. Like retirement had taken years off him.

'You're looking well, Ray. About ten years younger,' I said as I slid into the chair opposite him. 'What are you having to eat? Are you ready to order?'

He waved me off. 'Nothing for me, thanks, love. Tanya's making a curry.'

I decided to skip food too. It seemed easier that way. There were bigger things on my mind than a plate of grub. The small talk was already wearing thin, and as soon as my eyes met his, I felt the emotion rising. I blinked hard against it, swallowing down the lump in my throat. 'I'm struggling, to be honest, Ray,' I admitted. 'Halliday's been an *absolute* nightmare since Aitken's release. And now the bastard's talking about referring me for a psych assessment. Says I'm not up to the job.'

Ray jerked his head back, eyes narrowing. 'The man's a *prick*. Always was, always will be. I'd be tempted to tell him to fuck off if I were you. You're a better copper than he'll ever be.'

He leaned forward, elbows on the table, his expression darkening. 'There was a *lot* of evidence against Aitken when we nicked him. *A lot*. So what if we got it wrong? So did the CPS. So did the jury. It's easy looking back, picking holes, but at the time? We *all* thought he was guilty. And I don't remember Halliday raising any objections back then. He was only too happy to take the credit when the conviction came through.' He shrugged, lifting his glass. 'Aitken will get his payout, and that should be the end of it.'

I wrapped my hands around my coffee cup, letting the warmth seep into my fingers. 'It's more complicated than that.'

He pulled a face. 'What are you talking about?'

I hesitated, then said it out loud. 'Aitken keeps turning up. Outside my house, near Ed's school. It's like he's watching.'

Ray's brow furrowed, his entire body tensing. '*Watching?* What the hell's that about?'

'I don't know,' I admitted. 'At first, I thought Jan was imagining things. She was convinced she'd seen him multiple times. I told her it was probably just coincidence, but now? Now I've seen him for myself. I'm convinced he's trying to intimidate me. You saw his search history, same as I did. And I *don't* believe for one single second that he was *trying* to revive Holly Larkin when he was found with her body. There was far more to it than that. I have to accept he didn't kill the girl – no choice there. But he bit her corpse. That's for damn sure.'

Ray nodded, jaw tight. 'Aitken's a psycho. I said it from the start.'

I hesitated, pressing my fingertips together before looking up again. 'There's something else.'

'What is it?'

'Do you remember Megan Morgan?'

'Of course I do. I interviewed her myself after she was stabbed. Saw her in hospital.'

'She's missing.'

His eyes narrowed. 'Yeah, I heard. *Poor cow*. As if she hasn't already been through enough shit for one lifetime.'

I exhaled slowly. 'She came to see me a short time before she disappeared. And this is the bit that's really getting to me. She'd seen Aitken on TV. And she said she thought *he* was the man who stabbed her.'

Ray's fingers tightened around his glass, his face hardening as I continued.

'I didn't take it seriously at the time. We both know she's made false accusations before. But now I keep thinking... what if she was *right* this time? And what if Aitken *had* something to do with her disappearance?'

I let the question hang between us before continuing.

'I know it's a big jump. And I've got *nothing* to support it. No evidence, nothing at all. But it's nagging away at me. I keep seeing red flags everywhere I look. Aitken could be dangerous.

'Or maybe...' I swallowed, barely able to force the words out. 'Maybe Halliday's right. Maybe I am getting paranoid. Perhaps the pressure's getting to me.'

Ray shook his head, a thin smile crossing his lips. 'Don't be so daft, love. The man's a fool. Trust your gut. Mine rarely let me down.'

He leaned in, lowering his voice after a few seconds of silence.

'If I were you, I'd pay Aitken a visit. Let him know he's been seen watching. Mark his card for him. And mention Megan. See what his reaction is. That could tell you something.'

I dropped my chin to my chest before looking up again, frustration weighing heavy. 'Wish I could,' I muttered. 'But it's more than my job's worth. I *can't* go anywhere near Aitken. Halliday made that *perfectly* clear.'

Ray exhaled, drained his glass, then sat back in his chair, looking full of thought. 'Do you want me to make a few unofficial enquiries?' he asked, his voice measured. 'Off the record. See what I can find out. No one else needs to know. Just between you and me.'

Relief flooded through me, almost knocking the breath from my lungs. 'Would you?'

'Course I would. Just say the word.' His eyes sharpened. 'Does he still live in that big detached place outside town?'

I nodded. 'Discreet enquiries, yeah?'

A slow grin spread across his face. 'Goes without saying.'

I let out a slow breath, some of the weight on my shoulders easing. If anyone could dig up something useful, it was Ray. He still had his old contacts, still knew how to ask all the right questions without raising alarm. 'Thanks, Ray. I owe you one.'

He waved a hand, dismissing the notion. 'You don't owe me a thing, love. Just be careful, that's all. If Aitken's half as dangerous as you think he is, we're playing a risky game.'

I met his familiar gaze, steady and unflinching. 'I don't have a choice.'

Ray nodded twice. 'Then neither do I. We're a team, you and me. I'll make a start in the morning.'

32

THE SURGEON

The day had finally arrived. The day of days. The moment I'd been counting down to with an anticipation so fierce it felt like fire in my veins, crackling, surging, threatening to consume me if I didn't act soon.

The day I would take her. Kesey's love interest – her precious Janet – lured into the abyss, into my world, where pain and fear aren't just certainties; they're law.

Entertaining Megan had been a positive enough experience. Informative. Enjoyable. A necessary step in refining my craft. But Janet? Oh, Janet would be something else entirely. The culmination of all that had gone before.

Megan was a fragile little thing, already fractured long before I even got my hands on her for a second time. But Janet? Janet would have fight in her. She's older, tougher in some ways. Not in body – no, her body is soft, weak in all the ways that matter – but in mind. And that's a very good thing. A broken toy is no fun to play with for very long. The novelty wears off all too soon.

I have no doubt Lab Rat Two will hold out for as long as she can, clinging to whatever pathetic sliver of hope she has left, telling herself someone will come for her. That someone cares.

And I will enjoy shattering her misconceptions as only I can. This isn't just about the delicious thrill of peeling back her flabby, trembling flesh, stripping it from the bone, and watching her blood seep onto the concrete floor like thick, syrupy ink. Because Janet's suffering won't end with *her*. No. Her agony will stretch far beyond the bunker walls, reaching out like a disease, infecting Laura Kesey, poisoning her, seeping into every corner of her pathetic little life.

And she will feel it. Every scream. Every tear. Every last ragged, desperate plea.

Sadness. Guilt. Regret. Each will consume her. Eat her alive from the inside out, as I've longed to see. And that knowledge – that absolute certainty – will heighten my pleasure.

Kesey put me through so very much. She humiliated me. Hunted me. Treated me like I was less than her. Like I was *nothing*. And now? Now, it is time for payback. Balance will be restored.

Cream always rises to the top. And righteous vengeance will be mine. Soon. Very soon. The game will begin. And this time, I will win.

I had a sudden change of heart after Megan's demise. Using my Mercedes for Janet's capture is out of the question despite my original proposal. Too risky. Too recognisable. I can't afford to let a single miscalculation ruin everything. Another example of my flexible genius.

Seemingly insignificant details have the potential to upset even the best-laid plans. And I was never going to let that happen. So instead, I rented a car. A white saloon. Ordinary. Unremarkable. A model the local police sometimes use. It won't turn heads, won't draw attention. And that is precisely the point.

I'll still make use of the false plates, of course. Why wouldn't I? A true professional takes advantage of every angle. Enough waiting, It's time for action.

With the final preparations complete, I took my time adjusting to my new persona – checking my uniform in the mirror, ensuring my disguise was flawless. The crisp black tunic. The stab vest. The stiff cap pulled low over my tinted glasses. The transformation was remarkable. Janet wouldn't suspect a thing. And soon, she would be *mine*.

I drove cautiously through the quiet streets, keeping to the speed limit, obeying every traffic law as though I were exactly who I appeared to be. A dedicated officer on official business. The perfect illusion.

As I approached Kesey's home, my pulse remained steady, my focus absolute. I had rehearsed every step of this in my mind. Prepared for every possibility. Failure was not an option.

I slowed as I turned onto their street, my eyes scanning for any potential threats, any nosy neighbours, any wandering dog walkers who might remember a white car parked outside the DI's house.

Nothing. The road was still, the suburban quiet settling over the houses like a soft, suffocating blanket. And then I saw it. Janet's car. Sitting obediently in the driveway. And the TV was on in the lounge. She was home. Perfect.

I pulled up smoothly outside, adjusted the peak of my cap, and took a deep breath, composing myself before stepping out into the cool morning air.

I stood at the front door, my tinted non-prescription glasses shielding my eyes, the black peak of my police cap pulled low, shadowing my freshly shaven face. The uniform was immaculate and utterly convincing. To any casual observer, I was nothing more than a figure of authority, just another officer on official duty.

But beneath the calm exterior, my pulse beat with a dark exhilaration. And even I had to admit it – there was a flicker of nerves buried beneath the layers of control. Not fear. Never fear. But the kind of tension that comes when so much is on the line, when the success of the moment determines everything.

Because this wasn't just about execution. This was about possession. I *had* to get my hands on the bitch. I needed to own her.

My breath came slow and steady, the rush of anticipation sharpening my senses as I raised my fist and knocked. Once. Twice. And then I waited. Poised. And above all, ready.

And then, finally, my prospective lab rat appeared.

The door swung open, and there she was – Janet, standing in the hallway, staring at me like I'd just delivered the worst news in the world. As if she knew. As if some primal part of her sensed that the moment she crossed that threshold, her life would never be the same again.

Her mouth parted slightly, her eyes scanning me from head to toe, moving over the uniform, the cap, my authoritative stance.

But it was her expression that thrilled me most – wide-eyed, full of nervous energy, a flicker of something raw and unsettled bubbling just beneath the surface. Shock. Fear. A slow realisation that something wasn't right.

Janet was visibly trembling when she spoke, her voice unsteady, barely above a whisper. 'What, err... what can I do for you? Is everything okay?'

Predictable. Oh so very predictable. I'd anticipated that exact response, rehearsed for it. And so I straightened my shoulders, softened my gaze, and adjusted my voice – adopting the thick, unmistakable lilt of a Scottish accent I'd practised and perfected over recent days. Far removed from my usual educated tones. I had to appear genuine, trustworthy, and most of all – concerned. 'First things first, ma'am,' I began, keeping my voice low, measured, 'I need to be sure I'm talking to the right person. Are you Janet Webb? DI Kesey's partner?'

She blinked repeatedly, confusion swimming behind the fear. And then I saw it. The first glistening tear, welling in the corner of her eye, threatening to spill over. Beautiful.

My lab rat's shoulders sagged, the weight of whatever she thought was coming next pressing down on her, forcing her to lean into the doorframe for support. She looked very close to panic now. And that? That was quite the turn-on. But I found the strength to ignore it. For a time.

Her lips barely moved when she spoke again.

'Is... is Laura all right?' she asked, her face draining of colour. Such a happy sight to see. *Oh, Janet,* I thought, picturing her bruised and bleeding. *Poor helpless Janet. If only you knew.*

I let the moment *stretch*, watching as the weight of uncertainty settled onto her shoulders. She was already unravelling. I could *see* it – the way her fingers curled tighter around the doorframe, her breath coming just a little faster, her pupils widening as fear slithered beneath the surface.

I kept my expression composed, concerned.

'I'm very sorry to have to tell you...' I paused, exhaled slowly, as though the words were difficult to say. 'DI Kesey has been in a serious accident.'

The air shifted. Her body stiffened, a sharp intake of breath forcing her upright, as if she were bracing herself for a physical blow. '*An accident?*'

'A crash. She's alive, but had to be resuscitated at the scene. An ambulance rushed her to casualty.'

Lab Rat Two swayed slightly. It seemed her instinct was to

panic, to run inside, grab her things, and hurry to the hospital. But she fought it, forcing herself to stay composed. 'I'll get my car keys,' she said quickly, turning on her heels.

Car keys? What the hell? The bitch! That was never part of the project. A flicker of irritation twisted in my chest. *How dare she? She'd pay for that.*

For a brief second, I considered grabbing her, slamming her against the doorframe, knocking the breath from her lungs, shoving her inside and raining down blow after vicious blow, feeling her soft flesh bruise beneath my fists.

But no. Not there. Not yet. Too high a risk to take. I smothered the thought, forced my focus back. 'I can take you there,' I called after her, stepping forward slightly, positioning myself so she couldn't shut the door on me. 'We won't need to worry about speed limits. Come on, it'll be *quicker*. Leave your car where it is.'

She hesitated. A tiny pause. Just for a fraction of a second – but long enough for her mind to race through the possibilities, for her instincts to whisper that something wasn't quite right.

I thought her suspicions might be raised. But then she nodded and I knew I was winning. 'I'll just put on some shoes and grab my phone.'

Yes. She was already mine. I knew it. I kept my breathing slow as she stepped away from the door. Seconds stretched endlessly as she disappeared from sight, returning moments later with her phone in one hand and a pair of trainers in the other. She slipped her feet into them hurriedly, her hands shaking slightly.

'All set?' I asked, watching her closely.

She nodded again. No more questions. But she would ask. Soon enough. And by then, it would be far, far too late. Her fate would be sealed.

Janet sat stiffly beside me in the passenger seat, hands knotted in her lap, her body wound tight like a coiled spring. She didn't speak. Didn't even look at me.

Her breath came in short, uneven bursts, every exhale sharp – like she was holding herself together by sheer will alone. Pathetic. And every now and then, she gave a small, dry cough, clearing her throat, as if she wanted to say something but couldn't quite bring herself to do it. As if *that* would make a difference now.

I guided the car smoothly along the familiar roads, keeping my speed steady and my hands loose on the wheel. The route was second nature to me – mapped, rehearsed. I knew it so very well. My plump, pink lab rat believed we were heading for the hospital. And why wouldn't she? The uniform, the car, the air of authority – I had played my role to perfection.

But the road we travelled wasn't leading her to Kesey. It was leading her to *me*. To my world. My kingdom. Where I am god. And as we neared the hospital turn-off, I pressed down heavily on the accelerator pedal, feeling the car surge forward, sailing straight past the entrance without so much as a flicker of hesitation.

And that's when the bitch reacted. Such a regrettable inconvenience. Her head turned towards me, confusion giving way to alarm. 'Wait – what are you doing? The hospital's back there!'

The first stirrings of real panic. Another thing I'd anticipated. Because I am nothing if not meticulous. I kept my voice calm, neutral, letting the lies slip from my lips as smooth as silk. 'There's been a change of plan. I've been instructed to take you somewhere else.'

She blinked, her forehead creasing. '*What?* Where? Instructed? I didn't hear a thing. What *on earth* are you talking about?'

The suspicion in her voice sent a rush of satisfaction through me. Finally the realisation was creeping in.

But it was too late. Far too late. I let the silence stretch just long enough to let fear take hold, and then I made my move. I sped up to sixty, took one hand off the wheel, reached across, and – *click*. I unfastened her seatbelt.

Her head jerked towards me, mouth parting – ready to scream – but before she could even process what had happened, before the first syllable could leave her lips – I slammed my foot down hard on the brake.

The car screeched to an abrupt and sudden stop.

Janet was thrown headlong, her body snapping forward like a ragdoll, her head smashing into the windscreen with a glorious crack. A sound I thought wonderful.

My new lab rat slumped back into the seat, her body now limp, her breath coming in soft, shallow gasps. I exhaled slowly, pulse steady, and reached over to brush a strand of hair from her bloodied face. It really couldn't have worked out any better. I'd excelled. And now, she was ready for the next stage.

Within ten minutes or so, I was guiding the car through the entrance of my estate, my domain, where I hold absolute power.

The two tall electric gates hummed as they closed behind the car, locking us in, sealing her fate.

I drove to the back of the house, well away from potentially prying eyes, and pulled up on a large area of gravel bordering the lawn. I switched off the engine and paused, savouring my moment of victory.

Then I stepped out, stretching, breathing in the cool Welsh air – high on anticipation.

My lab rat still sat, slumped in her seat, head tilted at an unnatural angle, blood trickling from her hairline. She let out a weak moan, her body twitching slightly. Still conscious, but only just.

I pulled open the car's passenger door, gripping her by the

collar of her coat and dragging her out. Her limp form collapsed onto the hard ground with a thud. No need for further force. Although, that time would soon come.

I watched her for a moment, taking in the sight of her trembling, broken, and helpless. Then, with deliberate power, I drew back my leg and kicked out – a sharp, precise blow straight to her ribs.

A strangled yelp escaped her lips. She curled in on herself instinctively, her arms wrapping around her stomach as she writhed. So looked so very broken. And I laughed. Because she had no idea. No idea that the pain had barely begun. No idea that far worse was yet to come. No idea that she was about to enter a world of suffering she could never have imagined.

I grabbed a handful of her hair and dragged her across the lawn, her body jerking and twisting as she tried – pathetically – to resist.

Each whimper, each weak struggle, was met with a sharp, open-handed slap, the satisfying crack of flesh against flesh cutting through the air. Slap. A muffled sob. Slap. A useless plea. Slap. Yet still she resisted. Her hands scrabbled at my grip, her feet kicking out, a final, instinctual act of defiance.

And I let her fight. Let her believe, for those few, fleeting moments, that she had even the slightest chance. Then, when I tired of her pitiful struggles, I finally snapped. Because everything she'd done was worthy of punishment. I pivoted, drove my fist into her face, hard. Once. Twice. Then a third time.

The impact sent her sprawling on the damp lawn, a strangled cry slipping from her mouth before she lay still, her breath coming in shallow, shuddering gasps.

Blood – warm, thick – trickled from her nose, pooling at the corner of her mouth. Much better. There are limits to my patience. And she was already testing them.

The entrance to my bunker was right where it had always been, hidden beneath a perfectly camouflaged area of manicured grass – seamlessly blending into the landscape.

It had been painstakingly designed to conceal what lay beneath. My kingdom. My sanctuary. I lifted back the grass-covered, reinforced-steel hatch beneath. The metal hinges creaked slightly as I wrenched it open, the fetid scent of decay rushing up to greet me. And I have to say, it was rancid. A thick, cloying stench of rot, clinging to the air like damp wool.

Even I found it somewhat overpowering. The body below had been marinating for some time now. And as I lowered my Janet down through the opening, watching her drop ten feet to the concrete, I allowed myself a slow, satisfied smile. Because I knew exactly how this would unfold. The air thick with the scent of death. The walls pressing in.

And then? Soon. The music. A single, mournful note at first, stretching through the silence, slow and deliberate. Then the funeral march at full force, rising in volume, filling every corner of her new concrete hell.

And I would watch. Every reaction. Every panic-stricken moment. I would record it all, for Pig Kesey's later consumption. Because this wasn't just about Janet. No. It was about Kesey, too. And it would consume her. Destroy her mental state. Initiate a spiral of decline. The punishment she so rightly deserves. That will be my greatest pleasure of all.

33

THE SOULMATE

I knew. The second I glimpsed that house – looming, monstrous in its silence – I *knew*. Aitken was my captor. Of course he was. The signs had been there, right in front of me, and I'd walked past them blind. This was why he watched. Why he hovered just out of reach, patient as a spider. This was his revenge. A prison masquerading as a home, elegant on the surface, rotting underneath.

Then came the violence. Sudden. Relentless. I tried to twist free, but he was too fast, too precise – every blow calculated, brutal. Fists hammered into me as he dragged me across the gravel and grass, my hair clenched tight in his grip like reins. I kicked, scratched, screamed, but it made no difference. He was a force of nature, and I was nothing beneath him.

By the time we reached the centre of the lawn, I was barely conscious – blood in my mouth, knees bruised, vision tunnelling. He stopped. Just for a moment. Then came one final, savage kick – ribs, maybe. I don't know. Pain bloomed white-hot through my chest.

And then he knelt. The grass shifted beneath his hands,

peeling back like skin to reveal a circular opening – metal, black as a grave. I tried to stand to run. God, I tried. One last desperate push. But I was broken. He lifted me with ease, arms like vices, and began to lower me down. At first, it was almost gentle. Then he let go and I fell to the floor.

The metallic clang of the hatch slamming shut tore through the air like a rifle shot – violent, final, absolute. The sound ricocheted off the walls, fracturing into a dozen jagged echoes before dying abruptly, smothered by the thick, unmoving air.

I lay beneath it, my bruised and battered body aching, lungs already clawing for breath. Panic took hold fast and hard, coiling tight around my chest. My breaths came shallow and rapid, dragging the stench deeper with every gasp. Fine dust drifted down from the edges of the hatch in a lazy, grey fall – coating my hair, clinging to my lashes, settling on my tongue like ash.

Then – silence. Not the silence of peace. Something else. No voice called down. No footsteps moved away. Just stillness. Dense. Oppressive. The kind of silence that feels watched. Listened to. Held. As if the earth itself was crouched above me, waiting.

I lifted my body into a seated position, blood thundering in my ears, my heartbeat pounding out a desperate rhythm – too loud, too fast. The room pressed in from all sides. Walls of raw concrete, unforgiving and slick with damp. The cold bled from them, seeping into my skin. Four walls, seamless and sterile, streaked with long-forgotten stains that leaked downward like old tears. The ceiling loomed above, out of reach, split only by the now-sealed hatch – no ladder, no handle, no mercy.

There was nothing else. No furniture. No window. No escape. Nothing but walls. And *her*.

I smelt her before I saw her. The reek curled through the air – hot, putrid, with a sickly-sweet edge that made my stomach twist and my vision blur. It clung to the inside of my nose, the back of my throat, like syrup mixed with sewage. Like rotting meat dipped in sugar.

Megan? Could it be Megan? She was crumpled in the far corner, a grotesque parody of sleep. Her limbs were wrong – bent in ways that defied anatomy. Legs splayed wide, toes blackened and curling. Her skin had bloated to the point of tearing, stretched and cracked, weeping fluids that stained the floor beneath. Her neck was peppered with burst blisters – angry yellow boils that had ruptured and hardened into crusted wounds. Her hair was no longer hair – just oily clumps of decay plastered to a slack, misshapen skull.

But it was her face that undid me. One eye gone – just a sunken, wet hole where it used to be. The other remained. Wide. Glazed. Staring straight through me with the glassy vacancy of the dead.

I recoiled, bile rising fast, a scream buried deep in my throat. It took everything I had not to let it out.

The stench thickened. Tangible now. Alive. It wormed its way into my pores, wrapped itself around my lungs. I gagged and backed away, my hand over my mouth, stealing breaths like they were borrowed.

All of a sudden the walls felt closer. The shadows deeper. They stretched and breathed with me, moved when I didn't. No windows. No air vents I could see. No steps. Just concrete. Just her.

All I could think of was escape. But the hatch may as well have been the moon – distant, unreachable. I scanned the room again, frantic. Not even a loose stone.

The floor beneath me glistened – slick and sticky where Megan had leaked into the cracks. A black puddle expanding like an oil spill, lapping at her feet. And in my desperation, I was on the verge of losing all hope.

This wasn't a room. It was a tomb. A concrete coffin waiting for its next tenant.

I dropped hard. Back against a wall. Palms scraped raw. Pain flared, sharp and real – but distant. I barely registered it. Every nerve inside me was firing, panic short-circuiting reason. Still no sound from above. No voice, no footsteps. Just silence. And the smell of death.

My hands shook in my lap. Dirt embedded under my nails. Blood smeared across my knees from where I'd hit the floor. But none of it mattered. The pain was fading. It didn't feel like mine any more. Like I was already slipping out of myself.

Megan hadn't moved. Of course she hadn't. But I kept checking. I couldn't help it. Her eye still stared. The hollow socket still gaped. A warning. A mirror? A prophecy?

I pushed myself deeper into the wall, wishing I could vanish inside it. Wishing I could peel away from my own skin and melt into the concrete. My thoughts circled, frantic and raw, then slower. Heavier. Numb. Megan's body, nestled in my mind, pushed beneath my skin.

Suddenly a scream tore from my throat, raw and strangled, smothered by a new sound. I clamped my hands over my ears, nails digging into my scalp. But it didn't stop.

The music rose, solemn and unrelenting. It filled the bunker.

I collapsed to the floor, curled tight against the concrete. Shaking. Rocking. Sobbing without breath. The funeral had started. And I was the only one to attend it.

And in that moment, curled on the cold floor with death staring from across the room and music scratching at my skull, I realised the most terrifying truth of all. I'd never really known fear. Not real fear. Not until now. Not until I knew I wouldn't die quickly. Not until I understood that being buried wasn't the end – it was the beginning.

34

THE DETECTIVE INSPECTOR

Over a week had passed, and still nothing significant had developed since my meeting with Ray. The chaos that had consumed my life seemed to be settling – or at least that's what I kept telling myself.

I'd been given the date and time of my first session with the force psychiatrist, a meeting I had no choice but to attend. Just another hoop to jump through, another box to tick to keep Halliday off my back. But beyond that, things had been quiet. Maybe too quiet.

Neither Jan nor I had seen Aitken again. No sign of him lurking outside the house, no sightings near Ed's school. And I found myself hoping – however foolishly – that that might be the end of it. That maybe, just *maybe*, Aitken had moved on. Perhaps he was a far bigger risk to my career than to my family.

Ray, true to his word, was still following up on his own leads. He wanted to speak to an elderly woman he knew, someone who lived on a farm bordering Aitken's land, but she was away in Scotland, visiting family. And he didn't have her number. So that conversation would have to wait.

And then there was Megan. Still missing. Still nowhere to be found. Despite every effort, despite every resource thrown at the case, we were no closer to finding her than we had been on day one. The so-called mystery man, the one reported by our unreliable witness, remained just that – a mystery. No ID, no leads, no real evidence he had anything to do with Megan's disappearance. And the more I thought about it, the more I suspected he was nothing more than a red herring.

Because maybe – just maybe – Megan had harmed herself as I'd first feared. Or maybe she hadn't. One hypothesis seemed no more convincing than the other. No trail to follow, no real gut instinct pulling me in any clear direction. And in all honesty, the investigation was going nowhere.

That's the brutal truth about policing. The reality they don't show you on TV detective dramas. We don't always find the answers. We don't always join the dots. And sometimes, no matter how hard we push, no matter how much we want the breakthrough, it just doesn't come.

And sometimes, like everyone else, we're not in control at all. We like to think we are – we tell ourselves we're the ones making the decisions, shaping our own futures. But the truth? More often than not, we're just passengers, driven by the storm. The unexpected hits, relentless, pounding us down without warning. One moment, life is plodding along, mundane, predictable. And the next?

Everything changes. One event – one phone call – can rip the foundations out from under you, leave you staring into the abyss, wondering how the hell you got there.

And that's exactly how it was *that* day. An afternoon I'll never forget. I was sitting at my desk, reports, the same old bullshit swirling in my head. Then my phone rang at 3.55 p.m. And from that precise second nothing would ever be the same again.

Miss Sally Oakes, Ed's teacher, had an irritated edge to her voice the moment she spoke. Sharp, the kind of tone that suggested she'd had just about enough for one day. And to be fair, so had I.

Miss Oakes had never contacted me before. Not even once. And that set alarm bells ringing straight away. Teachers don't just pick up the phone for no reason. It had to be something. An accident, maybe? A playground scuffle? A fight over a football or some silly falling-out with another kid? Something minor. Something manageable. At least, that's what I wanted to believe. And I was right about one thing – something was wrong. I just had no idea how wrong.

'I've got Ed here with me,' she began, her tone clipped, impatient. Not just irritated any more – concerned. 'All the other children in his class have long since gone home. He should have been collected *twenty-five minutes ago.*'

I sat bolt upright, my grip tightening around the phone. Surprise jolted through me, followed by a creeping wave of confusion. Jan is *never* late.

And I do mean *never*. She's one of the most reliable people I know – obsessively so. She plans everything down to the last detail, loathes lateness with a passion. It's one of her biggest pet hates. If she hadn't shown up, if Ed was still sitting there, waiting – then something was wrong. *Badly wrong.* Because Jan wouldn't just forget. She *couldn't*. Not unless there was a *very* good reason.

'I'm so very sorry,' I said, my voice tight, my mind already racing. *What the hell was going on?* 'I really can't understand what could have happened. If you could just keep him there, please, I'll be with you in fifteen minutes. Ten, if the traffic's on my side.'

Miss Oakes seemed satisfied with that, at least. The irritation in her voice softened, again replaced by something closer to concern. 'I tried ringing Janet first,' she said. 'Several times. And I left messages. But there was no reply.'

That hit me like a punch to the gut. 'Really? That's not like her at all.' My throat felt dry. 'I'll be with you as quickly as I can.'

I ended the call, grabbed my car keys, and was out the door in seconds. By the time I got to the school, Ed was sitting there, confused and quiet, his backpack at his feet. He wasn't crying – Ed rarely cries – but his face was pale, his eyes flickering between me and Miss Oakes like he was searching for reassurance.

I gave him a tight smile, ruffled his hair. 'Come on, mate. Let's get you home.'

About fifteen minutes later, I pulled into the drive, Ed silent beside me in the passenger seat.

And Jan? Nowhere to be found despite her hatchback still parked where it had been when I left for work that morning. And no note in the house. Believe me, I looked. No explanation at all. Just an empty house and the kind of silence that makes your stomach clench.

I didn't hesitate. I picked up my phone and dialled the station, reporting Jan missing right there and then. The words felt foreign, unnatural, like they belonged to someone else. *Jan is missing*. It didn't fit. It didn't make any sense at all.

And then I rang Ray because I needed to hear his voice. Needed something solid to hold on to, someone who could keep me from spiralling. And Ray? He said all the right things, of course. He always does. Steady, practical, reassuring. 'Try not to panic, love. There has to be a reason. It's early days. She'll probably walk through the door at any second, full of apologies and with some perfectly reasonable explanation.'

But his words didn't change a thing. They didn't bring Jan home. And as I ended the call, a cold shiver ran through me, cutting straight to the bone.

Some strange, distant voice in the back of my mind whispered what I *didn't* want to hear. *Maybe you'll never see Jan ever again. All your fault. Perhaps you should have left the police force long before now.*

I pushed the thoughts away and forced myself to focus. There had to be an answer – something simple, something logical. But no matter how hard I tried, I couldn't find one. Jan wouldn't just vanish. She wouldn't leave Ed waiting, and wouldn't ignore her phone. That wasn't who she was.

I checked the house again, going from room to room, forcing myself to stay calm, looking for anything – any sign that might tell me where she'd gone. But there was nothing to find.

The silence suddenly pressed in, thick and suffocating. And as I stood there in our bedroom, mobile still clutched in my hand, one sickening thought took root. Something had happened to her. Just like Megan. Something beyond her control.

35

THE SURGEON

They say time passes differently underground. And I suppose that's true. Down there, the minutes stretch like wire, long and thin and cruel. Every breath echoes. Every sound becomes something more.

Janet's been down there for three days now.

And she doesn't scream any more. Not as often as she did. Not out loud, anyway. I sit in the study most nights, sipping a single malt or a glass of wine and watching the monitors – the feed from the cameras placed in the ceiling of the bunker. She's curled in the corner now, knees drawn tight to her chest, as if the walls might stop closing in if she just makes herself small enough. Pathetic, really. But human.

It's remarkable, the things people will endure when they think there's still a sliver of hope. That someone's coming. That the cavalry is just around the corner. What a deluded lab rat she truly is.

She still believes in rescue. I'm certain of that. I see it in the way she glances up at the hatch every time the air pipe creaks or she calls out Kesey's name. She hasn't quite accepted the truth yet. Not fully. That no one's coming. That no one even knows she's there but me.

It was almost too easy, taking Janet. The press had their eyes glued to Kesey, the role she played in my conviction, feasting on the fallout like crows on a carcass. The public were hooked on the drama, my release, the headlines. And while they argued over my innocence, over her obsession, I moved in plain sight. Walked the streets. Smiled at passers-by. Held the door open at the post office. All while planning something far more intimate.

Retribution isn't just rage. It's not only blood or screaming or chaos. It's patience, too. Control. And Janet's disappearance will scream louder than anything I could ever say.

As for how long I'll keep her alive... well, that depends. She's not entirely useless. Yet.

There's a rhythm to suffering. Peaks and troughs. You can learn a lot by watching someone break. The way they cling to routine, to memory, to faith in things that are long gone. And every moment Janet spends in that concrete tomb adds another thread to the noose tightening around Kesey's neck.

Because eventually, the questions will start.

Why wasn't Kesey watching her own family?

Was she too distracted by her obsession with me?

And when those questions start, they won't stop. Bella and her like will make sure of that. That's the thing about doubt – it spreads. Infects everything it touches. Even the strongest reputations rot from the inside when the wrong seeds are sown.

So I'll keep Janet alive – for now. Not out of mercy. Out of purpose. And when that purpose runs dry – when the silence grows louder than her sobs – I'll make a decision. Not *if* she'll die but *how*.

36

THE DETECTIVE INSPECTOR

I've faced tough times before. Both personally and professionally. I've seen and dealt with things that leave a mark, that never quite fade, no matter how much time passes. But *this*? Jan's disappearance? This is something else entirely. A different kind of hell. By far the *worst* time of my life.

She's been gone for a little over seventy-two hours now and it's impossible to process. My mind refuses to accept it, like some cruel joke I haven't been let in on. Like I'll wake up at any second and she'll be there, rolling her eyes at me, telling me I've been overreacting, that I need to get a grip.

But that's not going to happen. Because *this* is real. That's the brutal truth of it. She's gone. Just like Megan. And I have no idea where. That single thought churns in my gut, sickening, relentless.

And the worst part? I keep circling back to *him. Aitken*. It's crossed my mind more than once that he might have something to do with this. That he might have taken Jan after all his watching. But is that just paranoia creeping in? Am I losing perspective?

Seeing monsters in every shadow? Looking in the wrong direction? Maybe. Perhaps Halliday's right. Maybe I *do* need to see that psychiatrist after all.

My lovely mum is staying now, sleeping in the spare bedroom, stepping in, in the way she *always* does when life falls apart. She's here to help with Ed. To keep things as normal as possible for him, whatever that even means any more. And she'll stay for as long as it takes. Until I bring Jan home. Because I *have* to believe she's coming back. She's everything to me.

The love of my life. The centre of my world. The person who knows me better than anyone, who sees the worst parts of me and loves me anyway. And I *will* find her.

Right now, that's all I care about. All I can *think* about. And in truth, every other case, every other responsibility, has slid further and further down the list. I'm not proud of that. But family is everything. That's just the way it is.

I'm not leading the search. Not officially, anyway.

Thanks to Halliday, that privilege has been handed to DI Mike Phillips, an outsider from the Llanelli division. The so-called senior investigating officer. But let's be clear – I'm not sitting on the sidelines. Not when it's Jan. Not when every second counts.

I'm keeping myself informed, making damn sure I know *everything* that's going on. That nothing is being missed. That every lead, every tiny scrap of information is being handled properly. Because trusting other people to do it right? That's not something I'm comfortable with. Not when it's personal.

There was no significant evidence at first. And then, finally – *a break*. A lead. A real, tangible step forward. And the best part? *I* found it. Not Mike. *Me*. While he was preparing for his carefully rehearsed appearance on the Welsh evening news, making the usual appeal for information, I was getting on with the investigation. I dug deeper and made things happen. And now, for the first time since this nightmare began, we have something real to work with. A major *positive*. And I'll be damned if I let anyone screw that up.

I knocked on every single door in my street. One by one, working methodically, forcing myself to stay patient, to push through the rising frustration as I was met with the same useless responses, over and over again. *Nothing*. No one had seen a thing. No unusual activity. No strangers lurking. No cars pulling up where they shouldn't be.

And then – finally – *something*. Sharron Glazer.

A twenty-something children's nurse, currently on maternity leave, looking pale and tired when she answered the door, a baby's cry drifting from somewhere inside the house.

And she *had* seen something. Her words made me stop in my tracks, stand there and stare. 'I was looking out of my lounge window waiting for the Tesco van when I saw Jan step outside. Saw her get into a white saloon car with a uniformed police officer. A tall, well-built, *clean-shaven* guy with light hair and wearing tinted glasses.'

A good description, detailed. And the last thing I'd expected. *A police officer? In full uniform? Really?* A man who didn't sound like Aitken at all.

My stomach clenched. Sharron gave a statement, wrote down everything she'd seen, and I passed it straight to Mike. But it made little sense. I checked immediately – no officers had been to my home. No official visits, no legitimate reason for an officer to be there at all.

Which meant one of two things. Either Sharron was mistaken – her mind playing tricks on her, twisting the image into something it wasn't. Or someone had been wearing a uniform they had no right to wear.

And Sharron? She seemed pretty damned sure of what she'd seen. She'd put it in writing. Committed to it. Which meant the latter scenario was far more likely. It seemed Aitken was no longer a suspect. Maybe I had to accept that.

My mind had never been more troubled. I've made a *lot* of enemies over the years. Some the kind who don't forget. The kind who wait for an opportunity. And if this was the worst-case scenario? If someone was taking their revenge? Then Jan was in more danger than I'd even begun to imagine.

I went through *every* second of available CCTV footage at the earliest opportunity, scouring the screens with a relentless focus, my jaw tight, my fingers clenched. And at first, nothing. A slow, morale-sapping trawl through the mundane. Cars passing. Pedestrians strolling by, oblivious. A world that carried on as if nothing had happened.

And then – *there*. My breath hitched, my pulse spiked. A white saloon car. Exactly as Sharron Glazer had described. It glided into frame, unremarkable to anyone else, but my gut screamed at the sight of it. A man at the wheel – uniformed, light haired, his shaven face partially obscured by tinted glasses.

I couldn't recognise him however long I looked at the grainy image. But the woman seated beside him? *Jan!* Her profile, her shape, the tilt of her head – no question about it. It was *her*.

I leaned closer to the screen, fists clenched, my mind racing. Who the hell was he? And where was he taking her? Two crucial questions I couldn't answer.

I ran a computer check on the car. *Shit!* False plates. A Mercedes registered to an owner in the south of England. I was more confused than ever. And that scared me. Jan's disappearance was far more complex than I could ever have thought.

Whoever had her had planned her abduction. No way was it a spontaneous act.

I was able to follow the car on screen through the centre of town. But then I lost sight of it due to the limitations of the system. The driver could have gone in almost any direction at that point. Our evidence was a lot better than nothing. We had the make and colour of the car. But it wasn't the decisive break I needed. Too many questions remained unanswered.

I barely made it to the women's toilets before I threw up, my stomach rejecting the pitiful attempt at a light lunch I'd forced down. The bitter taste of bile burned my throat, my body trembling as I grabbed the sink. *Get a grip, Laura. Come on, girl.*

But I couldn't. Not this time. Not with my Jan still out there somewhere, in the hands of a man I didn't recognise. What were his intentions? Why had he taken her? I had no idea. Aitken again came to mind. But I quickly ruled him out despite every instinct. The man in the driver's seat looked so very different. It seemed it wasn't Aitken at all.

By the time I dragged myself back to my office, my head was pounding and my limbs heavy. I needed something – *someone* – to ground me. So I called Ray.

I didn't even let him speak at first, just launched straight in, voice raw, spilling everything. I told him about the CCTV, the car, the man. Told him I was now certain – *absolutely certain* – that pursuing Aitken was a mistake.

But Ray? He didn't seem nearly so sure.

I could hear it in his voice, that quiet, measured hesitation. And it annoyed the hell out of me because I couldn't see the sense in it. Not with the new evidence staring me right in the face.

'I've got a bit of good news for you, love,' he said gently when I finally stopped crying.

I wiped a hand over my face, trying to steady myself. 'Yeah? What?'

'That neighbour I mentioned. The one living in the farmhouse bordering Aitken's land. I was driving past late last night after a meal out with Tanya, and there was a light on. Seems she's back from her travels. I'm going to call in and have a chat with her later this morning. Fingers crossed she might have something useful to tell me.'

I swallowed back another wave of nausea, frustration prickling under my skin. I thought perhaps retirement had blunted Ray's edges. Or maybe he was just clutching at straws because he *wanted* Aitken to be involved. I often used to tell him to follow the evidence, not rely on instinct. Not that he ever listened. And he got it wrong sometimes. This seemed like one of those times. 'What the hell are you talking about? What's the point in seeing some old woman?' I muttered, my voice thick, snivelling. 'Have you been listening to a single word I said?'

But Ray wasn't having any of it. Not for one second. He didn't seem the slightest bit rattled by the intensity of my words.

'Best cover all the bases, love,' he said, firm now. 'You know how I like to rely on my gut. And this time? It's doing cartwheels.'

I rubbed my temples, exhaling sharply. 'Ray—'

He cut in. 'Aitken could be working with someone else. Some scrote he's paying or owes him a favour. A nasty little fucker he met in prison. Let's rule that out before we go writing him off as a suspect, yeah?'

I sighed, staring at the wall, my mind spinning. 'I suppose.' But the truth? I agreed more in hope than expectation. I was at least 90 per cent sure he was wasting his time.

In all honesty, Ray's stubbornness grated. But I knew better than to argue because it wouldn't get me anywhere. If he wanted to chase dead ends, then so be it. And meanwhile, I had to stay focused – needed to keep pushing forward. Jan's life depended on it. I felt sure of that.

I scoured the CCTV footage yet again, staring at the blurred profile of the man in uniform, my mind twisting with helpless rage. He was a ghost – calculated, cautious. No mistakes. No identifiers. Who the hell was he?

37

THE RETIREE

My gut instinct rarely lets me down. And my visit to the farmhouse and my interview with Mrs Myra Jones was a testament to that.

It took an age for her to answer the front door, and for a moment, I wondered if she'd even heard my loud knock at all. But then, finally, the latch turned, and there she was, smiling warmly, her face lined with the years but her eyes as sharp as ever.

She took one look at me and grinned, revealing slightly yellowed teeth that were clearly her own. 'Well, *Raymond Lewis*, of all people!' she said, shaking her head in apparent disbelief. 'I haven't seen you for *years*. Come on in, I'll put the kettle on. I hope this is a social visit?'

Her warmth was genuine, the kind that made me feel instantly welcome. I stepped inside, inhaling the scent of freshly baked bread, of tea brewing, of a house that had known decades of family life.

'I wish it was, love,' I said as she led me into the kitchen, her big tabby cat slinking past my legs.

I took a seat at the old oak table as she busied herself at the counter, filling the kettle, setting out cups and saucers. Myra had always been one for proper tea – none of that bag-in-a-mug nonsense.

'I was hoping for a chat about one of your neighbours,' I said, keeping my voice light. 'Professor Aitken – who lives in the big house.'

She hesitated, just for a fraction of a second, barely enough to notice. But *I* noticed. Then, without turning around, she poured the boiling water into the teapot. 'How about a nice slice of fruit-cake?' she asked casually. 'All homemade, fresh this morning. I do love my baking.'

There was something almost pointed in the way she said it, like she knew exactly why I was there but wasn't going to dive straight in.

I hesitated for a beat, then nodded. It seemed rude to say no. 'That would be *lovely*, ta. But just a small piece for me.' I patted my stomach with a wry smile. 'My wife's got me on a diet.'

Myra chuckled, slicing into the fruitcake with practised ease. 'A diet, is it? Ah, well, we'll see about that.'

I watched her carefully as she set the plate down in front of me, her hands steady, her face giving away nothing. I already had a feeling this chat was going to be *very* interesting.

I leaned forward slightly, keeping my voice casual, easy. 'So, tell me, what do you think of Aitken?'

An open question. Best to let her take it where she wanted.

Myra tilted her head, lips pursed in thought. 'Well, I heard all about him going to prison. But I never really believed he'd hurt that girl. Not an important doctor like him. Such an eminent man.' She paused, staring somewhere past me, as if plucking memories from thin air. 'I've not seen much of the professor over the years,' she went on. 'But when I have, he's always been polite enough. A real gentleman. Not like that *awful* man who owned the big house back in the eighties. You wouldn't believe some of the crazy things he got up to. A real punk type, totally mad. Spikey, he used to call himself. He'd been on *Top of the Pops*. Not my sort of thing at all. My husband would tell you the same if he was still with us.'

I took another sip of tea, watching her. She spoke with certainty, but there was something in her tone, a flicker of hesitation beneath the words. It seemed she liked Aitken. Respected him, even. Or at least, that's what she *thought* she should say.

I was keen to steer the conversation back to the professor as soon as possible, but I knew better than to push. Rushing people can shut them down. And right now? I needed her to keep talking. So, I played along.

I took another slow bite of the fruitcake – rich, moist, still warm from the oven – and washed it down with a gulp of tea. Delicious.

'So, tell me more about this *Spikey*,' I prompted with a forced grin, keeping my voice casual, light. Letting her set the pace. People reveal more when they don't feel pressed or squeezed.

Myra chuckled, clearly enjoying the attention. A people person. 'Oh, he was quite the character, I'll tell you that much,' she said, shaking her head. 'Blue haired, always rattling on about *changing the system*, whatever that meant. One of those types, you know? But his real obsession was the Cold War. He was absolutely convinced we'd all be blown to bits in a nuclear blast before the decade was out.'

She reached for her own cup of tea, blowing and taking a slow sip before continuing. 'He even had that bunker built because of it, you know. Thought it would be the only safe place left when the bombs dropped. Must have spent a fortune on it. Massive job. He had JCBs going for days, workmen swarming all over the place. And none of them local, either. English accents.'

I sat more upright in my chair. I'd searched Aitken's place at the time of Holly's murder. I saw the plans for the house. And no bunker! All of a sudden I was interested. Something cold settled in my gut, but I forced myself to keep my expression neutral. 'You're *certain* Spikey had a bunker?'

Her eyes widened. 'Oh, yes, of course I am. I'm old, not senile. He had it dug right there under the lawn.'

'And it's still there?' I asked, keeping my tone conversational.

She gave a small shrug. 'Well, I expect so. As far as I know. He used to brag that the thing was built like a fortress. Reinforced concrete walls, steel door in the roof, the lot. If you ask me, the loony did a better job of it than half the council houses they were slapping together back then. But he lost interest in it after a few years. Think he realised he'd spent all that money for nothing. Sold up and buggered off to America.'

She gave a short laugh, but I barely heard it. My mind was doing somersaults. *A fully reinforced underground bunker*. And now, decades later, who owned the land? *Aitken!* If that bunker was still intact... If Aitken *knew* about it... *This could be it*.

A slow, creeping dread slithered down my spine, though I kept my face still. 'And it's right there under the lawn?'

Myra nodded, her lined face creasing in thought.

'I used to be able to see the entire area from my bedroom window, clear as day. But the professor planted those evergreen trees not long after he moved in about fifteen years ago. Fast-growing leylandii. Thick. Dense. Practically a wall now.'

She sniffed, her disapproval clear. 'I'm not too keen on them myself. Too dark, too unnatural looking. But I suppose he likes his privacy. Doesn't want people snooping. He's an important man, after all.'

Her eyes flicked to me as she said it, like she was weighing something up, waiting to see how I'd respond. Or perhaps I was reading too much into it. Seeing things that weren't there.

I just nodded slowly, as if absorbing the information with mild curiosity. As if I wasn't suddenly fighting to keep my breathing steady. Because my gut was already screaming the truth at me. If the bunker was still down there, beneath that grass, behind that canopy of trees – if Aitken knew about it – then Jan could be down there. Trapped. Scared. Alone. And maybe running out of time. Megan too, maybe.

I forced my expression to remain neutral, though my hands clenched tight. No need to give myself away – not yet.

'Do you mind if I have a wander about outside, love?' I asked, keeping my voice casual, easy, like I wasn't already bracing for what I might find.

Myra nodded without hesitation. 'Look as long as you want, Ray. It's no bother to me. And keep an eye out for my sheepdog, Polly. She should come if you call her.'

I stepped out of the farmhouse, the crisp air thick with the scent of damp earth and wood smoke. I kept my movements slow, careful, as I crossed the yard. And Myra hadn't been exaggerating – the trees loomed ahead, thick and gnarled, twisted together like skeletal fingers, forming a fortress of tangled darkness.

I pushed through the undergrowth, branches snagging at my tweed jacket, whipping against my face. The silence was heavy, unnatural, pressing in around me as I moved along the boundary of the lawn, stopping just beyond the treeline.

The big house stood still, indifferent, its dark windows giving nothing away. Aitken's black Mercedes was parked on a patch of gravel near the door, its polished surface reflecting the light. But there was nothing else. No movement. No sign of him watching me.

I stayed hidden, crouched in the undergrowth, eyes locked on the building. Ten minutes passed. Then twenty. My muscles ached, but I held my ground, waiting, watching. I considered leaving – coming back after dark, when I'd be less likely to be spotted. But then I saw Jan's face in my mind's eye. Pale. Frightened. Trapped. And I knew I had to do more.

Glancing left and right, I scanned the house again, my gaze shifting from one window to the next. No sign of movement. No flicker of light. As sure as I could be that Aitken wasn't watching, I climbed the fence, cursing under my breath as the barbed wire tore through my trousers, slicing into my knee. Pain flared, hot and sharp, but I ignored it. Adrenaline dulled the sting, pushing me forward as I stepped onto the damp grass.

I moved methodically, my boots barely making a sound as I swept my eyes over the grassy ground, searching for anything – anything at all – that might indicate what I was looking for. But there was nothing to see. No disturbance in the earth, no concealed hatch, no sign of a hidden entrance. And in all honesty, I was close to leaving, reporting back to Laura, and deciding on the best next step from there.

I gritted my teeth. Decided on another five minutes. One last sweep before leaving. And then... suddenly, something shifted. Ten feet or so ahead, the ground moved, barely perceptible at first, but enough. And then a hatch lifted, revealing a dark, circular opening beneath.

My breath caught in my throat. Then, movement. A head. Aitken. His eyes met mine, wide with shock, his face illuminated by the bright light spilling from the entrance. He scrambled, reaching for the edge, trying to slam it shut before I could react. But I was faster. I lunged forward, stamping down on the fingers of Aitken's hand with every ounce of force I could muster. A howl of pain split the silence, his grip slipping. No more second-guessing. I knew now. This wasn't just a hiding place. It was his hunting ground.

I shouted down, my voice raw with fury. 'I'm coming for you, Jan!'

Then, from the depths of that suffocating place, I heard her. Weak. Trembling. But alive.

'I'm down here, Ray. Help me, please, for God's sake, help. Aitken's totally insane.'

And that was all the motivation I needed.

The moment locked into place – pure instinct, sharpened by years on the job and the raw jolt of hormone flooding my veins. I knew the risks. Knew that stepping into that bunker made me a target.

But there was nothing else for it. Jan was down there. And even calling for backup would take time I didn't have. Time *she* didn't have. Every second wasted might cost her more than I could bear to imagine. I'd always been impulsive – that old-school breed of copper who trusted gut over protocol. Never much cared for waiting around in the comfort of procedure while people suffered. Retirement hadn't dulled that. If anything, it had made it worse.

I knew, even as my fingers clung to the rim of the hatch, that I might not climb back out. This wasn't heroism. It was necessity. Raw, reckless instinct. And Aitken was waiting.

The blade came from nowhere – low, fast, and merciless. A flash of steel, followed by a searing pain as it tore through my flesh. Both legs, slashed open in a heartbeat. I felt the warm rush of blood soaking into my ripped trousers, trickling down in thin, hot streams. I lashed out, my right foot connecting with his chin in a sharp, brutal arc. The crack of impact was dull but satisfying, jerking his head back violently. He staggered back, teeth bared, blood on his lip – but he didn't go down. Not yet. Just rocked on his heels like a man too stubborn – or too deranged – to fall.

I dropped the last few feet, landing hard on the concrete floor, the impact rattling through my bones. Pain shot up through my knees, my spine, but I quickly forced myself to stay upright. No time to feel it. No room for hesitation. The bastard had drawn first blood, but he wasn't finished. And neither was I.

The stench truly hit me as I raised both fists – thick, putrid, a sickening cocktail of damp decay and death. And as my eyes focused, in a fraction of a second, I saw why. A corpse. Slumped beside Jan on the far wall, a lifeless body curled in a mockery of sleep, the skin pale as wax.

And then – Aitken. Just feet away, positioned between me and Jan, he was waiting and ready to attack for a second time.

A scalpel glinted in the surgeon's hand, its blade catching the harsh light overhead like a sliver of ice. He held it with the calm precision of a man who knew exactly how deep to cut – and how quickly. His grip never wavered. Not even slightly. His chest rose and fell in a measured rhythm, unnervingly composed, like he was preparing for a lecture, not an act of violence.

And then as I caught my breath, the bastard smiled. Not with warmth. Not even with triumph.

It was the dead-eyed smile of a man lost to his own delusions – cold, clinical, utterly detached. The kind of smile you'd see behind a glass partition, in a locked ward.

'Now it's your turn to die,' he murmured, almost lovingly. Then he came for me again. He moved with terrifying speed – unnatural, almost – lunging like a striking snake, the scalpel arcing towards my throat with surgical precision.

I twisted instinctively, but not fast enough. The blade sliced across my cheek and the bridge of my nose, a searing line of fire that brought the taste of blood instantly. Hot. Metallic. Familiar.

He snarled, low and animalistic, and clawed at my face with his free hand, wild now with rage. But I wasn't one of his victims. I knew how to fight. And I had far too much to live for.

I met the bastard head-on, slamming my shoulder into his chest, driving him back into the concrete wall with a thud. The impact knocked the wind from him, but only for a breath. His eyes flared with something primal – feral, unrelenting – and the scalpel came again, slashing towards my eyes.

But this time, I was ready. I drove my knee up – hard, fast – burying it in his gut. He choked on the impact, folding slightly, but he didn't drop the blade. Still, he was off balance. That was all I needed. I grabbed his collar and yanked him forward, then smashed my forehead into the bridge of his nose with every ounce of fury I had left. The crunch was brutal. Blood sprayed from his face as he reeled backwards, disoriented and gasping.

Aitken dropped to one knee, crumpling like a marionette with cut strings – but even then, he clawed at the air, still trying to rise. Relentless. Inhuman. I'd put men down for good with far less. Broken them clean. But Aitken wasn't like the others. He was wired differently – driven by something colder than hate. He was rising like a phoenix from the flames.

I sucked in a long, ragged breath as I tired, close to exhaustion, the fetid air thick with the stench of sweat. My body ached, every joint screaming in protest. My bloody injuries throbbed in time with my heartbeat, leaking strength with every passing second. And I could feel it – my age, my limits – bearing down like a weight I couldn't shake. And for the first time, the thought took shape. Solid. Unavoidable. *Aitken might win.*

And not just *might* – he was the likely winner. The balance was shifting. My fists felt heavier. My vision swam. Jan was somewhere behind me, seemingly too weak or terrified to help, and far too precious to lose. And in that moment, I saw it – the real end. Her life. Mine. Snuffed out down here in the dark, beneath Aitken's blade, beneath his madness. He was rising. And I didn't know if I had anything left to stop him. And then, as I stood there panting, he came at me again.

38

THE SOULMATE

I wanted to look away as I pressed myself against that concrete wall next to Megan's corpse. But my eyes were locked on the scene in front of me, unable to blink, unable to breathe. The bunker was a hell of echoing shadows and blood-slicked concrete, and in the middle of it all, Ray was losing the fight.

I could see it in the way he moved – slow, sluggish, every breath a battle. He'd come for me. Risked everything. Put his life on the line. And now he was on the ground, sprawled like a broken doll, blood leaking from somewhere deep, his strength bleeding out with it. I wanted to scream, to cry out, but my throat felt stuffed with sand.

And Aitken... He was above him, towering, not even winded. Calm. Precise. Like the whole thing had gone exactly as he'd planned. His fingers clenched around the scalpel – small, gleaming, terrifying. The blade caught the light, a cruel little flash, and for a second it didn't seem real. None of it did. I could've been watching a film. But then I saw Ray try to lift a hand, weak and trembling, and the truth hit hard. This wasn't a film. There was no pause button. No rescue on the way. Ray was going to die. Aitken was going to kill him before he killed me.

Something inside me suddenly shifted as I pictured Laura's and Ed's faces in my mind's eye. A quiet kind of madness. A fury I didn't know I had, thick and cold and absolute. It burned through the exhaustion, through the fear and the days of horror. It erupted up from the pit of my stomach and took over. I was a roaring lioness now, not a cowering mouse.

I stood and my legs almost buckled, rubbery from too long without food or hope. But I didn't fall. I *wouldn't* fall. Because Aitken was raising the blade now, his hand steady, his face a mask of focus. That same clinical detachment I'd seen when he first opened the hatch, like this was just another task to complete. Another line to cross.

And I screamed. It ripped from my throat like fire, raw and animal. Not my name. Not his. Just sound. Fury given voice.

Aitken turned, frowning, confused – and that was enough. I launched myself at him with all the power I possessed. And the impact knocked him sideways, unbalanced. I climbed his back like a rabid thing, legs around his waist, arms around his chest. He bucked and twisted, his hands flailing for a grip, but I clung on. *Tighter.* Teeth bared. I didn't think. I couldn't. Primal instinct had taken the wheel now. And then I bit him. Hard.

My teeth sank into the side of his neck – through skin, through sinew – until I tasted salt and iron. He shrieked, high, his composure shattered in an instant. I bit deeper, harder, until something tore beneath my jaw. Something warm and vital.

Aitken howled – a raw, guttural sound, more beast than man – and the scalpel slipped from his grip, clattering across the concrete. The noise echoed, sharp and final. He staggered beneath me, legs buckling, arms flailing for balance as I clung to him like a second skin.

Blood poured from the wound in his neck – thick, hot, and fast – coating my chin, my throat, seeping into my hair. I felt it on my lips. In my teeth. The copper tang of it filled my mouth.

But I didn't stop.

I bit down again. And again. Tearing at him like an animal, jaw clenched, teeth ripping through flesh. His skin gave way beneath me, warm and slick and awful. He bucked and thrashed, but it was different now. He was slower. Weaker. The fight was draining from him like the blood soaking the floor. He wasn't superhuman after all. He bled like any other man. And just like Ray had moments earlier, Aitken was starting to fade.

After what seemed an age, Aitken went down hard. I hit the floor beside him, elbows scraping on the concrete, pain flaring up my arms – but I didn't care. I spat out the taste of him, wiped my mouth with the back of my hand, and smiled as I saw Ray looking across at me as he struggled to his knees. He was still breathing. Shallow. Ragged. But alive.

I was on my feet before Aitken even knew I'd moved. He floundered, slow and crawling, blood pouring from his neck in thick, sluggish rivulets. But he was still a threat – still dangerous. The fight wasn't over. Not yet.

My rage still burned white-hot, keeping me upright when my body screamed to collapse. I saw his hand reach out, fingers trembling, clawing across the concrete towards the scalpel that had skittered out of reach. Desperate. But still capable of murder if I let him get there.

I didn't. I drove my foot hard into his ribs. The crack of impact was sharp, satisfying, his body jerking sideways with the force of it. A pained grunt tore from his throat. He rolled, disoriented, and I didn't give him the chance to recover.

Another kick – this time to his head – flipped him onto his back, his arms flailing weakly. And then I saw the opening.

I stepped forward and stamped my foot down between his legs. *Hard.* Again. And again.

I kept going – ruthless, relentless – until he stopped moving. Until the breath rattled in his throat like broken glass. Until there was nothing left of the smug, surgical precision that had haunted my dreams and my every waking moment. Just a wreck of a man, groaning on the floor, his hands now curled inwards like claws.

From the corner of my eye, I saw Ray rising slowly – wobbling, bloodied, but grinning. His phone was in his hand, screen glowing. And then as Aitken whimpered, Ray spoke, one of the sweetest sounds I'd ever heard.

'Help's on the way, love,' he said quietly, like it was nothing. Like we hadn't nearly died down there.

I stood over Aitken, just out of reach, my chest heaving, fists shaking. The scalpel was there, a few feet away – its blade streaked with blood, glinting in the light like it wanted to finish the job. And God help me, I was tempted. One slice. That's all it would take. Throat to ear. Make it quick. Final.

But I didn't. That's not me. That's not who I am. Instead, I turned away from the monster on the floor and staggered away. My hand found the cold steel of the ladder and gripped it like a lifeline.

Ray limped to my side, wincing with every step.

'You go up first, love,' he insisted, voice raw with pain but firm.

And then – the sound of sirens. Distant at first, but rising. Wailing like ghosts. The sound of salvation.

Together, we slowly climbed – bloody, broken, but alive – towards the world outside the bunker's walls. Towards the light of day.

39

THE DETECTIVE INSPECTOR

It's been a tough few months since Aitken's arrest. For Jan, the stress is obvious – I hardly need to say more. She suffered terribly and was a heroine down there. But for me, too, every day carries its own heavy load.

In quiet moments, my thoughts often turn to Ray. He didn't hesitate when Jan was in danger. He risked his life for hers. So very typical of the man. And I still remember our conversation, word for word, two days after Aitken's trial, when we sat together in my kitchen, his face lined with scars. Jan had a counselling appointment, so Ray and I could talk freely over a coffee.

I looked him in the eye and said, 'I can never thank you enough. And I'll always be grateful.' And I meant every word.

Ray's tired smile was all the answer I needed. 'That's what friends do, love,' he replied. 'I couldn't stand by and watch Jan suffer. You'd have done the same for me. No thanks needed. And don't forget. It was Jan who saved me in the end.'

Those words struck me deeply. Ray's loyalty wasn't just a gesture – it was a lifeline. He found Jan when I failed. And because of him, she has a future. My family has a future. I owe him everything, and that gratitude is something I'll carry with me every day.

And yet even as I felt thankful, a dark cloud hung over me. The events of Aitken's recent trial ate away at me. The outcome seemed a slap in the face of real justice. 'How could they do that?' I asked Ray during a quiet moment, frustration lacing my voice.

And his reply was entirely predictable. Because I knew the answer even before he said it. 'You can't beat the system, love. It is what it is. Best let it go. Try to focus on the future. It's time to get on with your life.' And Ray was right as usual. He has a knack of summing things up in a way that makes sense.

The very same week, I found myself in conversation with Halliday. And I can say the information I gleaned was a definite positive. He'd been on the defensive, naturally. He got things badly wrong.

And so I was in a buoyant mood when I stepped into his office without bothering to knock. I would never have done that before, and it felt so very good.

The room had an air of order as usual, cultivated and precise. Picture windows allowed the afternoon light to filter in, casting clean lines and shadows across the polished wood floors. Papers were stacked neatly in corners, organised and ready for review. A single chair sat across from him, positioned just so, facing him like it had been placed for one purpose alone – confrontation or conversation, but always under his careful attention. But not this time. I remained standing. Now I was in control.

Halliday sat behind his desk, the kind of desk that spoke of years of authority, his silhouette framed perfectly by the room's clean lines. His posture was rigid, ever the professional, even when the walls – the same walls that had served as the backdrop to countless criticisms – seemed to whisper their unspoken thoughts. And despite all that, I could tell his usual self-assurance was flagging. He was striving to retain his dominance without any real hope of success.

'I'm very glad to see you, Laura. I've been rethinking the whole Aitken matter,' he began, breaking the silence. His voice was unusually measured; he wasn't fully there, lost somewhere between his reluctance and the unwelcome truth creeping in. 'Maybe there were certain matters I overlooked.'

I sat down across from him now, the chair's soft creak breaking the weight of his words. There was a sense of victory in me. Every muscle in my body on alert, surprised to hear him admitting fault.

'I told you from the beginning,' I said, my voice steady but pointed, 'Aitken was watching my family. I never trusted him. And you called me paranoid. Questioned my ability. You should have listened to me all along.'

Halliday paused, his fingers drumming against the top of his desk. A single file, slightly out of line, caught his attention. He straightened it with a subtle motion but didn't immediately meet my eyes. 'Look, Laura, I'm not saying I was completely mistaken. I trusted the system... and I didn't want to see the gaps. Maybe you had a point. About Aitken. Perhaps I should have handled things differently.' His words didn't flow easily, like a reluctant confession. 'I admit that much.'

I leaned in slightly, feeling the shift in the air, but pressed him further. 'I told you of the danger. And you were blind to it. More concerned with the force's reputation than your officer's safety.'

I caught the fleeting frustration in his eyes, but he controlled it quickly. There was a long pause. When he spoke again, it wasn't about Aitken – at least, not directly. 'I'm moving on,' he suddenly said, that same dark edge to his voice that made it clear this was his decision, and not one taken lightly. His eyes steeled, a look of resolve masking any embarrassment. 'I've accepted a senior management position back with the Met.'

The news hit me like a lottery win. London! The bastard was leaving. I'd dreamt of the day. As Ray had when in the job. I couldn't hide the pleasure in my voice, that mix of elation and surprise.

Halliday nodded, lifting his gaze from the desk to meet mine, his expression firm. 'Yes, it's time for a change. A fresh start, and the Met... it offers something different. A place to pursue justice without all this – without the compromises a small force inevitably brings.' He waved a hand as if dismissing the local area surrounding us.

I tried to find my grounding, but the betrayal of his words left a taste of something unspoken, an emptiness mixing with the growing pile of unresolved justice. I could have told him exactly what I thought of him. I'd wanted to often enough. But when the time finally came, I decided not to waste my breath. Halliday seemed insignificant when compared to recent events. He was going. That's what mattered. I'd raise a glass or two to that.

I didn't offer my hand, didn't thank him for anything. There was nothing to thank him for. Instead, I turned and walked out of his office without looking back, already feeling lighter. Life was finally looking up.

40

THE SOULMATE

The memory of Aitken's bunker haunts me like a recurrent nightmare – at times, a surreal, hazy dream from which I awake with a start, and at others, dark thoughts crash over me with the brutal clarity of a midnight assault when I least expect it. The sight of Megan's remains is imprinted on my memory, never to be forgotten. And the stink of decay seems forever in my nostrils.

The oppressive gloom of that underground cell and the ever-present echo of unspeakable deeds have etched themselves into my mind. I've tried to ease the torment through talking therapy, each session a feeble attempt to exorcise the demons of my past. Yet the events I endured have left an indelible mark, changing me in ways I am only beginning to understand. In all honesty, I fear that I may never fully escape the grip of that time.

Laura has been my steadfast companion throughout this ordeal, her unwavering support a bright light in an otherwise dark world. And Ray – my hero – stands as a living testament to bravery, having risked everything to rescue what little goodness remained amid the chaos.

Yet neither Laura's gentle reassurances nor Ray's gallant deeds can erase the relentless spectre of my recent past. Ray's scars are visible reminders of his physical pain, a story written upon his skin; and mine are etched into the very fabric of my mind, hidden yet ever-present. I often find myself wondering which wound is more grievous: the one you can see, or the one that festers in the shadows of your soul.

But despite the dark echoes, I still find solace in life's quieter blessings. Laura's recent promotion fills our home with a renewed sense of pride – she's now a detective chief inspector, a title earned through grit and unwavering determination. I watch her stride through her days with a quiet confidence, and I know that in her success lies a piece of hope for us all. And then there's our dear Ed, thriving at school, his youthful laughter and earnest curiosity a daily reminder that life, in its simple moments, continues to flourish.

I work each day to mask the inner demons that still rage within me. I bury my suffering beneath a careful smile, fearful that revealing its depths might cast a shadow over my loved ones' joy. Yet even as I hide my pain, a small ember of anticipation has been kindled – a promise of respite in the shape of a long-awaited holiday.

Laura has arranged for an extended period of leave this coming summer, gifting us the prospect of a three-week villa escape in Lanzarote. I imagine the island's stark beauty: sun-soaked days unfolding beneath an endless blue sky, evenings where the warm breeze carries away the weight of my thoughts. The villa, with its quiet corners and gentle rhythms, beckons like a haven from the relentless demands of our world. In that foreign landscape, perhaps the repeated drum of memory will soften into a distant sound, replaced by the gentle murmur of the ocean and the subtle rustle of palm fronds.

I cling to this vision as a promise of relief – a moment to

reclaim the fragments of joy that remain. Even in the midst of enduring pain, these simple pleasures remind me that life, with all its trials, still offers grace in the most unexpected corners.

Yet even as I look forward to this respite, a part of me remains uncertain – unsettled. Trauma isn't something you can outrun, no matter how many miles you put between yourself and the place it took root. I worry that even under the golden sun, in the stillness of warm, tranquil nights, the ghosts will follow. That I'll close my eyes and still find myself in the depths of that bunker, gasping for breath against the suffocating stench of death.

But Laura is right, of course. I need the break. We all do. A fresh start. And maybe, just maybe, healing will finally begin.

41

THE SURGEON

Almost thirteen endless months have now passed since that day – the arrest that shattered everything I once believed indestructible. The day I thought I'd never see. And I won't lie; if freedom is to be my prize again, it won't come from proof of innocence. That ship has long since sailed, sunk beneath the weight of ill-informed misconceptions.

I'm not behind bars, or at least not the kind you think of when you picture a prison. No, I'm locked away in a secure hospital for the criminally insane. It's laughable when you think about it, a mockery. Me, the great man of medicine who's pushed the boundaries of science, my intellect sharp as a razor, labelled a lunatic.

My actions should have been celebrated. Applauded. And yet, the so-called justice system, so blind to progress, decided the narrative. My legal team, ever the eager puppets, shoved me into this box, advising a plea of diminished responsibility to escape a murder conviction. As if I were insane.

Can you believe it? Ludicrous, I know. But I played the game with a cold smile, threw the dice with a steady hand, knowing there were angles in this madness. A twist to the tale, a way to navigate the limits of my captives' minds.

So, here I sit – convicted of manslaughter, not murder. A reduced charge, they say, thanks to *madness*. But still serious. Too serious for a system that can't see beyond its own ignorance. The very people who sit in judgement, unable to even grasp the need for the work I've done. Work that could change everything, if they'd just stop their incessant, misguided fear of the unknown.

But there are, of course, some positives to my situation that shouldn't be ignored. I've been granted an abundance of time in which to craft my written thesis – a labour of precision and perfection, one I've diligently honed through sleepless nights and solitary contemplation. And to say I'm pleased with the outcome would be an understatement. It is nothing short of magnificent for what it is.

Yet I am a man of science, ever diligent in my pursuit of truth. And I know – perhaps more than anyone – that the conclusions I've drawn, bold though they may seem, are still fragile. Two lab rats – suitable subjects – are but a mere whisper of what is required to cement my findings in the eternal annals of scientific achievement.

All that seems so very obvious to me. And I made the mistake of trying to enlighten them. The doctors. The nurses. The pathetic little functionaries who scurry about in their sterile white uniforms, convinced they possess even the vaguest comprehension of the human mind. Of my mind. But it was a wasted effort. Of course it was. You can't teach brilliance to the blind. You can't explain Beethoven to a monkey.

The fools file into my room like clockwork, their dull, vacant eyes flickering over me, skimming the surface, seeing nothing of substance. They mistake their clipboards for authority, their scripted questions for insight, their rigid little protocols for knowledge. It's almost amusing – this feeble charade of competence. Almost.

They nod, they murmur their rehearsed pleasantries, they pretend to listen, but it's all meaningless. They lack the intellectual fortitude to grasp the magnitude of my work, the depth of my genius. And how could they? They are lesser beings. Inconsequential, replaceable, utterly devoid of the vision that sets men like me apart.

Yet they have the audacity to observe me. To study me, as though I were some peculiar specimen under glass, as though they could ever begin to understand what it is to be me. It's laughable.

And so, I now find myself forced to play the long game. No more will I speak of my research in these sterile halls. Not a single word of its promise will grace my lips from this moment forth.

No. Instead, I will offer them what they want, what they *need* to hear, with my most convincing mask of contrition. Their counselling and their drug therapy, their ineffectual tools of the trade, will all be credited with unprecedented success. I will apologise for my *crimes*, not with any true remorse, of course, but with practised precision. I will claim that, were it possible, I would undo the past, erase the moment where my genius went so badly astray.

And I will repeat it all. Again and again, in a steady rhythm, with a feigned sincerity so convincing that even I might begin to believe it. Their gullibility will be their undoing. They are idiots, every one of them, and soon, they too will be caught in the web I weave.

And when they finally release me, when the facade is complete, they will see no more in me but a man rehabilitated – no longer a dangerous anomaly, but a model of the system they so dearly want to believe in. And I will be free. Unshackled once more, destined to continue my work on a stage far beyond the confines of this pitiful institution.

And when that great day dawns – when they finally deem me no longer a menace to society – I will seize my long-coveted release. Yes, I am certain that day will come. If that bitch Kesey thinks she's escaped me, she's very sadly mistaken. And now I have others on my list for righteous revenge. Janet and Lewis deserve no less.

Patience is my most powerful ally. I have studied the delicate balance of persuasion and deception, and I will wield both with surgical precision. Every therapy session, every carefully curated display of remorse will serve its purpose.

The hospital staff think they are reforming me, moulding me into something safe, something contained. But I am neither. I am simply biding my time. I will kill again. My research demands it. It's only a matter of time.

* * *

MORE FROM JOHN NICHOLL

The next book from John Nicholl is available to order now here: https://mybook.to/JohnNicholl18BackAd

ACKNOWLEDGEMENTS

With heartfelt thanks to my editor, Isobel Akenhead, and to the entire team at Boldwood Books for their unwavering support and expertise.

ABOUT THE AUTHOR

John Nicholl is an award-winning, bestselling author of numerous darkly psychological suspense thrillers. These books have a gritty realism born of his real-life experience as an ex-police officer and child protection social worker.

Sign up to John Nicholl's mailing list for news, competitions and updates on future books.

Visit John's website: www.johnnicholl.com

Follow John on social media:

- facebook.com/JohnNichollAuthor
- x.com/nicholl06
- instagram.com/johnnichollauthor
- bookbub.com/authors/john-nicholl

ALSO BY JOHN NICHOLL

The Sisters

Mr Nice

The Cellar

The Student

The Cop

The Victim

The Bride

The Holiday

The Boyfriend

The Surgeon

The Carmarthen Murders Series

The Carmarthen Murders

The Tywi Estuary Killings

The Castle Beach Murders

The Dryslwyn Castle Killings

The Galbraith Series

The Doctor

The Wife

The Father

THE *Murder* LIST

THE MURDER LIST IS A NEWSLETTER DEDICATED TO SPINE-CHILLING FICTION AND GRIPPING PAGE-TURNERS!

SIGN UP TO MAKE SURE YOU'RE ON OUR HIT LIST FOR EXCLUSIVE DEALS, AUTHOR CONTENT, AND COMPETITIONS.

SIGN UP TO OUR NEWSLETTER

BIT.LY/THEMURDERLISTNEWS

Boldwood

Boldwood Books is an award-winning fiction publishing company seeking out the best stories from around the world.

Find out more at www.boldwoodbooks.com

Join our reader community for brilliant books, competitions and offers!

Follow us
@BoldwoodBooks
@TheBoldBookClub

Sign up to our weekly deals newsletter

https://bit.ly/BoldwoodBNewsletter

Printed in Dunstable, United Kingdom